LIAR LIAR

BOOKS BY JAMES PATTERSON
FEATURING HARRIET BLUE

Never Never (with Candice Fox)
Fifty Fifty (with Candice Fox)
Liar Liar (with Candice Fox)

A complete list of books by James Patterson is at the back of this book. For previews of upcoming books and information about the author, visit JamesPatterson.com, or find him on Facebook.

LIAR
LIAR

JAMES PATTERSON AND CANDICE FOX

Little, Brown and Company

New York Boston London

Copyright © 2018 by James Patterson
Excerpt from *The Chef* copyright © 2019 by James Patterson

Hachette Book Group supports the right to free expression and the value of copyright. The purpose of copyright is to encourage writers and artists to produce creative works that enrich our culture.

The scanning, uploading, and distribution of this book without permission is a theft of the author's intellectual property. If you would like permission to use material from the book (other than for review purposes), please contact permissions@hbgusa.com. Thank you for your support of the author's rights.

Little, Brown and Company
Hachette Book Group
1290 Avenue of the Americas, New York, NY 10104
littlebrown.com

First North American edition: January 2019
Originally published in Australia by Century Australia, a division of Penguin Random House Australia, July 2018

Little, Brown and Company is a division of Hachette Book Group, Inc. The Little, Brown name and logo are trademarks of Hachette Book Group, Inc.

The publisher is not responsible for websites (or their content) that are not owned by the publisher.

The Hachette Speakers Bureau provides a wide range of authors for speaking events. To find out more, go to hachettespeakersbureau.com or call (866) 376-6591.

ISBN 978-0-316-41824-9 (hc) / 978-0-316-41834-8 (large print)
LCCN 2018953815

10 9 8 7 6 5 4 3 2 1

LSC-H

Printed in the United States of America

LIAR LIAR

CHAPTER 1

SOMETHING WAS NOT RIGHT.

Doctor Samantha Parish noticed an odor as she pulled the door of her Prius closed. An earthy, almost metallic smell, the distinct reek of male sweat. As soon as the lock clicked, she knew one corner of her world was out of place.

When he spoke from the back seat, a part of her wasn't even surprised.

"Try to stay calm," he said.

But his deep, soothing tone made staying calm impossible. His self-assurance told her he was speaking from experience. This was the moment his victim usually panicked.

Doctor Parish's first impulse was to push open the door and roll out of the vehicle. The quickly darkening parking lot was full of cars where other mothers waited. Teenage girls in black leotards, matching pink silk bags hanging from thin shoulders, were filing between the vehicles from the door of the nearby hall. When Samantha tried to move, she found her body was frozen.

"Don't make a sound," the man said. "Put your hands on the wheel. Eyes straight ahead."

Her shaking hands moved to the steering wheel, gripped hard. She smelled blood. Rain or stagnant water, something almost swampy.

She chanced a look in the rearview mirror. He was silhouetted against the sun setting beyond the nearby park. Shaved head. Tall. Broad, powerful shoulders.

"What do you want?" Her voice was far smaller than she had intended.

A click. The sound of a gun.

Doctor Parish felt tears sliding down her cheeks. "Please, just take the car."

He said nothing. *What are we waiting for?* she wondered. Then it hit her, hard in the chest, like a punch. She'd forgotten all about Isobel. She turned, her mouth twisted in a silent howl just as her eleven-year-old daughter opened the passenger-side door.

"No!" Doctor Parish could hardly form the words. "Isobel, ru—"

The child didn't even look at her mother. She was wearing those little white headphones, cut off from the world around her. She flopped into the car and pulled the door shut behind her with a *whump,* locking her inside their nightmare.

When they arrived at the clinic, Isobel gave a moan of terror, huddling against her mother as they exited the car. In her ballet getup, she was the frightened black swan, shoulders bent forward, trying to disappear under her mother's wing.

They walked to the doors, and Samantha swiped their way into the darkened space.

She guessed where he wanted to go and turned and walked through the consulting room into theater three. They passed a large poster of a woman with perfectly symmetrical breasts, a chart showing liposuction before-and-after shots. *Parish Lifestyle and Body Enhancement Clinic* was embossed in thin letters on a stainless-steel plate above the door.

What he wanted from them was becoming clear, at least to Samantha. She watched him undressing carefully in the surgery room, easing a messily bandaged shoulder out of the torn shirt. His clothes were filthy, his skin covered in a fine sheen of sweat. She could smell already that the wounds were septic. Trying to control her shaking, she straightened, let go of her daughter, and took a step toward him.

"You want me to help you," she said. It was the first time such a concept had ever repulsed her.

She helped him peel away the bandages. Three puncture wounds, one in the side, two in the shoulder. The wound in his side had an exit hole at the back. A bullet. It was the ones in the shoulder that bothered him the most. The bullets were still in there. As he peeled the last of the blackened bandages away, blood began seeping from the wounds.

"Lie down," she instructed, gesturing to the operating table.

He didn't lie, but sat on the edge of the table with some difficulty, the gun pinned under one hand, a finger on the trigger guard. Samantha went to the shelves and began filling a tray with tools.

"I'll need to administer an anesthetic," she said.

"No," he answered. He was panting now with pain. "No injections."

"But I can't—" She whirled around, gestured to his wounds. "I can't perform surgery on you without a local anesthetic at least."

"You'll have to," he said. She waited for more, but there was none. He wasn't willing to let her inject him with something—didn't trust her not to administer a general anesthetic and knock him out. But he trusted her with a scalpel. Why? She could slash him. Stab him. Then, of course, what good would that do? A nicked artery would put him down in three minutes, maybe longer. Long enough for him to fire the gun at her, or Isobel. Long enough for him to swing one of those huge fists.

The wounds were days old. He'd clearly been hiding somewhere filthy, waiting for the strength to enact his plan.

"You're him, aren't you?" she said, low enough that her daughter couldn't hear. "The one they've been looking for. Regan Banks."

He didn't answer. She watched his cold eyes appraising the scalpel in her hand.

"You're not going to let us live, are you?" she said.

Again, no answer came.

FIVE WEEKS LATER

CHAPTER 2

I DIDN'T SLEEP MUCH. But when I did, my mind turned in circles, repeating their names like a mantra, connecting them end to end. When I was really tired, my lips moved. I sometimes woke to the sound of my own whispering.

Rachel Howes, Marissa Haydon, Elle Ramone, Rosetta Poelar.

Regan's girls. The innocent lives he had taken. He had left their bodies ruined on lonely stretches of sand, horrors to be discovered by strangers.

Tox Barnes, my friend, left for dead in my own apartment.

Caitlyn McBeal, a smart young American woman reduced to skin and bones, traumatized, crawling on her belly out of Regan Banks's grasp.

"*Samuel Blue,*" I whispered through my dreams.

My brother. All I'd had left in the world. The only man who would never abandon me, never judge me.

I didn't know why Regan Banks had seized on my brother. But my research, my gut instinct, and what my friends had been able to determine was that Regan Banks was obsessed with him. Regan, a boy from the suburbs, a foster kid like me, had spent fifteen years in prison, incarcerated for the brutal murder of a young woman when he was just seventeen. Regan had found Doctor Rachel Howes working late in a veterinary clinic and unleashed his first deadly passion on her, paying for it with hard time. Not long after his release, girls began appearing on the shores of the Georges River, beaten and strangled, sexually violated. I had wanted in on the case, but no one would approve my assignment. Soon enough, I found out why. My colleagues already had a suspect for the murders, and he was my own flesh and blood.

I knew Sam was innocent. But I was the only person making that claim. There had been evidence in my brother's apartment, put there, he said, by someone else. While I'd fought to secure my brother's release, I'd managed to convince two friends to help me, Tate "Tox" Barnes and Edward Whittacker. Together we'd found the man we'd believed to be the real Georges River Killer. A man who'd set out to destroy my brother's life. Tox had taken Regan on and almost got himself killed. Whitt had got achingly close to catching him, only to have him slip away, wounded and wild, into the night.

I'd thought it was over. That once we caught Regan, my brother would be set free.

But that dream was snatched away from me. My brother was stabbed in prison and died only hours before I'd planned to visit him and tell him the good news.

I was the only one left to speak for Sam now. For him and all of Regan's victims. But my plan had changed. I wasn't just going to clear my brother's name by forcing Regan to admit to framing him. Regan deserved to die for the lives he had taken.

I, Detective Harriet Blue, needed to be the one to kill him.

A sound broke through my dreams. I snapped awake, bolted upright in the stiff motel bed. For a moment, I had to orient myself. I had been on the run for five weeks, shifting from motel room to motel room, trying to stay under the radar while I hunted my brother's killer. I had looked for him where I knew bad men felt safe. I'd wandered homeless camps, where armies of wanted men hid their faces in shadowed hoods and blankets, huddled around campfires. I'd squinted into the corners of blackened, stinking barrooms and drug dens, the basements and attics of city brothels. I had searched for Regan through the underworld, following whispers between depraved men, chasing rumors through the streets. In five weeks, I hadn't found him, but I hadn't given up.

There were no warrants for my arrest. But to my colleagues in the Sydney police, my intentions were clear. I had gone off the map so that Regan couldn't find me, so that I could get my revenge for what he had done to my family. I had disappeared because I knew that if my colleagues in the police discovered where I was, they'd try to convince me not to commit that final devastating act. The act that would mean giving up everything. My career. My life. My freedom.

And I couldn't let them do that.

As I sat listening in the dark, I knew someone was coming.

CHAPTER 3

THE ROOM WAS a strange T-shape, narrow in the stem so that the end of the bed almost touched a dresser against the opposite wall. At the rear, the room turned left to an old chipboard closet and right to a moldy bathroom. The front window looked out into a parking lot stuffed with cars. I'd left the heavy curtains open a crack so that the red light from the motel's NO VACANCY sign poured in through the lace. The light flickered as a figure passed before it. I heard the telltale blip of a police radio.

"Yeah, Command, we think we've got her. Have that rover stand by for our call. Over."

Patrol officers. I could hear the squeak of their leather boots. Shadows moved under the door. Three men. Two cops and the motel's owner, most likely. My backpack was zipped up, ready to go, as always. I'd slept fully dressed. I threw myself out of the bed and dragged on my shoes as a heavy fist began to beat on the door.

"Harry, we know you're in there. Open up!"

I slipped the backpack on and went to the end of the T-shaped room, tucked myself into the corner by the closet, and waited. Before me, the open bathroom door, the shower and toilet beyond. I heard the jangle of the motel owner's keys.

"Harry?" one of the officers called. "Go easy, all right?" I heard a subtle tremor in his voice.

He knew my reputation.

CHAPTER 4

THEY'D BEEN STUPID. The patrol cops had told the backup car to hold off, wanting to be heroes. Big men who had grabbed the snarling feral cat Harriet Blue and finally shoved her in a cage where she belonged. Their first mistake.

Their second mistake had been coming into the room and leaving the lights off, thinking they'd have a tactical advantage over me in the dark. They probably expected to catch me in my underwear, still half asleep.

Wrong. I knew the room, they didn't, and I'd set the place up for a situation just like this. I listened as they ran into the drawers I'd left pulled out at the bottom of the bed, blocking their path forward. In the red light from the motel sign, I saw them separate as I'd hoped they would, one climbing over the bed while the other tried to shut the awkward, rickety wooden drawers. I took the small packet of soap I'd left on the carpet in front of the closet and tossed it through the bathroom door. It made a clattering sound on the toilet lid.

The first officer jumped off the bed and leaped forward at the sound, into the bathroom. I popped up, grabbed the handle of the door, and pulled it shut on him, slipping the slide bolt closed. I'd set the same trap in every motel room I'd stayed in, taking the lock from the inside of the door and screwing it onto the outside with a screwdriver I kept in my backpack. I'd never used the trap before, but now it worked like a charm. I smiled in the dark.

"Hey! Hey! What the fuck?" he yelled.

I turned, left him beating on the inside of the bathroom door, and faced the second officer, who was blocking my path to freedom.

"Don't," he said, his arms out, as though to catch me. "Harry, come on. Give us a break."

I didn't know this young officer. Didn't want to hurt him. But I was on a mission to bring down a killer, and I would do what it took to stay free.

He was backing up toward the exit. I couldn't let him get there. I made a leap for the bed, and that encouraged him. He came forward, grabbing at my legs while I tucked into a roll and landed on the other side of the mattress.

His arm came around my shoulders. I jutted my elbow hard into his ribs, got nowhere, kicked the wall, and shoved myself backward, propelling him onto the mattress. The shock of it was enough to loosen his grip.

The motel owner, a squat, hairy man, was standing helplessly just outside the doorway as I sprinted out into the night.

CHAPTER 5

CHIEF TREVOR MORRIS sat at his cluttered desk and gripped his head, looking at the report from two patrol officers in Lidcombe. In the early hours of the morning, the pair had briefly encountered his rogue detective, Harriet Blue, and predictably failed to bring her in. In five weeks, it had been the only confirmed contact.

Oh, Harry, he thought. *I'm so sorry.*

He should have been the one to tell her that her brother was dead. He had a special kind of relationship with the unpredictable, hotheaded officer he'd found in his local boxing gym fifteen years earlier. The new kid on the block in Sex Crimes, his only female detective in that department. Chief Morris had agreed to train her in the boxing ring. She'd started calling him Pops, and yes, he'd felt almost like her father. He'd found she could already hold her own in a fight. It had been her fury he'd had to tame, her fast, clumsy rage.

It hadn't been much of a leap for Harry's rage to evolve into a need for revenge.

He turned in his chair and perused a collection of articles he'd pinned to a nearby corkboard detailing the city's reaction to Regan Banks's escape.

Police bungle Regan Banks arrest, deadly serial killer still at large.

Two found dead; scene suggests Regan Banks alive and well.

Where is Harriet Blue? Speculation rife detective is in league with killer.

The public had never liked Harry. Had never believed that a Sex Crimes detective didn't know her brother was a serial killer. Sam Blue had been in the middle of his trial when Regan Banks had surfaced. Harry and her few supporters had been claiming Sam was being framed by a tall, broad-shouldered man with a shaved head. They knew Regan was a killer. He'd killed as a teen, and now a woman had only barely escaped his clutches, telling investigators Regan had spoken about Sam Blue. Had Sam been innocent all along, the victim of a setup? Or was the Georges River Killer actually a two-man team? The answers weren't coming anytime soon.

"What a mess." Morris shook his head as he turned and looked at another corkboard, the various crime scenes touched by Regan's hand. The pictures of his pretty victims, pale and still on morgue tables. "What a fucking mess."

"Yes, it is an incredible mess," someone said.

Pops looked toward the doorway. Deputy Police Commissioner Joseph Woods stood there with his hat in hand, the various buckles and attachments to his jacket gleaming in the harsh overhead light.

Pops stood, smoothing down his tie, feeling sweat already beading beneath his shirt. Before he could begin the necessary greetings, Woods cut over him.

"Get your things together," Woods said. "You're out, Morris. I'm taking over."

CHAPTER 6

THERE WERE NO WORDS. Pops eased the air from his lungs.

"I'll need this office as an operations center for the Banks case," Woods continued. "You can start working on that after we brief the crew about the command change."

"Deputy Commissioner Woods," Pops said finally, "this is my investigation. You can't take it over without approval from—"

"All the approvals have been given, Morris." Woods patted the smaller man on the shoulder, the gesture stiff and devoid of warmth. "You've done your best, I'm sure. But this"—he waved at the corkboard—"this isn't just a mess. It's a fucking catastrophe. It has to be taken in hand immediately by someone with suitable experience."

Pops's eyes widened. "Joe, nothing like this has ever—"

"You've got a vicious killer on the loose." Woods leaned on the edge of the desk. "Eight dead. A rogue policewoman running amok, refusing to come in. Another rogue officer in a coma. Am I missing anyone?"

"Detective Barnes is out of his coma," Pops said. "And he never—"

"Don't try to defend him, Morris. Tox Barnes is a lunatic. Always has been. He wanted to play with Regan a bit before handing him in—be a hero. He almost became a casualty. Well, that's not how we do things in this job. We don't take matters into our own hands, no matter how good it feels. I'm here to make sure that Blue woman doesn't do the same as Barnes and add herself to the already numerous body count."

The two men glared at each other. Morris and Woods had been at the academy together, more than thirty years earlier. It was precisely these interactions that had got Woods to the rank of Deputy Commissioner while Morris remained at Chief Superintendent. Woods railroaded people. When he spoke. When he acted. When he went for promotions. He was a tall, thick-bodied battering ram of a man, charging in and taking over when he decided good publicity might be available.

Pops felt a pain in his chest, scratched at the anxiety creeping up his insides.

"Detective Blue is refusing to come in," Woods said. "To me, that's not only professionally unacceptable, but it's deeply suspicious."

"She's not in league with Banks."

"Then why won't she come in?"

Morris didn't answer.

"Because she wants to kill him," Woods said. "If she's not in league with him, she must be hunting him. That's premeditated murder. It's just as critical for us to bring her in to save Banks's life as it is to investigate her involvement in his past crimes. We don't condone vigilantism, Morris. I want her found and arrested."

"That's a big mistake." Morris shook his head. "You cannot approach her with force. She will kick arses, Joe. I'm telling you. If you try to bully her, you better prepare to clean up the mess. I've been trying to establish contact so I can lure her in. I had two officers early this morning who found her, and they were supposed to call me. Instead they went in, and they're lucky they didn't get hurt."

"All the more reason to get her into custody."

"No," Morris said. "I won't support an arrest warrant without a criminal charge." He shrugged stiffly. "And you have nothing to charge her with. She was not in league with her brother. She's not in league with Banks. Right now, she's an official missing person, and we have concerns for her welfare. End of story."

"This is not your decision," Woods said. "There has been a change of command. It's out of your hands."

Pops grimaced, turned away.

"I'll offer a reward," he said suddenly.

Woods gave a quizzical frown.

"I have a hundred grand in my personal savings account," Pops went on. "You continue to play her to the media as a missing person, as a good cop we have grave concerns for, and I'll offer the money as a reward for her whereabouts."

"This is ridiculous."

"I guarantee you'll find her faster that way. If the public thinks she's dangerous, they'll run from her. If they think she's one of us, and better yet, their ticket to a fat pile of cash, they'll be drawn to her. You'll get more hits with a reward."

Woods looked down at the man beside him.

"I'll hand over the investigation to you, no questions asked." Pops put his hands up in surrender. "But I'm asking you now not to put out a warrant on Harry. Don't do that to her. She doesn't deserve it."

Woods snorted, unconvinced. "When we get her in, we'll see what she deserves."

CHAPTER 7

DETECTIVE EDWARD WHITTACKER barely made the briefing on time, jogging to the mirrored door to the boardroom and stopping to tuck in a loose corner of his shirt. He hated to be late. Actually felt a burning anger in his throat at the thought of it. He opened the door and walked stiffly to the back of the room, determined not to react to the eyes of other officers following him. As he took a seat, a detective he knew from Robbery turned and leaned over the back of the chair in front of Whitt.

"How's Barnes?" the younger detective asked. "Still kickin'?"

Whitt felt his face flushing. His former unofficial partner, Detective Tate "Tox" Barnes, was deeply reviled across the Sydney metropolitan police department. His grievous wounding in a fight with Regan Banks was hardly tragic news. Whitt knew it wouldn't be long before this hatred for Tox, and for Whitt's partner before him, Harriet Blue, would turn on him.

"Detective Barnes is recovering well," Whitt said. "He's not receiving visitors. But the doctors tell me he'll likely be up and about in a couple of weeks."

The young Robbery/Homicide detective gave a theatrical sigh. "Well, you know what they say. Only the good die young."

The officers around them sniggered.

A senior detective came in and began the progress check on the Banks investigation. There were sightings of Banks all over the city to run through. Most were unsubstantiated, panicked calls from elderly women after hearing bumps and thumps in their yards in the early hours. There were a few legitimate, interesting calls about big men with shaved heads acting suspiciously, but they were not clustered in any particular place. It seemed that, like Harry, Regan had gone to ground since his last killings: the vicious slaughter of a mother and her eleven-year-old daughter in a Mosman plastic surgery clinic.

Whitt took a file out of his bag and selected his manila folder on the Parish murders. There were crime-scene photographs of the once-immaculate surgery room, bloodstains and spatters found to be from Isobel and Samantha Parish. And some blood that matched the DNA profile of Regan Banks. The detectives had determined that Banks had abducted Doctor Parish and her daughter and forced the skilled plastic surgeon to attend to wounds Banks had acquired in a shootout with police.

Whitt had been there when Regan was shot by police,

had heard Regan's cry as the bullets tore through him. It didn't escape Whitt that if he'd just been faster, smarter, more prepared, *he* might have been the one to take Regan down before he escaped. Before he killed the mother and child.

Whitt flipped quickly through the photographs of the bodies, the mother curled in a corner of the surgery, her throat cut. The little girl still in her dance leotard, her arms splayed and head twisted back at an unnatural angle. The killings had been swift but violent. Whitt wondered whether Doctor Parish had known when she was helping Banks with his wounds that he planned to kill her. There were indications the woman and the child had both put up a vigorous fight, completely trashing the surgery room. They'd died at opposite ends of the building, the child making it all the way down the hall to the front reception room and grabbing the phone off the hook. No call to emergency services had come through.

Whitt looked at the photographs of the mangled bullet Doctor Parish had removed from Regan's body, the clippings of stitches that had fallen on the floor after the surgery table was upturned. Doctor Samantha Parish had got a broken killing machine up and running again and paid for it with her life. And her daughter's life.

Whitt wondered how many more names he would have to write on identical folders before the killing machine was taken out of operation for good.

CHAPTER 8

WHEN THE BRIEFING was done, Whitt walked across the busy bullpen to his desk, coffee in hand. The desk was new, a delay in his official transfer from Perth, meaning he had spent his first couple of weeks at the department working out of his car or a briefing room. A group of detectives was gathered nearby, watching the large glass window of Chief Morris's office with interest.

Whitt looked over to see what they were all focused on.

"It's him," a detective said, his arms folded, leaning on Whitt's desk. "It's Big Joe Woods."

"That's the guy who caught Elizabeth Crassbord's killer?"

"And Reece Smart, the Farmhouse Killer," another detective said, nodding. "Dude's a big-case bandit. Swoops in after all the hard work is done, trying to get the press. He's got a lot to prove. You hear about his daughter?"

Whitt scoured his desk for his folder. He thought he'd

just put it down on the desk when he passed to get his coffee, but now it was gone. He straightened and turned to the group of men beside him still focused on the office across the room.

"Did someone take my...?"

The detectives turned toward him and smiled. Whitt sighed. One of the woes of being associated with Tox Barnes was that other detectives in the department were given license to harass, belittle, and prank any detective partnered with him. It was a tradition dating back to Tox's entry into the force. Rumors spread, almost as soon as he was badged, about violent killings in his childhood. Tox had been responsible for the death of a mother and son, but it was a freak accident that got the pair killed. The police didn't want a murderer in their midst and punished anyone who aligned themselves with Detective Barnes. Tox might have cleared up the rumors about his past, but he wasn't the world's most social guy. He liked to work alone, and his reputation, however false, kept people away.

Even with Tox holed up in hospital, out of sight and out of mind, Whitt was still being messed with for befriending the department's most hated detective.

"Seriously? That's my only copy of the Banks case file in its entirety," he said.

"Well, then!" the nearest detective said cheerfully. "We know how you'll be spending *your* morning."

Whitt appreciated the prank for its subtlety and effectiveness. He would have to go down to "the dungeon," the records department in the bowels of the building, and print himself a whole new file. He took his coffee to the sink and poured it out without drinking it. He knew by the time he returned, it would be unsafe to drink.

He rode the clunking, shuddering elevator down to the darkened car park and traversed the concrete floor lined with police vehicles to another elevator down to the lowest floor of the building. Records was housed where the command center held its armory, and it had the added benefit of being a suitably dark, damp, and cold place for insubordinate officers to be sent as punishment. Officers who stepped out of line were sent to do time either in records, where they could wither away filing paperwork, or in the armory, where cleaning and servicing the weapons would allow them sufficient time to think about what they had done.

Whitt knew who was in the records department now—a young patrol officer named Karmichael, who had been filmed dancing suggestively in uniform with a couple of ladies in a nightclub in Kings Cross. Constable Karmichael's movie had made it onto YouTube and, inevitably, to the top brass's e-mail in-box. And then there was a long-term inmate of the dungeon, Inspector Mia Fables. Fables was in her fifties and had clawed her way to inspector through decades of shoddy police work and bad attitude.

Whitt exited the elevator and pushed open the door of the long hall leading to the lowest floor of the building.

The lights were off. It was his first clue that something was amiss.

CHAPTER 9

WHITT STOOD HOLDING open the heavy door. He seemed to recall that there had been some mention of the lights and electrics on the dungeon floor playing up. He called out into the infinite blackness and received no reply. Surely Karmichael and Fables weren't working in pure blackness? The door at the other end of the hall must have been shut. Whitt let the door close behind him, sealing him in the dark. The sound of his shoes on the concrete as he walked seemed so loud now, his eardrums pulsed.

A smell. Gunpowder. Not the lingering reek of the armory up ahead, but a whiff of it, a cloud suddenly enveloping him. Whitt felt the hairs on the back of his neck stand on end. He stopped short, his hand reaching instinctively for the gun in his shoulder holster.

"Hello?"

No answer. Whitt wouldn't have put it past his colleagues to try to give him a fright in the dark down here. He cleared his throat, trying to ease a little of the fear out of his words. "Is someone here?"

Nothing. He kept walking and, with relief, opened the door at the other end of the hall.

He would have looked back, just to check, to see if the strange sense that someone was in the hall behind him had been correct. That in the blackness someone had waited as he passed.

But he didn't check.

He was distracted by the blood.

CHAPTER 10

JUST ONE DROP. A big drop, searing red in the fluorescent light.

Whitt looked back into the hall. No one. He crouched, squinted at the bloodstain. It was wet. He pulled out his weapon but didn't call out this time.

It was only one drop of blood, but the feeling he'd experienced in the dark hall had put him on edge. His back teeth were locked, muscles tensed.

Whitt walked silently to a T-intersection in the hallway and peered around the corner. To the right of him, the door to the armory. To the left, the door to the records room. He looked down before he reached for the records-room doorknob. He noticed another drop of blood on the floor.

From inside the room, a moan.

Whitt threw open the door. The small reception space before the caged records room was empty. He went to the barred door and peered in, saw a pair of legs jutting from behind a filing cabinet.

"Karmichael?" Whitt tried to see more, but there was only blood—not single drops of it now but smears and streaks, a dark pool. He rattled the door. There was no sign of Mia Fables. He climbed atop the counter and slid his body through the gap across which the records were usually handed, landing almost on top of Constable Karmichael.

"Oh, Jesus," Whitt breathed, spreading his hands instinctively on the officer's bloodied chest, trying to stem the flow from two gaping holes. "Oh, Jesus!"

The young man had been shot three times, twice in the chest, once in the throat. He was alive. Trying to speak. His mouth moving open and closed, a gasping fish on a riverbank.

Whitt hit the panic button under the counter, the one Karmichael had dragged himself across the floor trying to reach. A shrill electronic tone split the air.

"I'll be back," Whitt assured the dying man. "I'm coming back, I promise."

He grabbed his gun from the counter and ran to the farthest aisle. Lieutenant Fables lay on her side at the very end of the row, papers fallen all around her, her mouth hanging open as though giving a pained howl. Whitt could tell, even from a distance, that she was dead.

He checked the other aisles, one at a time, sweeping his gun before him. No one. He heard running footsteps, shouting. His colleagues arriving at the distant hall.

"I'm here!" Whitt went back to the dying constable on the ground. "Karmichael, I'm—"

He was gone. The blood that had been gushing from his throat had stilled. Whitt stood, listening to the alarm, blood dripping from his fingers onto the floor, sliding down the barrel of his gun. On the ground nearby was another collection of files and papers, a heap lifted from an open drawer nearby and dumped. Whitt went to the cabinet where the drawer stood open and looked at the sign above it.

PERSONNEL: A–F.

He didn't touch the files scattered near the body of the dead officer. He read the names he could see as though in a dream. *Brummer. Brown. Blake. Billett. Benson.*

He knew which file was missing.

CHAPTER 11

A DOUBLE SHOOTING in their own command building. Whitt couldn't fathom it. He sat dumbfounded at the table in an interview room after giving his statement. He'd been told the CCTV had switched off ten minutes before the shooting. The concrete walls had suppressed the sound of gunfire.

"Harry's personnel file is missing, isn't it?" Whitt asked his chief.

Chief Morris and Deputy Commissioner Woods were the last detectives to interview Whitt. He had given his statement three times over. They sat across from him, reading his statement.

"Details of the crime scene aren't your concern right now, Detective," Woods said. "You're signed off for the day. Go home. Walk it off. We'll resume interviews in the morning."

"It was him." Whitt couldn't stop the words tumbling

out. "Banks. I think I passed him on his way out. He came to get Harry's records. That means he's got every-thing we have on her. Her childhood. Her academy results. Her disciplinary—"

"Whitt," Morris said.

"He was here. Banks. He was *in the building*."

"That's enough, Detective." Woods stood, towering above the men still sitting at the table, his bulk casting a shadow over Whitt. "Shut up and go home. That's an order."

In the men's change room, while collecting his belongings, Whitt jumped at the touch of a hand on his shoulder.

It was a female detective he'd not met before, her black cotton top cinched at the underarms by her holster.

"Edward Whittacker?" she said.

"Oh, yes, hi." He closed his locker. "Sorry—you're from Forensics? Is there more I need to—"

"No, I'm Detective Vada Reskit." She put out a hand. "I'm your new partner on the Banks case."

A partner. That made sense. Someone to lean on while he dealt with the events of the morning, someone to keep an eye on him for the top brass as he carried on with the case. Leave time was not in abundance right now. He'd be expected to suck it up and keep looking for Banks and Harry.

Whitt shook the offered hand. Vada's grip was firm, warm. The first comforting thing he'd felt in hours. He focused on her bright white teeth. Her red hair. Her ponytail. "I see. Chief Morris assigned you, did he? Or was it Woods?"

"Woods. But Morris approved it."

"Right, right."

"Come on, let's get going. You've had yourself a pretty hard day. We all have. We'll have a few drinks, blow off some steam. You can talk about it, or not talk about it, as you like."

"Oh," Whitt said. He never had "a few drinks." Not anymore. It had taken years to climb his way out of the hole drinking had sunk him into after a bad case he'd worked on back home in Perth. A little girl had died, and Whitt had not been able to bring her killers to justice. Worse yet, he'd planted evidence and all but secured their freedom.

Old tingles of desire rippled through him at just the mention of a few drinks. He said nothing about his problem. It was too awkward to bring up at the outset. His ritual was to allow himself a single standard glass of red wine at 5:30 p.m. Not a drop more. Sometimes, on his worst days, he had a Scotch. Just one.

He'd have that drink with his new partner and explain it all to her then.

"Let's go," he said, the dread almost choking off his words.

CHAPTER 12

I SAT AT the back of the bar in a shadowy corner, my eyes on my glass, listening to the talk of the men at the counter. The tumbling and crashing sounds of the poker machines. The cars rushing by in the wet street.

In the time I'd been on the run, I'd learned plenty of things, but the most important had been how essential the sense of hearing is to a fugitive. I kept my ears pricked for mentions of my name at all times. For sirens, or the unmistakable stern, direct talk of cops. I made eye contact with no one. I'd kept my head so low in my first week in hiding, my neck had been stiff and sore at the end of each day.

On the television screens above the bar, a cricket game, a cooking show, and the national evening news. I listened as the bartender howled above the general din of conversation from the men crowded at the tables nearest the bar.

"Shut up, you guys! I wanna hear this!"

The men's volume lowered. The sound of the news program rose. I turned my drink on the tabletop before me, watching the ice melt.

"...*shocking scenes. Police are saying they have no reason to believe the shooting at Sydney Police Center in Surry Hills is linked to the ongoing search for Regan Banks*..."

I dropped my head, realizing I'd almost risen out of my seat, eyes glued to the screen, my cover forgotten. My thoughts were racing. A shooting at the police command center. Did they mean *inside* the building? How was that possible?

I realized with sudden, shocking clarity how many people I cared about had probably been in the building that day. Pops. Whitt. I thought briefly about Nigel Spader. He was a jerk, a jerk who had been partly responsible for my brother's incarceration. But I didn't want him dead. There were others—old partners, people I knew from the academy. Who was dead? Who'd done the shooting?

"...*in total lockdown, as you can see. The names of the two officers who were killed have not been released, but sources are saying a shootout inside the station records room resulted in*..."

The records room. I chanced another look at the screens from under the ball cap pulled low on my brow. The reporter was standing outside a barricaded command center, his face demonstrating his shock at the story he was reporting. Rage flickered in me. Regan Banks. Why had the reporter mentioned Regan Banks at all? Of course, the country was in terror at the idea that Regan was running around, ready to kill again. They were horrified at the police's apparent inability to capture him. But a shooting at the station—nothing about that brought Regan Banks and his crimes to mind. Banks was a rapist. A strangler. A stabber. A torturer of women. He was not someone who entered buildings crowded with cops and shot people.

But there was one possibility: the reporter had mentioned Regan Banks because someone had mentioned it to *him*. A press release from police headquarters might have specifically said the shooting was *not* linked to Regan Banks.

Which meant, of course, that it was.

Regan. Why would he break into the records department? Was it to kill the people working there? The records room was a dumping ground for the department's bad kids. I'd worked there plenty of times myself. The room was a weak access point for the building, now that I thought about it. If Regan just wanted to kill a cop, any cop, the records staff were sitting ducks.

Or had the records room *itself* been the target, and the staff there collateral? But what in the records room could Regan possibly—

I knew, even before I'd completed the thought.

I drained my drink and rose from my seat.

Two could play at that game.

CHAPTER 13

BEING ON THE lam is harder than you think. It takes a lot of setup. I'd been given the news of my brother's death only minutes after landing at Sydney Airport, coming home from my last case. From there I'd walked out, got a cab to my apartment, which was a crime scene, taped and locked up after Tox's showdown with Regan. I'd taken no time to survey the chaos, the smashed coffee table and the blood pool where my friend had fallen. Numb, working purely on cold, calm directions coming from somewhere deep in my subconscious, I'd packed a bag with some clothes, the cash that was lying around my home, my phone, and all my IDs. I'd locked the apartment, gone straight to a bank, and emptied my accounts of the few thousand dollars I had left after my brother's trial. This I'd put straight into the backpack.

I'd copied essential numbers from my phone, switched it off, dumped it, and got a taxi back to Kings Cross, where I'd spent many of my first cases in Sex Crimes taking statements from working girls abused by their pimps or clients. I found someone I knew and, on her recommendation, headed for a back-alley phone dealership where I purchased an untraceable sim card and handset. Standing in the alley under blinking LED lights strung over the battered doorway, I'd called my boss. In the small, dark storage room where I'd bought the phone, a Chinese family was sitting down to dinner surrounded by unopened boxes of phones in every shape, color, and size. The laptop that served as their television set was being pawed at by a toddler in pajamas. My brother's face was warped by the angle of the screen, the banner under his chin half hidden by Chinese subtitles.

Breaking news: GRK accused Samuel Jacob Blue dead after prison fight

I'd been so out of it, Pops was on the line for a long moment before I spoke. I barely remembered dialing.

"I can't let him get away with it," I'd said finally.

"Harry? Harry, listen." Pops had sounded puffed, the way I'd always known him, an old man trying to control a much younger, much angrier fighter in the ring. "I know this hurts. But don't do anything. I'm warning you. Don't—"

"I'm sorry," I'd said.

I'd never stopped being sorry. I was sorry for every night that I didn't come in, for every phone call I knew Whitt and Pops were making to my original, switched-off phone, leaving messages that would never be picked up, hoping to talk me down. I was sorry that I had not gone to Sam's funeral. That I had not called our mother. That I had not visited Tox in hospital. I regretted what I was about to do now, as I sat in the darkened car park of the Department of Family and Community Services, smoking a cigarette and watching the automatic back doors opening and closing as workers left for the night.

I'd committed plenty of crimes since I went underground. Theft. Fraud. Fare evasion. The crimes were getting worse.

Resisting arrest. Assaulting a police officer.

When there was one car in the parking lot, I stood and flicked open the blade on my pocketknife.

I was about to commit my worst crime yet.

CHAPTER 14

THE REMAINING CAR was a brand new Toyota Corolla, rose red and shining in the light of the moon. I snuck up to the side of it and punctured the front passenger-side tire with my blade before dashing behind a row of bushes.

Only minutes passed before a plump woman in a long denim skirt came wandering out of the back doors of the building, locking the glass door behind her and shouldering a heavy handbag. She was typical of the child-services women I'd traipsed after for most of my childhood in foster care. The long skirt was good for a little kid to hide behind, and the handbag, if squeezed, would crackle with the sound of lolly bags. I waited while the woman crossed the lot and slid into the car, dumping her handbag on the seat beside her with the crackle I'd expected. For a moment or two, she appreciated the new feel of the car, the strange slant toward the front left side. When she exited the vehicle and walked around the front of it, I crouched, ready.

"Oh, shit," she wailed, looking around the empty lot. *"Shiiiiiit!"*

I waited. She grabbed her phone and dialed while she popped the boot and went around the back. As she began speaking, I snuck forward and went for the driver's-side door.

"It's me," I heard her saying. "I've got a flat tire. Can you believe it? No, I'm just gonna change it myself. But stay on the line with me, will you? I'm all alone out here. I'll put you on speaker."

I squatted in the doorway as the car shifted all around me, the FACS woman unloading the tire from the boot. The keys were in her handbag on the passenger seat. I snuck away as the sound of another female voice came from the phone's speaker.

"Just call roadside service! There's a serial killer running around out there, haven't you heard?"

"Why do you think I called you, Mum?" The FACS woman sighed. "If you hear me scream, you'll know he's got me. Hang up and call the police."

"Maria, if I hear you scream, I'm gonna have a stroke!"

The key to the back door of the FACS building was the biggest and thickest on the key ring. I closed the door quietly behind me and stood in the dark, listening. It had been nearly two decades since I had been here, but it smelled the same. Baby powder and sterilized plastic toys, soiled nappies, and sour milk. In the hall were posters with happy, smiling teddy bears and elaborately illustrated dinosaurs giving advice on how to be brave if you're feeling scared. How nobody should ever make you keep a secret. How the police and your care workers were to be trusted above all others, how they would always keep you safe.

Bullshit.

I passed a wall displaying domestic-violence pamphlets and rounded the corner of a service desk.

Behind it I found the computer still turned on and gritted my teeth at the password system, until I found a Post-it note on a nearby shelf with the login details helpfully written out. I logged in and went straight to a record search. I realized how sweaty my hands were when I began to type in Regan's name.

The sound of my phone ringing in the silence made me yelp. I looked instinctively back toward the hall that led to the rear door, expecting to see Maria the FACS worker standing there, drawn by the noise. No one had the number of this phone. I'd never heard it ring, never bothered to turn the sound off. I assured myself it was some kind of mistake and rejected the call. But as I was switching the phone to silent, it rang again.

"Hello?" I answered.

"It's me," Regan said.

CHAPTER 15

IT WAS IMPOSSIBLE that it was him. This number was unlisted, untraceable, unobtainable by anyone but the man in Kings Cross who I'd bought it from.

It was impossible that he would call to speak to me, after everything he had done to me and my brother and my friends. Impossible that I would know it was him, having never heard his voice.

But I did know. It was him. Every cell in my body confirmed it. I couldn't speak. My hands shaking, tears already rising, I threw the phone from my ear as though it were red hot and scrabbled with it on the counter, fumbling for the button to hang up.

I was panting. Making faint whimpering sounds. Regan's name was on the computer screen in front of me, his voice still in my brain, searing itself into my memory.

It's me. I'm back. I've found you, Harry.

The phone rang again. The computer screen went dark, timed out. I caught a glimpse of my own horrified face, lips trembling.

"Get a grip, bitch," I snarled at my reflection.

I grabbed the phone and answered.

CHAPTER 16

I DIDN'T LET him speak this time. I hadn't known I had anything I wanted to say to Regan Banks, but apparently there was plenty. I squeezed the phone so that the plastic creaked with the pressure, and I spewed vitriol at him down the line. I called him every name I could think of, trying with each new sentence to make him understand how much I hated him, what a vile and worthless creature he was. Slowly I realized that the words were weak. Nothing I said came close to expressing what I felt. I gasped for breath at the end of my tirade, rounding it off in the only way I knew how.

"So *fuck you*," I said. "Fuck. You. Regan. Banks."

"Harriet," he said, after giving me time to regain my composure, which I failed to do, "that was some impressive speech."

I didn't answer. I wasn't going to take his bait, acknowledge a compliment from the man who had ruined my life. I woke the computer, hit the search button, and started running through the findings, the phone wedged between my ear and shoulder.

"Your brother called you Harry," Regan said. His voice was heavy, slow. Unflappable. "Can I call you that?"

"You better call me the Grim Reaper, arsehole," I said. "Because I'm going to find you, and I'm going to *end you*. I'm gonna put you in the *ground*. And I'm gonna come back to visit you every year on the anniversary just so I can tell your rotting, worm-riddled corpse to go *fuck* itself."

I glanced toward the doorway, hearing my own voice rising and being unable to stop it. I'd bitten the inside of my cheek in my fury. The hatred was intoxicating.

He was laughing softly. I felt something wild inside me throwing itself about inside its cage, yanking painfully hard on its chains.

"I believe you, Harry," Regan said. "There's not an instance here in your personnel file that makes me believe you're not a woman of your word."

My file. I'd been right. He'd killed two cops to get what he could on me. I ground my teeth, selected his record on the screen, and hit print.

"I see you've been questioned multiple times about revenge attacks on the men you've dealt with on the job," he said. I heard papers being shuffled. "You were questioned after a luxury Mercedes belonging to a man who was accused of molesting his teenage daughter was set on fire."

I remembered the case. The daughter had been too scared to testify. I recalled the warmth of the flames as I stood in the dark across the street. The man was trying to put out the fire with a blanket as his neighbors slowly emerged from their houses.

"Here's another one," he said. He was having fun with this now. "A couple of teenage boys accused of raping a girl at a high-school party. You did your best, but there was not enough evidence to convict. Three weeks after the charges were dropped, the two were found naked, bound to a tree on the school grounds. Neither would identify their attacker."

I gathered up the wad of paper on Regan and shoved it into my backpack. The phone was sweaty against my ear. I turned back into the hall and saw through the glass doors that the FACS woman was nearly finished securing the new tire on her car.

"Seems to me," Regan said, "you like your scores settled. You like vengeance. You see yourself as a powerful being, sometimes the only person powerful enough to bring down justice."

"Oh, please." I went to the glass door. "Give me a fucking break. Don't do this. Don't try to *relate* to me, Banks. I'm not going to be the one to finally understand you. We're not going to cry on each other's shoulders about our sucky lives and how we're justified in being violent because the world owes us something. You want to hold up a mirror to someone? Do it to yourself. If you have any sense at all, you're not going to like what you see." I grabbed the doorhandle. "You're a monster," I told him. "I am *nothing* like you."

I could almost see his smile, heard it lingering in his warm voice.

"You sure?" he asked.

I hung up, jabbing the phone screen too hard in my fury.

I jogged on my toes out into the car park, making a wide circle so that I didn't alert Maria to my presence. I snuck to the car, chucked her keys back into her bag, then took off into the night.

The night air was unseasonably cold. However, a part of me wondered whether the trembling in my bones was not from the cold but from Regan's final question. *You sure?*

The realization hit me, crushing, becoming heavier and heavier with every step.

I wasn't sure at all.

CHAPTER 17

WHITT KNEW HE was in dangerous territory, wandering along the line he'd drawn in the sand, from the moment he sat down at the bar beside her. The whole situation was seductive. In the corner, an old-style jukebox was playing Miles Davis, just the kind of soft, rolling jazz that usually loosened Whitt right up. The lights were low, and the place was almost exclusively theirs. Burgundy leather armrests on the bar top, Vada's deep-red hair glossy, shimmering. She smelled good. Expensive perfume. They ordered a couple of wines, and Whitt was drawn out of his fantasies when the bartender drained the end of a bottle into his glass. Whitt didn't say anything, but even from where he sat, he could see the sediment at the bottom of his glass. Disappointing.

"How are you coping?" Vada said without warning, fixing her eyes upon him. "You want to talk about it?"

"Uh. I'm not sure." Whitt was startled as he realized that his glass was already a quarter empty. "It's just hard not to blame myself for it all."

"Blame yourself for what?" she asked.

Whitt drew a deep breath, doubting he could possibly explain it. And then suddenly it was all flowing out of him, beginning right back at the start, when he'd sabotaged an investigation into a child's murder. Vada watched him, coaxed him gently with occasional questions. Whitt didn't speak to people like this. He didn't dump all his problems on strangers in bars without asking them a single question about themselves. But the words went on and on. He spoke about seeing his friend Tox Barnes near dead on a hospital stretcher. About having to tell Harriet her brother had been killed.

When the words finally dried up, Whitt felt his face had grown hot. He scratched the back of his neck, embarrassed.

"Edward," she began.

"Most people call me Whitt," he said, and cringed. It was Harriet who had branded him "Whitt," against his will. Vada was not "the new Harry" in his life. He had to remember that. "Sorry. I interrupted you."

"It's fine." She put a gentle hand on his. "Whitt, I feel like what you might be experiencing is something called survivor's guilt."

"Oh, I haven't survived anything," Whitt said. "It was Tox who got himself stabbed. And now Harry's out there, running around, putting herself right in harm's way. I've never been in the middle of the danger."

"Exactly," Vada said. "Your friend was stabbed. Harriet's

brother was killed. But what have you actually suffered? The guilt comes from *not* participating in the pain. Feeling like you haven't taken your share."

Whitt thought about it. He felt the stirrings of relief in his chest. Vada's hand was still on his.

"How are you sleeping?" she asked.

"Terribly."

"And you feel anxious?"

"All of the time."

She sat back, folded her arms, her theory confirmed. Whitt chanced a tiny smile and played with his wineglass.

"You need a support system." Vada returned the smile. "You've got me now. I may not be the most experienced detective around, but I'll be right by your side from now on."

"How new to the rank are you?"

"I just got the promotion a few weeks ago. I'm out of North Sydney metro. This will be my first major case."

"Oh, wow." His eyes widened. "That *is* new."

"I'm the rookie," she said. "But I feel like I'm going to be an asset to this case. I did a bachelor of psychology at the University of Sydney before I joined the force. My thesis was in personality disorders. I think the key to catching Regan will be to get into his head. Understand the way he thinks."

Whitt couldn't help but like her. Vada was sitting upright on her bar stool, gesturing with one hand as she explained the various aspects of her degree. She had a lot of confidence. Whitt tried to guess her age. Early thirties. She'd made detective long before he had. He was broken from his reverie by her hand, slipping a wineglass into his.

"Oh, no." He pushed the glass away. "I only ever have one. I'm not a drinker."

"Come on." Vada rubbed his arm. "You look like you need it. It's okay to take a break every now and then, Whitt. It's called self-care. You need to be kinder to yourself."

She excused herself and went to the bathroom. Whitt turned the glass on the bar before him. His first glass had been soured by sediment, the dregs of the bottle. A waste, really, of his one and only daily treat. He'd had a hard day. He deserved an extra reward. Perhaps he could have one more. *Only* one more. He didn't want to be rude.

He lifted the glass to his lips.

CHAPTER 18

I STOOD IN the queue at the soup truck, hoodie pulled up around my face, the gathered homeless men and women grinding the heels of their battered shoes into the dirt. With my face downcast and hands in my pockets, I was, I hoped, no more remarkable than the gaggle of down-on-their-luck prostitutes standing nearby—freelance girls banned from the glittering red-light district only streets away, park dwellers who stood on corners and took rides in dark cars. Kings Cross's parks were full of young women like these, girls who had come from the country to make their fortune and instead found themselves on a waiting list for over-crowded brothels.

The roller door on the side of the van went up, and a young man with lip piercings began handing out trays of food, no questions asked. A styrofoam cup of steaming brown soup topped with floating cubed pieces of ham and potato, two slices of toast, and a coffee. I took my tray and moved off toward a low sandstone wall in the middle of the park. A decent dinner that wouldn't eat into my already substantially diminished funds. I ate as I spread Regan's papers out before me, reading them for the third time.

Regan had my police personnel file. In it, details of every promotion, every infraction, every unusual occurrence during my eighteen years in the police. He had my medical records, my yearly physical results, and details of every case I'd ever worked on. He also had a duplicate of my Department of Community Services file, which the police had dragged out to question me about when I applied to join the force. I was a state-care baby. They'd been concerned about my time "in the system."

I didn't have nearly as much on Regan. But I had his childhood in my hands. It was clear to me that there had been something wrong with Regan from the moment he entered foster care.

At his first institution, a group home for children in Blacktown, a seven-year-old Regan Banks had set fire to a young girl's dress. The girl's injuries had been cataloged in the report—second- and third-degree burns to her legs and torso. The institution's manager had put the incident down to a young boy's curiosity, a mischievousness he didn't think warranted isolating the boy from the other children. Three weeks later, Regan had dropped a full can of house paint on a toddler's head, fracturing her cheekbone. He'd been shipped out immediately to a foster home.

When Regan was nine he'd been moved out of a foster home after a girl of similar age complained he'd choked her. When he was ten he'd been moved again after cutting all his foster mother's clothes to shreds with a pair of scissors.

He was not only violent, it seemed, but also manipulative. There were a host of mysterious nonviolent explanations for Regan being moved from one foster home to the next. One report read, "Foster mother reports Regan coming between her and husband, creating marital problems." Another read, "Regan's nighttime activities scaring foster parents." Yet another, "Foster father fears Regan's influence on young sons."

I flipped all the way through the reports to the back stack of pages, looking for the report that would explain why Regan had come into the care of the state in the first place. I'd seen my own Care Initiation Report, the accompanying photographs of my brother and me, our undernourished, bruised bodies, the filthy drug den where the police had found us. But in place of Regan's CIR, I found a scan of a yellow sheet of paper signed with a flourish by a Judge Edgar Boscke.

The report on Regan's parents was missing.

CHAPTER 19

MY PHONE RANG. Some of the girls in the posse of prostitutes nearby gave a whoop of excitement out of habit, thinking one of their own had been summoned for a job. I answered the call, trying to swallow the white-hot rage that immediately rose.

"Good evening, Harry," he said.

"Good evening, Mr. Sick Fuck," I sneered. "Set any little girls on fire today?"

"Not yet," he said. "How are you enjoying my files? Find anything surprising?"

"No." I gathered the files against my chest, as though he could see them. "Nothing at all. I knew from what you did to those women that you weren't right in the head. I just don't see where my brother comes into all this."

He didn't answer. My stomach dropped. I hadn't seen any mention of Sam in the paperwork, but his silence

made me feel as though I was missing something obvious. Regan had spent plenty of time in the suburbs of
Sydney, moving from house to house as foster parents
gave up on him. Had he been in care with my brother?
And if so—what did that mean? I realized I was bracing
for Regan to reveal what I'd dreaded all along: that I
had been wrong about Sam. That they had indeed killed
together. That my brother *was* the monster everyone
thought he was.

"Were you in care together?" I asked. "Did you meet
him then?"

"It's hard for me to talk about Sam," he said.

I was lost for words. Some homeless men were watching me from a picnic table nearby, one with his beard in
tiny braids.

"I'd rather talk about you," Regan said. "Did you note
that we were in the same Risk Category?"

I looked at the papers in my hands. Regan's RC across
his time in foster care had come down to 5 out of a possible 5. The assessment indicated how volatile he was—
how much of a threat he was to other children, how
many infractions he had in group homes, how many
homes had outright rejected him as too difficult to deal
with after only a short period. My score had been the
same.

"There's a big difference between what you did in foster care and what I did, Regan," I said.

"Is there?" I heard him shift. "You've got a total of
twelve assault reports. Fourteen failed short-term placements. Says here you stabbed one of your foster fathers
in the leg with a corkscrew."

"Does it mention he was climbing into my bed at the time?" I snapped.

"You were defending yourself." Regan's sarcasm was gentle. "All those times."

I said nothing. I wasn't going to let him feel like he knew me, even though he was right. Most of the time when I'd been violent as a kid, I'd been defending myself against predatory men or boys, or girls my age who wanted to steal my stuff or recruit me into a gang of bullies. But yes, some of the time I'd just plain had enough. I'd been angry. I'd picked on other kids. Caused trouble to get attention.

I'd been a bad kid. But didn't I deserve to be?

"What happened to your parents?" I shoved the papers into my backpack. "Your file was sealed when you were seven years old by a court order. They must have done something really bad to you. Is that why you go after girls? You got mummy issues?" I made a sooky baby voice as I stood and paced before the wall. *"Did Mummy spank her Reegsie-Weegsie too hard and give him a big nasty boo-boo?"*

He laughed. "I like it when you do that voice. Do it again."

"Go fuck yourself."

"I like the way your mouth pouts," he continued. "You've got good lips, Harry."

I stopped in my tracks. The prostitutes were looking over their shoulders at me, their cigarettes leaking smoke.

"Are you watching me?" I asked.

He didn't say a word.

CHAPTER 20

I WENT TO my bag, drew out my gun, and stuffed it into the pocket of my hoodie. But I was sloppy, too busy scanning the street for a tall man with a shaved head and a phone to his ear. One of the girls saw my gun and stepped out of the circle.

"Aww, shit!" She pointed at me. "We got a narco over here!"

She thought I was one of the undercover cops who regularly patrolled Kings Cross in hoodies and jeans, doing hand-to-hand buys and busting dealers, or simply hanging around, listening, trying to keep a finger on the pulse. The girls were all looking at me now.

"Hey, bitch!" one of them shouted. "We know you're five-o!"

"Fuck the po-lice!"

Regan said something in my ear. I couldn't hear it over

the group of girls all now pointing, shouting, throwing threats. A fire-engine siren started up at the nearby station.

"Get out of here, bitch." One girl shoved my shoulder. "Go back to the fucking pigpen, narco piece of shit."

"Hey!" I returned the shove, squeezing the phone to my ear. "Back the fuck up."

She pushed me again, encouraged by her friends, who now surrounded me. But they weren't important. *Regan was here.* These people were in danger. A phone rang nearby. I thought I heard it on the other end of the call. Had I heard the siren through the phone, too? Was he that close?

"Where are you?" I said into the phone. "Come on. Come out, you bastard."

"Look at them," Regan said. "These are the people you spend your life protecting."

A hand on my shoulder. I whirled around. The girl who'd noticed the gun, a round, pasty creature squeezed into a short skirt, knocked the phone from my hand and came at me again, her chest against mine.

"I said get moving, bitch!"

I bent and picked up the phone, used the distance between the ground and her face to build momentum in the swing. I punched her hard in the jaw, heard crunching teeth. She staggered backward, head wobbling. They all backed up.

"Anyone else?" I asked, setting my feet. "Anyone else wanna go?"

No one did. I swung my bag onto my back, was about to run when I spotted one of the girls from the circle. She was across the park, impossibly far away, arm in arm with a big man. A big man with a shaved head. They were just heading through the doorway of the female public toilet. I tried to run, but someone was holding the handle of my backpack.

"He's here!" I cried. "Let go of me!"

But they yanked me down onto the ground.

"I got her," the homeless man with the plaited beard said.

I didn't have time for this. I'd seen Regan, seen him with his next victim.

I rolled, tried to kick out from underneath him, but someone else had my legs.

I looked up through the forest of legs around me and saw the young man in the food truck trying to see what was happening over heads of the crowd. I did the only thing I could think of—I screamed as pathetically as I could.

"Help! Help! He's got me! Please!"

The young man burst out of the side of the truck, trying to shove his way toward me. The distraction was enough. I freed my hand from where it had been trapped under me, took the gun from my pocket, and fired it into the air above my head.

I was free, instantly, the crowd falling away in terror. I got up and bolted for the other side of the park, my phone still in one hand, my gun in the other. The door to the toilets seemed miles away, over pathways, behind bushes.

I ran for my life. For her life. The phone clattered from my fingers as I lifted the gun with both hands and skidded to a halt through the doorway.

"Police!" I roared. "Hands up!"

CHAPTER 21

THE DOOR TO the cubicle was open. His jeans were pooled around his boots, his white arse clenching as the tremors pulsed through him. The girl leaned out from her position in front of his crotch, shock in her eyes, standing and putting her hands up with a wail.

It was not him. Just some tradesman getting a blow job on his way home from work. He turned and I cringed. He, too, put his hands in the air.

"I'm sorry!" he gasped. "I'm sorry! Don't shoot!"

The gunshot had brought more people into the park. In the distance I could see the homeless men pointing in my direction. Another siren. I grabbed my phone from the ground and took off at a sprint across the road toward the hospital. I'd lose them in the underground car park, come up on the other side of the building, disappear into the winding streets and alleyways around Surry Hills. As I ran, I remembered the phone. The line was still open. I put the phone to my ear and listened, my face burning with embarrassment.

"Harry?" Regan was saying. "Are you there?"

"You've fucked with me for the last time," I promised him. Even to me, my voice sounded weak. Rattled.

"I'm sorry," he said. "I couldn't resist. I have considered following you around, watching you from afar, reporting your whereabouts back to you. It wouldn't be hard. You're not exactly the world's hardest person to track."

"Bullshit," I sneered.

"How do you think I got your number?" he asked. "I followed you to that back-alley shithole in Kings Cross where you got the burner phone."

I swallowed. "Did you hurt those people?" I thought of the family sitting around the boxes, watching their laptop screen. The toddler.

"I don't have to hurt people all the time to get what I want," he said.

"What do you want from me?" I asked. "What the fuck is all this? Why Sam? I need to understand."

"You'll understand one step at a time," he said. "I'm not going to follow you. *You're* going to follow *me*. And I think that, as you do, you'll learn to understand both me and yourself. Things are about to get very personal, Harry."

"I don't want to play stupid games. Just come at me," I snarled. "I'm ready. If you have any guts at all, you slimy little coward, you'll tell me where you are and we'll have at it."

"I'll tell you exactly where I am," he said. "When the time is right."

CHAPTER 22

WHITT WALKED QUICKLY toward the front steps of the station, his coat pulled tightly around him, partly to ward off the cold, partly as a shield against curious eyes. He knew that if he looked as terrible as he felt, there would be rumors. His past relationship with the drink was public knowledge across the police department. Everything was. He'd slipped off the wagon the night before.

Not so much slipped as leaped, arms out. Swan-dived. He had no memory of how the evening had ended, but that morning as he dressed gingerly, stopping now and then to be sick, evidence of his fall was all around him. Glass smashed in the kitchen. Vomit in the sink. The fridge hanging open, beeping in protest. Disarray. Whitt didn't *do* disarray. It was not him. Some other person had crept into his body after the second glass of wine and had refused to relinquish their hold.

Whitt gripped the handrail to pull himself up toward the front doors of the station.

Vada was at the doors waiting for him. He glared at her as he walked into the foyer.

"Je-sus." She strained to see his face over the collar of his coat. "Looks like someone pulled up rough!"

"I didn't *pull up rough*," Whitt said. "I haven't pulled up at all. I think I'm still drunk. Last night was . . . well, it was completely inappropriate, is what it was."

They came to the entrance to the conference rooms. Vada juggled her folders of case files, rummaged in her handbag. Whitt waited, then searched his own bag and found his security card.

"You're being too hard on yourself." Vada put a hand on his shoulder as they walked the immaculate halls. "You saw two of your colleagues killed. You deserved to let off some steam."

There it was again. That word. *Deserved*. Oh, the things Whitt could justify to himself with that single word. All he had to do was think about how tired he'd become since the Regan Banks case began, how stressed and afraid he was, and he'd leap happily back off the wagon again. The temptation for another drink now just to take the edge off his sickness was overwhelming. It would probably help him work better. Ease his stomach, his nerves, stave off the full force of the hangover at least until the afternoon.

They sat at a table. Whitt held his head in his hands as Vada took her notepad and pen from her bag, setting herself up for their first briefing. Whitt liked her meticulous placement of her pen by her paper, her mobile at her elbow, a chilled water bottle directly between them. She was organized, ambitious, direct. Maybe if she said what he'd done the night before was okay, then it was. Whitt reveled in the sensation of having a partner to reassure him. He wasn't alone. She was going to be here for him.

Whitt spread out his own papers, a map with a winding river cutting through forest and suburbia.

"This was where we last saw him," Whitt said, pointing at the map. "After Regan was wounded in a shooting beside the Georges River, we believe he swam ashore here at Sandy Point, on the opposite side of the bank. He made his way through the national park and stole a car from a service station here, on Heathcote Road. We don't know the extent of Regan's injuries, but the officer who winged him thinks he got him at least twice. And I think I can confirm that. I saw him shot."

Vada was scrawling notes.

"Obviously the wounds were not life-threatening," Whitt continued. "We lost him for a couple of days. He dumped the car in Baulkham Hills, and then five days later turned up in Lane Cove. He abducted Doctor Parish and her daughter Isobel. He forced them to drive to her plastic surgery clinic in Mosman, where she treated his wounds. Then he killed them both."

"My God," Vada said. She sat looking closely at the crime-scene photos of the Parish murders that Whitt had offered her.

"It was clever," Whitt said. "Hitting a plastic surgeon.

We had eyes on vets, hospitals, medical centers, doctors' offices. We'd even put word out around the organized-crime community that he might try to use one of their underground doctors."

"He's an intelligent man." Vada nodded.

"Since then, we've had facial recognition at train, bus, and ferry stations on the lookout for him. The airports, too. Regan's face and description is circulating around police, security, and customs departments daily."

"Did CCTV inside the command building confirm it was Regan who killed the officers yesterday? Karmichael and Fables?"

"There was no CCTV of the incident," Whitt said. "But I'm sure it was him. Ballistics will have to see what they can do with the bullets removed from the officers." Whitt squeezed his eyes shut. A vision of Karmichael's face had appeared before him, blood gushing from the hole in the young man's throat. Karmichael had been pushing for approval to take the detective's exam before he was caught goofing off in a nightclub.

"So what are the current leads?" Vada asked, lifting her eyes to his.

"There aren't any. We've talked to as many foster parents, prison guards, teachers, and institutional carers who ever dealt with Regan as we can. There are some we're still tracking down. This is what I was working on yesterday." Whitt handed Vada a sheaf of documents. "Interviews with his former cellmates and prison associates. We're still waiting on the psych report. It's taking some time, apparently. I'm pretty sure I know what it's going to say, though. We've checked out everyone he knew who's still incarcerated, and everyone who's been released since Regan got out, to see if they know where he might be hiding."

"What about his phone? Bank accounts? Where was he living after his incarceration? Where was he born?"

"When he got out of prison, he secured a ground-floor apartment in Newtown," Whitt said. "Not far from where Sam Blue was living. We checked it. It was stripped—but apparently he didn't own much anyway. His cards and phone have been dead since he went on the run. We don't know what he's using for money. The house his parents owned when he was born was an ordinary little working-class place in Greenacre. It's industrial estate now. There's a paper factory there. We've had eyes on the place for weeks, but there's been no sight of Regan there or any-where near it."

Vada smoothed out the papers before her, seemed to want to absorb the images and words she was seeing with her fingertips. She was quiet for a long time, but when she spoke, Whitt was taken aback by what she said.

"Can we talk about Harry?"

CHAPTER 23

"UH." WHITT SHRUGGED. "Sure. What do you want to know?"

"I want to know where she fits into all this," Vada said. "Harry's personnel file went missing from the records room—so we can assume that Regan is interested in her now. Interested enough to kill two innocent police officers just for a snippet of information on her."

"It's so awful." Whitt rubbed his weary eyes. "She doesn't deserve this."

"You sound almost like..." Vada began. But when Whitt looked at her, she blushed and turned away.

"Like what?"

"I don't know." She said. "Like her boyfriend or something. You care so deeply for her. You feel her pain."

"Of course I feel her pain," Whitt said. "She's my friend."

"You moved all the way across the country for her," Vada went on.

"I did," Whitt said. "She needed someone to be with her during her brother's trial."

"But you'd only worked one case with her," Vada said. "You'd only known her weeks. That's a huge commitment, isn't it? For someone you've just met?"

Whitt hadn't thought much about the time before Sam Blue's trial, his decision to leave everything in Perth and transfer to the New South Wales Police Force to be beside Harry when she needed him. The move had seemed to come very naturally, had seemed almost like his only option. The right thing to do. No one had ever asked him to explain it.

"I guess I came because it didn't seem like Harry had any other real friends," he said. Only in voicing the words did he realize their sad truth. Yes, he knew Harry to have acquaintances, and she was close in a father-daughter kind of way to their boss, Chief Trevor Morris. There was Tox Barnes, but Barnes was so aloof and weird as to fail to count as being "close" to anyone.

Whitt was about to go on, to defend Harry's friendlessness somehow by explaining that she took some time to be understood, that she was damaged and volatile but loyal and clever in equal measure. But before he could speak, his phone rang. It gave them both a start. A private number. He picked it up.

"Detective Edward Whittacker."

"Whitt," Harry said, "we need to talk."

CHAPTER 24

SHE SOUNDED DESPERATE. On edge. He stood, exhilaration bolting through him.

"Harry!"

He couldn't help it. He'd not heard from his partner since she disappeared from the airport. Vada stood with him, her face tense.

"Harry, where are you? Are you okay? Tell me where you are. I'll come get you."

"I'm in communication with Regan," she said, ignoring his pleas.

Whitt's mouth became dry. *"What?"*

"He's started calling me," Harry said. "He was behind the shooting at the station. He went to—"

"—to steal your records. We know."

"He has everything on me, and he says things are about to get *personal*." She paused, trying to catch her breath. "We have to think about what that means. He's got information on all my former partners. You. Pops. Everyone there is at risk. I think he's going to try to come after someone I love. You better warn my mother, I guess."

"Why is he doing this?" Whitt asked. "What's the connection between him and Sam?"

"I don't know." Whitt could almost hear the fury rising in her voice. "He's doing this because he's got spiders crawling around in his shriveled little brain. Whatever the reason he chose Sam, Sam's gone now. He's shifted his focus to me. You've got to be careful, Whitt."

"I will, I—"

"He knows where you live. He knows...He knows everything."

"Harry, you've got to come in. We can work with you. We can put a trace on his phone."

"You won't be able to trace his phone any more than you'll be able to trace mine."

"Come in," Whitt begged. "Harry, please. We'll help you find him."

There was a pause. The line went dead. Whitt looked at the disconnect screen on his phone and felt an urge to throw it across the room.

"Fuck!" he snapped. Placed the phone down carefully. "Sorry. Sorry."

"This is so irresponsible." Vada shook her head. Her face and neck were flushed. "So reckless." Whitt didn't answer. He didn't have the strength to defend Harry now. Regan Banks did indeed know where he lived and had attacked him there before. He wondered if he should get a hotel room. If he should request an officer be posted to watch over Tox Barnes in hospital.

They sank slowly into their seats, the weight of the work before them filling Whitt with dread.

"Don't lose heart," Vada said. "We will find him."

"Or he'll find one of us," Whitt answered.

CHAPTER 25

KNOCK, KNOCK.

Bonnie Risdale looked up from her computer screen toward the hallway at the sound, a politely quiet rapping at the front of the house. *Charity door knockers,* she thought. It was the curse of working from home. At least once a month they came with their little pamphlets, embarrassingly happy to see her, painful cheerfulness on youthful faces. She put the laptop aside when the knocking came again, walking to the door in her slippers.

He was not what she expected. He was alone, his big fist raised for further knocking, and his chiseled face didn't spread into a smile as she opened the door. He was handsome, if in a tired, worn way. The glasses were inexpensive, almost ill-fitted.

"Hello, Bonnie," he said.

The first sparkle of fear. A silly thing she pushed aside immediately. There was nothing to be scared of. A tall, handsome man was standing on her doorstep, framed by the red rosebushes on either side of her stoop. His hair was short, neat, combed to the side in an almost boyish way.

"Um, hi?"

"I'm Detective Sergeant Richard Winslow." He waved a badge, but her eyes didn't focus on the silver shape in the leather; she was too distracted by his other hand, reaching for her own. He gave a flicker of a smile, really not more than a twitch. "I'm sorry to bother you. I'm here making inquiries into a matter of some importance, and I think you can assist me."

The hand was cold. A second pulse of fear, higher this time, a tightening in her throat. Bonnie had dealt with the cops long ago. This man's language was the same. Stern. Unnecessarily official. She glanced at the empty street. Something wasn't right, but she couldn't place it. His shirt was wrinkled. His shoes didn't match his trousers. Shouldn't he be with a partner?

"Where's your—"

"May I come in?" He took a step up onto the stoop, smiling. "The matter relates to someone you've been involved with in the past. A Detective Harriet Blue?"

Bonnie felt the fear in full now, an invisible choking grip around her throat. She stepped back. Harry. God, it had been so long. There were days, few and far between, when Bonnie didn't think about what had happened to her at all. A swift, violent attack behind a bar in the city six years ago. Harriet Blue had been Bonnie's investigating officer. Bonnie remembered the small woman with the keen blue eyes, a straight-to-the-point hunter of details. Harry had interviewed Bonnie over and over. She'd caught the guy. Of course. The detective had never allowed Bonnie to feel any doubt that she would. She'd seemed the over-the-top type, the kind of fierce, obsessive cop who would pursue the case without eating, without sleeping. A cop who took it personally. She'd been abrasive in the beginning. Almost rude. But Bonnie had grown to love the woman who'd solved her case.

Bonnie had seen something about Harry and that serial killer running around Sydney in the news a week earlier. She turned into the hall, hardly focusing on the man on the doorstep, her mind whirling.

"Oh, God," Bonnie said, her hand at her throat. "Yes, come in, come in."

The man followed her into the kitchen. She went to the sink and filled herself a glass of water. The shock of it all—remembering the rape, remembering Harry and those dark days during the investigation and trial. Bonnie told herself that those memories were where the fear was coming from. But as she looked over at the stranger in her kitchen doorway, the fear refused to go away.

She swallowed painfully. "Is Harry okay? She's...she's on that serial-killer case, isn't she? Something about her brother."

"Tell me about Harry." The man dragged a stool out from under the marble bench, blocking the door. He sat on it and folded his thick arms.

Bonnie felt hot all over. Her heartbeat was thumping in her ears.

"Can we go outside?" Bonnie asked. "I just need some air."

The smile he'd flashed on the front doorstep was nowhere in sight now.

"I'm sorry," she said for some reason. "What did you say your name was again?"

He didn't answer. Just sat there, staring at her. Bonnie had backed into the corner of the kitchen.

"I'm..." She rubbed her arms. "I'm uncomfortable with this. I'd like to go outside. I'd like to—"

"Bonnie," he said.

Her hand fluttered of its own volition toward the knife block on the countertop, instinct taking over. He watched coldly as she grabbed the biggest handle.

"Bonnie," Regan said, "don't be stupid."

CHAPTER 26

WHITT FOUND CHIEF MORRIS just outside his office, standing with a group of beat cops consulting a map. They seemed to be planning a cordon around Kings Cross. He tapped Pops on the shoulder.

"Harry's just called me," he said.

A bigger man whirled around, and Whitt stepped back to allow Deputy Commissioner Woods more space.

"Harriet Blue is in contact with you?" Woods seemed almost insulted. "I assume you told Detective Blue to surrender herself into custody immediately?"

Whitt explained the phone call, deciding to look at Chief Morris instead.

"She's rerouting her line," Whitt said. "I checked with IT before I came up here. Her calls are basically untraceable. She bounces her signal around a bunch of towers and networks, and doesn't stay on the line long enough for the signal to settle and for us to get a location. It's likely that's what Regan is doing to her."

"Regan Banks is calling Harriet Blue?" Woods sneered. "This is exactly as I was saying, Morris."

"It was the first time she's called me," Whitt said nervously. "She may call again."

"All right." Woods filled his barrel chest with air. "This is good news. You'll divert your line to the command-center phone, Detective Whittacker. I'll be taking all calls from Detective Blue from now on."

"I'm not sure that's the smartest idea," Pops intervened. "If Harry calls and it's not Whitt, she'll hang up and she won't call back. We need to keep the communication channels open. If Regan's talking to her, and she's talking to us, we have some chance of anticipating where Regan will be."

"No, thanks, Morris." Woods put his palm out toward Whitt, waiting for him to give up his phone. "I'm not relying on a rogue detective to intermediate communications with a killer. Give it to me, Whittacker."

Whitt gripped the phone by his side. "I think I agree with Chief Morris."

"I don't give a rat's arse who you *agree with*, Detective," Woods said quietly. "I'm giving you a direct order to hand over that phone so that your line can be diverted to—"

"It's my personal phone," Whitt said carefully. "I don't have to surrender it to you. Not without Harriet having been charged with a crime. Not without you having secured a warrant to listen to my personal calls. Legally, I don't have to do it, sir."

Deputy Commissioner Woods dropped his hand and straightened. Whitt thought he heard the dull click of the bigger man's teeth locking together in his powerful jaws. Pops clapped Whitt on the shoulder, hoping, it seemed, to signal the end of the conversation. He went back to the map, and Whitt tried to turn away, but Woods stopped him in his tracks.

"Whittacker," he said, "I read about you when they asked me to take over the investigation. You're Harry's former partner. From Perth, was it? Yes, I had a brief look at some of your past cases."

Whitt felt sweat breaking out at his temples. People were staring.

"The men who killed that little girl," Woods said. "The ones whose release from prison you practically handed to them on a platter. Have they killed again since they've been free?"

Whitt couldn't answer. He felt suddenly, unbearably sick.

"I don't suppose anyone knows," Woods said. "A kid goes missing. They never find her. Could have been your guys. No one's watching them anymore. You made sure of that."

Whitt walked toward the men's room. He barely made it through the door before the sickness came.

CHAPTER 27

LOOK AT THEM. These are the people you spend your life protecting.

I looked, keeping my head low, pretending to browse through a magazine in a convenience store while I filled my hoodie pockets with snacks for the road. Something told me I was going to be on the move soon. Regan was going to kill again. He was going to make things "personal." There weren't many people who meant anything to me anymore, not now that Sam was dead. I'd felt better after warning Whitt. But I needed to think laterally. Be smart. He might murder someone I cared about, or he might murder someone in front of me. Make the experience "personal" that way. Any of the people around me could be a target. Even the strangers. He'd said he wouldn't follow me, but Regan was a liar, a manipulator.

The shopkeeper was oblivious to my stealing. He stood

with a hand on the glass countertop, chatting to a young mother who was buying lottery tickets.

Mention of my name on the television in the corner of the store distracted me. The people at the counter had turned to watch. I pulled my cap lower as a picture of me flashed on the screen beside a video of my chief, Pops, reading from a piece of paper. He looked old, tired. A man I recognized as Deputy Police Commissioner Joseph Woods stood at the corner of the screen, looking bored. Was he on the case now? I knew little about Woods other than that he was powerful, a hard-arse who had influence and knew how to use it.

"She is an official missing person," Pops said. "We want to stress that the reward for her whereabouts does not imply any wrongdoing on Detective Blue's part. The reward is being offered by an individual, not the New South Wales Police."

One hundred thousand dollars for Harriet Blue's location, the banner read.

"Oh, no." I covered my eyes. I knew instantly that he had done this himself. Pops didn't care about money. He wanted me home. I was his pet project. His lost cause. He would never stop believing in me. He would not let me ruin my career, my life, by taking revenge on Regan.

"This'll flush her out," the shopkeeper commented as I shoved the magazine back onto the rack. "A hundred grand? Shit, everyone in the city will be lookin' for that woman."

Great, I thought. *Just what I need.*

My phone buzzed. A text from an unidentified number. Regan. It was a single word.

Nowra.

A suburb two hours' drive south of Sydney. What? Why was Regan so far away? I held the phone and tried to breathe. Who did I know in Nowra? How would I even get there?

I walked out of the convenience store and turned right, almost ran to the entrance of the train station I knew was on the corner. Stealing a car now in the broad light of day would be too risky. I snuck through the wheelchair-access ticket gate and headed down the stairs.

CHAPTER 28

DEPUTY COMMISSIONER WOODS didn't look up at the sound of a rapping on the door to his office. He'd spent a half an hour adjusting the space to suit his needs, removing Chief Morris's many distractions—the framed photographs on his desk, a misshapen clay mug a child had obviously made him, framed awards on the walls. Woods hadn't needed to take Morris's office as a command space—there were plenty of other offices in the building that would have suited his needs—but sometimes it was necessary to send a message to the gawkers outside the glass doors. Big Joe Woods was here, and he was cleaning house. Already a detective had stood up to him in front of the task force. He'd nail Whittacker in time, as publicly and ceremoniously as he had dumped all Morris's knickknacks in a box in the corner.

The officer at the door approached when Woods failed to look up from his paperwork.

"Deputy Commissioner," the officer said, "I'm Detective Inspector Nigel Spader. I wanted to take a minute to welcome you to the building, and to the Regan Banks task force."

Woods didn't answer. He liked making them uncomfortable, the underlings. It was far more effective than shouting at them, hurling things across the bullpen, as he'd seen other men of his standing do. His approach was psychologically deeper, less predictable. He felt the detective on the other side of his desk squirm.

"I really think we've wasted enough precious time in this investigation so far," Nigel said.

"Oh?" Woods straightened in his chair, finally looked up.

Nigel lowered his voice.

"If I may speak candidly, sir. I really feel that the Banks investigation has been tragically mishandled, and I'm looking forward to having someone with your experience and skill in command."

Woods felt a smile attempt to creep to the surface of his face. He pursed his lips, denying it, and gestured for Nigel to shut the door.

"I followed the Elizabeth Crassbord case closely," Nigel said, seating himself rigidly in the chair before the commissioner. "Very admirable work, sir."

"Spader, was it? Oh, yes. You were part of the original Georges River Killer task force, weren't you?" Woods said, glancing at his personnel pages. "You've been here since the beginning."

"Yes, sir," Nigel said. "And I think that yesterday's incident in the records room was indicative of the disaster this case has been from the beginning. A double murder in our own station?" Nigel shook his head, puffed out his cheeks. "We have a lot of reputation-saving to do. And I think that, when you bring down Regan Banks—and I know you will, sir—part of the cleanup is going to have to be making Harriet Blue accountable for her role in this."

"Now, there's an unusual standpoint." Woods plucked at his lower lip. "Everyone around here seems to be an avid Blue fan."

"Not me." Nigel sneered. "Harriet Blue is a disgrace to the badge, sir. She has physically assaulted me on a number of occasions. Well, I mean to say, she's attempted to. Unsuccessfully. I was there when her brother was arrested, and I can tell you straight up that rumors of his innocence are unfounded."

"Hmm." Woods appreciated the man before him. This Nigel Spader was a gifted arse-kisser, but Woods never tired of having arse-kissers around him in his work. They were good for morale. He tapped Spader's name on the list before him as though trying to make a decision and watched as the detective's eyes sparkled with excitement.

"Detective Spader, I like your style. I'm going to charge you with being my right-hand man in this investigation," Woods said. "Of course, on paper, my second-in-command has to be Chief Superintendent Trevor Morris. But, I think you and I will both agree, Morris has really fucked the dog on this one."

Nigel laughed, perhaps too hard.

"There will be a lot of recognition for the team involved in bringing Banks down," Woods said. "I've been offered six-figure publishing deals in the past for stories of my cases. I've been asked to appear on television, to act as a consultant on crime dramas. But I'm a reserved kind of man."

"Of course." Nigel nodded.

"I've always seen opportunities for promotion on the job as a far more valuable form of reward," Woods said. "And believe me when I say that, if you stick by my side on this, there will be such opportunities on offer. I guarantee it."

Nigel stood and straightened his shirt, trying to contain the excitement obviously flickering in the corners of his mouth. As he went to the door and grasped the handle, he paused, trying to decide whether to say what he said next.

"Deputy Commissioner." Nigel took a deep breath. "Before I go, I'd just like to add . . . Many of us experience family difficulties, and these can impact on our standing in the job. But I want you to know that I believe, and many of us believe, that your daughter's situation in no way reflects on your character as a police officer."

Woods had been just about to set pen to paper, and now the man sat frozen, staring at the pages before him, unseeing.

"Your daughter is—"

"That'll be all, Detective," Woods snapped.

CHAPTER 29

EYES EVERYWHERE. On my face, my hands, my bag as I tossed it onto the seat and slid over to the window, adjusting my cap to hide my eyes. The thousand-yard stare of commuters, tourists going down the coast to see the wineries, farmlands, national parks. I sat tensed as the train pulled away from the station, waiting for someone to recognize me. No one did. Catching my reflection in the window beside me, I could see why. I was a tired, thinned version of the Harriet Blue in the photos the television kept running. My hair was stringy, unwashed. I rubbed my eyes and watched the city shrink into suburbia. The train was warm. I eased out of my hoodie. The movement of the carriage lulled me into an uneasy sleep.

When I dreamed, I saw my brother. One of the many

times we were reunited at the Department of Community Services offices after months apart. He'd been waiting for me, looking oddly guilty, his fingers stained yellow from cigarette smoke and his shirt reeking of it as I pulled him close to me. He'd started smoking very young. It always annoyed the DOCS workers. A pair of them sat at the table near him in the wide, sterile meeting room, murals of kittens and bunnies painted on the walls. They were going to brief us on where we were headed next. Promises of longer-term placements, stability that would never come. They watched, bemused, as we hugged, knowing neither of us were huggers.

"You're getting taller," I told Sam, patting his greasy teenage hair.

"No, you're getting shorter."

"A dual placement," I'd almost squealed, punching him in the shoulder with glee. "This is awesome! God, I've missed you so much! How'd you swing this? Your last family kick you out? What'd you do?"

"Nothing." His face flushed with guilt. "Nothing. It was all good. I just...I asked to be removed. I needed a change of scene, you know. That's all."

I knew when my brother was lying to me. He'd never been very good at it. I remembered taking his arm, trying to meet his eyes.

"Bullshit," I said. "There's something wrong. What happened? Some fucking pedo try to mess with you? Did you tell your caseworker?"

"Nah, nah, Harry, it's fine." He rubbed my shoulder.

"Then what?"

"Nothing."

"What?"

"Look, I met this guy." His voice was low. Uncertain. "Another kid."

"In the same family?"

"No, another foster kid. His placement was near mine."

"What happened? What'd he do?"

"Nothing. I don't know. He was just..." Sam shrugged. Wouldn't look at me. "Just a bit intense for me, I guess. A bit weird. I got creeped out. That's all."

"What, the guy have a crush on you or something?" I snorted.

"Would you two stop messing around so we can get started over here?" one of the DOCS ladies said. "Harriet? Harriet. Harriet Blue..."

"Harriet Blue."

I was snapped out of the dream by the sound of my own name. My neck was sore from leaning my head against the train window at an odd angle. The voice was coming from the headphones of a young Asian man in a red cap sitting across the aisle from me, watching a news clip on an iPad. The volume was so high, I could hear every word of the broadcast.

"Much of their work, police say, has been chasing down false sightings of Banks across the state, some coming from as far away as Broken Hill. And while the public wonders where Banks will strike next, the search continues for Detective Harriet Blue, sister of..."

I'd been paying so much attention to the flashes of the program I could see on the screen, I didn't notice the man with the iPad looking right at me.

I nodded acknowledgment, trying to play it cool, but as I did, the screen in his hands was filled with a picture of me.

He looked at the screen.

Then at me.

CHAPTER 30

I GRABBED MY bag and walked quickly down the aisle toward the stairs. The other passengers seemed to sense my urgency and glanced up. When I turned, I saw the red-cap guy with the iPad following me. I cursed and sped up.

"Hey! Hey!" he called. "Excuse me? Miss?"

I ignored him, taking the steep stairs to the carriage entry two at a time. There were people here on the long benches beside the doors. I held on to the handrail, trying not to panic. It was one guy. I could fend him off.

"Excuse me?" he said as he got to the bottom of the stairs.

"Dude, leave me alone," I whispered.

"Is this you?" He lifted the iPad, pointed to the picture of my face, the video paused on the screen. "Are you Harriet Blue?"

At the mention of my name, and his excited tone,

more people looked up. I shielded my eyes, gritted my teeth, and snarled at the guy.

"No, I'm not. I just look like her. Now, *fuck off*."

"Is everything okay?" A man in a business suit standing by the doors turned toward us. "Is he bothering you?"

"Yes, he is." I tried to push toward the doors to the next carriage. The train lurched, and I grabbed an over-hanging handle.

"She's Harriet Blue," Red Cap said. "The one they're looking for. The police."

A woman nearby slipped her phone out of her pocket. She watched me, looking guilty, as she dialed what was obviously emergency services. I went for the doors again, grabbing the handle and wrenching them open. The gang-way between the two carriages was unsteady, the train thumping on the tracks. I shoved my way into the next carriage, but the two men were right behind me now.

The businessman grabbed my arm. "I think you really ought to come with me."

"Hey, I saw her first," Red Cap snapped. "You just want that reward."

"Someone get a guard!"

I shrugged my arm out of the man's grip and pushed him in the chest. He grabbed again, but the guy in the cap was with me now, a sudden ally, shoving him against the doors. Red Cap went for the strap of my backpack and I grabbed his fingers, wrenching them backward, causing him to drop to his knees. I put a boot into his side and hurled him to the ground. The train was slow-ing, rocking on the tracks. People were getting up from their seats, alarmed by the scuffle.

"Someone call the police!" the businessman yelled down the length of the carriage.

I turned and ran down the aisle, leaving the men to fight it out. "Hey, stop her!"

I burst through the doors to the next carriage and looked out the side doors, watching the rocks and gravel between the tracks rushing past me through the glass. I couldn't wait for the train to slow much more. Through the murky windows to the carriage I had come from, I could see a small crowd gathering in the aisle, pointing, passing on the story to one another. A couple more people grabbed their phones. In minutes, the police would be waiting for me at the next station.

I hit the emergency exit button and pried the automatic doors apart. The jump seemed higher, somehow, now that the doors were open.

I had no choice. I closed my eyes and jumped.

CHAPTER 31

WHITT TOOK THE on-ramp to the highway at break-
neck speed, causing Vada to grab onto the handle above
her window.

"Edward, you're driving like a crazy person. Can you
slow down? I know Nowra is a long way off, but I want
to get there in one piece."

"Sorry. Sorry. I'm just anxious to get to the crime
scene. You know." He pushed his hair back and tried to
ease off the accelerator.

Not even twenty-four hours, he told himself. The pre-
vious evening at 5:30 p.m., he'd relapsed, broken his
promise to himself that he would not succumb to drugs
or alcohol again. Now he'd stumbled once more, talking
himself into taking a couple of Dexedrine to wipe out
the hangover and get him moving. The great weight that
Deputy Commissioner Woods's words had dumped on

him had made it difficult to breathe. But as he'd cracked open the plastic baggie of pills he'd stolen from the evidence room, he'd felt the weight lifting. He deserved this, needed to take care of himself, needed to be kinder to himself. How else was he supposed to keep going? Regan was escalating—so Whitt needed to escalate, too, if only for one day.

By 5:30 p.m., he promised himself, he'd be sober again—mentally strong, emotionally impenetrable, ready to continue the hunt. The Dexedrine pills would have worn off. He would be clean. *Everybody gets a day off once in a while, right?* he thought. As long as Vada didn't notice he was high, he would be fine.

"Edward, slow down!"

"Sorry."

"What did the report say, exactly?" Vada gripped her seat belt. She'd had to take a phone call when Whitt was called up to the emergency briefing in the command center.

"It just said a woman's body was found in a house," Whitt said. "A big man, broad shoulders, white, late thirties, not a regular from the neighborhood was spotted leaving the scene in her car late morning. We haven't found the car yet, but we've got an alert out on it. They're erecting roadblocks, but they may be too late. Local cops say the scene was only discovered because a neighbor got curious about the door standing open for a couple of hours."

"What did they say about the scene?"

"Only that it was bad." Whitt glanced at his partner. Heard the tremor in his own voice. "Really bad."

CHAPTER 32

CUTS AND SCRAPES: I could deal with them.

The leap from the train had done something funny to the tendons in my elbow: nothing major.

The shoulder of my backpack had torn and it now hung crooked: that was all right; I'd get used to it.

But I'd left my hoodie on the train, and it was cold.

Goddamnit, I hate the cold.

The cold makes me unreasonably angry. Pair it with a strong wind, and I become near homicidal. I gathered my arms around myself and trudged, head down, through the rough, battered landscape north of Nowra station, keeping an eye on the highway in the distance. I decided overland on the isolated roads stretching between farms was the safest route. There was no need to make a spectacle of myself.

It started to rain. I ground my teeth, my fingers gripping my shoulder straps so tight, the tough fabric bit into my palms.

Regan called. I didn't answer. I was not his plaything. He didn't get to just call me up to whisper sadistic sweet nothings whenever he pleased. I was going to be this man's killer. His righteous punisher. It was all I could do not to throw the phone into the dry grass of a nearby field.

After an hour of walking through farmland, my phone rang again. I had a brief moment of weakness and answered.

"Hello, shit biscuit," I said.

"Hello, Harry," Regan said. "What are you doing?"

"Thinking about breaking all of your fingers." I sniffed and wiped my eyes on the back of my wrist. "With a hammer."

"Sounds windy where you are," he said. "Don't catch a cold, Harry."

"Thanks, I'll try not to. I hope you're snuggled up somewhere warm. Perhaps very close to a crackling fire, enjoying a steaming mug of gasoline."

He laughed.

"What are you going to show me in Nowra?" I asked. It was quiet where he was. I pictured him sitting in a car somewhere, maybe watching me. I glanced toward the highway. A big truck lumbering slowly along. "Are we going to take a tour of your childhood family getaways? *This is where baby Regan had his first swim. This is where teenage Regan disemboweled a cat.*"

"I do have something to show you," he said. "But it's not about me. It's about you."

"Well, I've got some sad news for you," I said. "I have no personal relationship with Nowra whatsoever. I think I might have had some excellent fish and chips here once. That's about it."

"We'll see," he said. I could hear the smile in his voice. I hesitated before I asked the next question, wondering if I would give the monster on the other end of the line any ideas.

"Does my mother live in Nowra?" I didn't want to tempt Regan to go after my mother, though something told me that he knew she wasn't the most important person in my life. My mother had taken $40,000 to do a magazine interview on Sam and me only days after his death in prison. She'd posed for pictures by the ocean, staring out at the waves, a single tear sliding down her drug-ravaged face. All my life, she'd been uninterested, unreliable, a junkie who popped up in my life periodically, looking for money or shelter and nothing more. I had no idea where she lived.

He gave no answer.

"Are you there?"

"I'm here," he said. "I'm thinking. Trying to analyze your tone. Do you want your mother to die, Harry?"

"No."

"No one would be surprised if you did," he said. "I've been looking at the reports on her in your records. On your fourteenth birthday, she turned up three hours late to the McDonald's where you were scheduled to meet. She was high as a kite, on the nod. She had a black eye, and some thug who wouldn't give his full name was with her. She stayed for fifteen minutes, then tried to punch a

DOCS worker when he accused her of being under the influence."

"I've tried to punch a few DOCS workers in my life," I reasoned.

"She did a good job of looking torn up about Sam," Regan said. "Did she even know anything about him?"

"Sure," I lied. "In fact, I think they were pretty close at times." I was hoping to bait Regan into talking about Sam, maybe revealing something about their relationship.

"Sam grew out of *nothing,* Harry," Regan continued. "That something so complex and beautiful and unique could grow out of the beginning that Sam had is just amazing to me. He was full of potential. He refused to be what he should have been, another scavenger. It took a long time to understand what Sam did to me." He struggled with the words. "*For* me."

"You loved him, didn't you?" I said. "You were in love with him. What did he do to you?"

Regan hung up on me. I saw a house through the trees before me, a car sitting in the gravel driveway. The lights in the house were off. With regret stinging in my chest, I approached the house and made a cautious circuit, looking for the best way in. I needed a car and a new jacket, and my food supplies were running low. I hated to steal from innocent people, but right now I had no choice.

As I shoved open a window left ajar at the side of the house, my phone beeped. The text message contained an address.

CHAPTER 33

KILLERS HAVE THEIR RITUALS. I'd seen them before. A murderer comes into a house and cuts the phone lines, turns all the family photos face-down, maybe tours the victim's underwear drawer as he waits for her to return home from work. He draws the curtains. Sits on the living-room sofa in the dark and gets a feel for the house. The ritual allows him to do the deed, move on, and do it again. A well-practiced routine.

Cops have their murder rituals, too. They unfurl blue-and-white crime-scene tape and festoon the house and surrounds like they're preparing for a party. They close off the street. Set up roadblocks. Video the cars, the people emerging curiously from their houses. They go in, turn the lights on, push back the blinds.

I crouched in the bush behind the house that had been identified in Regan's text and watched the goings-on, well acquainted with everything that was happening and the reasons for it. The Nowra police had the scene but seemed to be holding off processing it, waiting for someone. They'd set up a perimeter around the house and gathered in a neighbor's yard to smoke and chat under umbrellas. When a car arrived and two detectives got out, the most senior officer broke away and approached, hand out in greeting.

Whitt and a woman I didn't recognize walked up and identified themselves before being led into the scene.

I gasped at Whitt's appearance. Usually immaculate, his shirt and hair were rumpled and his eyes were restless, like he was afraid. He walked with a sharp, determined stride. It hurt to be so near to my friend and unable to go to him. I envisioned myself walking up from the back of the house and simply presenting myself to the Nowra officers. But I knew if I did that, I would be shoved in a patrol car and driven right back to Sydney, perhaps without even getting to talk to Whitt.

I had to know whose life Regan had taken. What he had done. I decided to wait.

The hours passed by with agonizing slowness. I knelt in the bush, huddling against a tree.

It was dark when three officers wheeled a stretcher from the house. I stood, resisting the urge to move closer. There was no telling who was dead—but the figure in the body bag looked to be female. Whitt and the red-haired woman he was with followed the body out, got into their car, and disappeared. If it was possible, Whitt looked even more awful as he walked toward the car, his head down, eyes searching the ground. I thought I saw a thin sheen of sweat on his brow, despite the chill.

As night fell, the Forensics staff left the house one at a time, taking with them their various envelopes and packages of samples. The lights flicked off. A pair of officers took up stations in the concrete driveway, visible from where I hid. The smoke from their cigarettes curled in the orange light of a streetlamp. As I expected, one of them walked away from his position at the front of the house and did a lap of the property every fifteen minutes, squinting into the dark, shining a torch over the bushes, causing me to duck. I counted off three of these patrol rounds and then crept forward into the yard to see what Regan had left for me.

CHAPTER 34

I WAS SHAKING as I entered the house. I paused in front of the crime-scene tape over the back doorway to the kitchen, telling myself I needed to be calm before I carried on, but already I could see signs of what had happened here. Everything had been left as the Forensics team found it, the debris on the floor scattered around stainless-steel steppers the officers had placed to pre-serve any footprints. I trod carefully across the little platforms, a tourist taking a path through a macabre art installation.

The fight had begun here.

There was no blood yet. But the dish rack had been upended from beside the sink, spilling a couple of plates and glasses and some cutlery on the floor. There had been a knife in the fray. A big one, probably taken from the block that sat overturned on the counter. A stab mark punctured the center of the fridge door, another wayward slash carving a chunk out of the doorframe that led into the living room.

I looked about desperately for some sign of who lived here, but there were no pictures on the walls. They had probably been taken down for release to the media.

I walked carefully into the living room.

His victim had been hit here for the first time. Blood on the wall, a small spray, then a handprint on the carpet as she tried to get up. He'd stabbed her, maybe a couple of times, just to take the wind out of her. Upward drip marks, flung up on the ceiling as the knife went up and came down. Drag marks in the hall. He'd taken her into the bedroom. I followed the invisible couple writhing and fighting before me, saw him shove her onto the bed. He'd made the effort to get her up onto the mattress, to do it there, to leave the sheets twisted and torn. So that I would know. So that we would all know what she had endured.

It hadn't ended there. I followed the blood trail back into the living room. Had she gotten up? Tried to get away? Or had he simply let her go, let her run for her life for a few paces, the cat playing with the half-chewed mouse? The television was lying flat on the carpet. Cushions off the couch. Broken glass. The blood pools here were bigger, the drag marks shorter and thicker. A big handprint on the wall, the fingers spread wide. A man's hand.

There was no sound. Only my own frantic breathing, the air struggling to squeeze through my throat into my lungs. I crouched in the doorway and closed my eyes.

In my terror, the questions kept coming. Who was this person, and how was she connected to me? How was this "personal"? Was this what Regan had planned for me when we finally came together? Was he giving me a preview of my suffering, or an insight into the last moments of the girls he had already taken?

I went back into the kitchen, retching, almost collapsing at the sink. I ran the tap and put a hand under the cold fount, washed my face. There was a collection of unopened pieces of mail on the counter, laid out for photography by the Forensics specialist. I looked at the nearest one in the dim light from the streetlamps outside.

Bonnie Risdale.

One of my old case victims.

CHAPTER 35

THE MEMORIES CROWDED forward, bursting into my mind through an unlocked door. Bonnie Risdale, a slim brunette, a website designer or tech-support person, I recalled—something with computers. Nerdy, sweet, naive. I'd been assigned to her case and called up to the Prince of Wales Hospital, where I'd found her sitting upright in a clean hospital bed looking broken and empty, the way victims often do. I'd sat by her bed and taken down her story.

She'd been out on a girls' night with a group of friends, got drunk, misinterpreted where they were all supposed to meet when she got back from the bathroom. She'd gone looking for her group in an alleyway behind the back of the nightclub, having spotted the taillights of a car through one of the windows. She'd thought it was a taxi waiting for her.

The man raped two other women before I caught him. I didn't kill him. But I'd wanted to.

Bonnie Risdale. A woman who had come into my life wanting justice. I'd assured her that I would find her at-tacker. And I had. I'd told her then that she was safe. That nothing like this was ever going to happen to her again.

She'd obviously believed me, moved here to Nowra, set up this beautiful home, lived in some semblance of the peace and happiness she'd known before her ordeal.

But I'd been wrong.

Because of me, she'd once again known the horror of a man's hand clasping her wrist, dragging her down. She'd once again fought in vain as he tore at her clothes. I found myself crouching in the corner of her kitchen, grip-ping my skull, trying to drive out the images. My brain pounded with the terrible truth.

This happened because of me.

Because of me. Because of me. Because of me.

When Regan called, I answered immediately. But I couldn't speak.

"She told me some things about you," he said.

I gripped the phone, shaking, my eyes wide in the dark kitchen.

"She said you'd been fierce." Regan's voice was soft. Al-most apologetic. "That's a good word for you, I think. *Fierce*. Bonnie told me that almost as soon as she met you, Harry, she felt like she was going to be taken care of. That meeting you was like taking an outstretched hand. You rescued her from the fear."

"You bastard," I managed. My voice was weak. "You . . . *evil* . . . bastard."

"I told her that I'd chosen her because she was one of

your cases," Regan said. "So she knew, at the end, that what I did was all because of you."

I couldn't breathe. All I could do was hold on to the phone.

"I'm not trying to torture you," Regan said. "I'm trying to unravel you. Do you understand?"

I bit my lips.

"Harry, you being a cop—it doesn't mean anything."

"Yes, it does," I breathed.

"Liar," Regan said. "Listen to yourself. You're lying. Deep down, you know it. Being a cop is just a protective layer of bullshit you wrap around yourself. When I killed Bonnie, I undid all your good work on her case. I destroyed one person's positive memories of you. They're gone now. It was that easy to erase the goodness you'd done in the world, Harry."

Outside, one of the patrol officers was making another round. I didn't know if he'd notice my presence. In the moment, I didn't care. I almost wanted to be discovered. To give up, to be taken away from the awful voice on the phone.

"If I wanted to, I could go on and on undoing all your hard work as a police officer, Harry," Regan said. "One at a time, I could cross off every woman, man, and child you'd acted the hero for. And then where would you be, without your shiny badge and your big gun? Without the gratitude of your case victims?"

"I—"

"What Sam did for me," Regan whispered, "is he got me thrown in prison."

"He *what*?"

"I was angry at first. But in there, I was stripped of all my bullshit layers. All the lies fell away. I was exposed, bare bones. I found out what's inside me, Harry. What's at my core. It sounds bad, but actually it was incredibly freeing. It was wonderful. I realized what Sam did to me was one of the greatest, most loving gifts he could ever have given. He released the real me, the one that had always been there. I've always been bad. Bad at the core. And every time I was beaten in prison, every time someone abused me, stomped on me, spat on me, used me for their perverted games, another layer came off."

I held tight to the phone.

"When I left prison, I was raw. Real. Reborn. It was a beautiful thing. I was so grateful. I thought the only way I could pay Sam back would be to do the same for him," Regan said. "I took his perfect little life. Sam had as many lies wrapped around him as you do. He was all bundled up in them. You should have seen him walking around the university campus. Mr. Design Professor. I wanted to take his pride. I wanted to strip away his friends, his colleagues, his stupid little apartment. Show him how free he could be. Give him back the gift."

I squeezed my eyes shut, fighting to hear every last word but unable to bear much more.

"The process had just begun," Regan said. "I wanted to take everything from Sam. I'd never planned for him to be arrested. He was going to join me on a journey, an unraveling. I had a girl waiting for him. It was going to be the two of us, discovering the real him together."

"Jesus Christ." I covered my eyes.

"I never got that chance," Regan continued. He sounded

on the verge of tears. Mourning my brother. "When Sam died, everything that he could have been died with him."

"You..." I struggled to find words.

"I thought it was all over," Regan said. "But then I discovered you."

"Don't do this," I said. "Don't play this game. Just confront me. Don't take any more innocent lives."

"I can't," he said. "Because when I look you in the eyes for the first time, Harry, I want you to really see me. And I want you to have the gift of seeing yourself."

"Tell me where you are, and I'll see whatever you fucking want me to," I snarled. "I'll gaze appreciatively upon all the magnificent horseshit you've constructed before I feed your internal organs to you one at a time."

"We can't meet yet," Regan said. "When we do, it's going to be in a place that helps you understand me, but along the way, you've got to learn to understand yourself."

"You've got a mystical fucking journey of self-discovery all worked out for me," I said. "But you're going to be sorely disappointed at the end when you realize that Sam was a good person, and so am I."

"We're going to find out," Regan said. "I think you'll be surprised. You're not a good cop, Harry. I took that away from you. I'm going to keep taking layers away, and we're going to see what we find inside."

CHAPTER 36

WHITT STOOD BEFORE the mirrors in the men's room, bracing himself against the sink. Reflected in the glass, he saw a failure. A man in pieces, wandering along the precipice of a gigantic fall. He took the packet of Dexedrines from his back pocket and threw a couple more into his mouth. Yes, he was over the twenty-four-hour mark of his relapse. But he needed to keep his blood pumping and mind sharp for as long as Regan was on his rampage. He would have to postpone his comedown at least until they had Banks cornered. Whitt could handle his addiction until then. He'd got sober before. It might even be easier this time.

He shouldered open the door to the bathroom and walked back down the hospital corridor to where Vada was waiting at the elevators, having escorted Bonnie Risdale's body to the morgue.

The press on the footpath outside the Shoalhaven District Memorial Hospital emergency room didn't recognize Vada, but they recognized Whitt.

Vada turned away from the cameras, slipping unnoticed toward the back of the crowd as the group assembled in front of Whitt, blocking his path.

"Detective Whittacker! Can you tell us about the woman killed in Nowra today? Is it him? Is Regan Banks in our community?"

"I can't comment on the case." He tried to wave them off. "Investigations are pending."

"Who was she?" The calls were defiant. The huddle of reporters followed him down the footpath. "Did Banks know her? Did Detective Blue know her? Do people have cause to be worried?"

"Members of the public are advised to take all usual precautions," Whitt said. It was an old line he rattled off with ease, but not something he easily believed. He was worried for the women here. For the men, too, for that matter. Regan was out there, probably moving on to his next target.

"Was Harry with Regan Banks?" someone asked. Whitt felt a chill run up his spine. "Are they in league with each other?"

"Who asked that?" Whitt snapped, looking at the faces around him, the polished countenances of the nation's news media. No one answered. He spied Vada looking guilty for having left him to the hounds.

"Detective Harriet Blue is trying to find Regan Banks," Whitt said, his face flushing as he felt himself wandering out of the bounds of professional conduct with the media. "She's a good police officer. She's on our side, and if any of you want to argue with me about it, you can put the cameras down and I'll meet you in the fucking parking lot."

There was a ripple of surprise from the crowd. The journalists turned to face one another, glancing uncomfortably at Whitt's clenched fists. The Chief Superintendent from the Nowra police station exited the emergency-room doors, and most of the gaggle ran toward him, microphones at the ready.

Vada came to Whitt's side as he walked to their car.

"You were really willing to punch a news journalist to defend Harry's honor?" she asked.

"It was never going to come to that." Whitt yanked open the door of the car. "At least I said something."

"You're right. I should have stood by you." Vada slid into the car beside him. "I'm really camera shy. I get all tongue-tied."

Whitt's phone rang. He picked it up quickly when he saw the unidentified number. "Harry?"

"She was one of mine," Harry said.

CHAPTER 37

IT WAS WINDY where she was. Her voice was un-characteristically shaky, and she sounded like she was walking fast. "Bonnie Risdale was a victim in one of my Sex Crimes cases a few years ago."

"Shit," Whitt seethed. "Are you here? Are you in town? Did he call you?"

"He called me. And I went to the crime scene."

"She *what*?" Vada's eyes widened. In the closeness of the car, she could hear Harry's voice over Whitt's phone. He frowned at her.

"How did you get into the crime scene?" Whitt asked. "Are you still there?"

"Whitt, I need you to look back through all my case files, get a readout of every victim I've ever dealt with. Prioritize the women—we know he likes them young.

Brunettes, late teens to midtwenties. But, Whitt, I have children whose cases I've handled. Maybe their mothers... We have to warn these people."

"I'm on it," Whitt said. He wanted to reach through the phone and grab Harry, draw her to safety.

"Do you have any guesses at all about who Regan might go after next?"

"I have no idea," Harry said. "I don't know why he chose Bonnie. I've had hundreds of cases. He would have had the pick of any of the dozens of young women living in and around Sydney. Why risk traveling two hours south to kill her?"

"He didn't say?"

"He said when we come together, it's going to be somewhere that shows me the real him."

"What does that mean?"

"I don't know," Harry said. "He's probably got a fucking dungeon somewhere full of victims he wants to show me. He wants me to see what he can do. He's called me a few times, rambling bullshit about discovering the real me."

"Did he tell you why he's doing this?"

"He said Sam was responsible for him going to prison," Harry said.

"Oh, my God."

"I don't know anything about that." She struggled for words. "Sam never told me anything about it. I think the two of them knew each other. Regan said he'd come after Sam when he left prison, and now he's after me. He said that this is my unraveling," Harry said. "He's pulling me apart. He's trying to undo everything good I've ever done in this life, Whitt. He's trying to hold a mirror up to me, to show me that deep down inside, we're the same."

"You're not the same, Harry. You're—"

"I'm a good person," she insisted. "I'm a good cop, and a good human being. Maybe I do bad things sometimes, and I enjoy doing bad things, and I wasn't the best kid in the world. And no, I don't have many friends. I'm weird. People don't like me . . ."

She didn't seem to be able to go on. The only sound on the line between them was the howling of the wind.

"His plan is not going to work," Harry said.

Whitt thought she sounded deeply uncertain.

CHAPTER 38

I RAN, THE BACKPACK thumping on my shoulders, back through the forest behind Bonnie's house and along a dark, deserted road. The rain had come and gone, but my shoes were soon drenched. Between the clouds, the moon was occasionally revealed, lighting the fields.

After the call with Regan, I'd turned on Bonnie's home computer and logged into the police database. It was an old computer, her laptop having been removed to search for evidence about her death. My case-file list was twenty-seven pages long. I'd only had the nerve to stay for the printing of twenty pages, watching through the front windows of the house as one of the officers guarding the crime scene patrolled the rear of the house again. I packed my bag and left through the back door, knowing that within seconds of my login to the police personnel system, an alert would have been raised at headquarters in Sydney. They would have tracked my login to Bonnie's IP address, known I was there. I called Whitt briefly at the edge of the forest and then sprinted into the dark.

As I'd predicted, after ten minutes of jogging down the road, I heard the sound of sirens on the wind. It would have been too risky to return to the car I'd stolen and drive it to the crime scene. Looking back across the darkened plains, I saw a police helicopter hovering over the distant highway, a searchlight picking through the trees. I'd once again lifted my criminal game. I'd lied. I'd hurt people. I'd stolen a car. Now I had breached an active crime scene and tampered with evidence.

I tried to call Pops, but someone unfamiliar answered his phone. A man with a hard, unyielding voice. I didn't speak. He sounded superior and annoyed, though he couldn't possibly have known who I was. I wondered if this was Deputy Commissioner Woods. If he had taken Chief Morris's phone in case I called.

When I was sure I was out of the search zone, I turned south and started heading back toward the highway in a long, slow curve. Luminescent eyes appeared now and then in the fields, watching me go by, some low and slanted—foxes or feral cats—others higher and wider—kangaroos. As the hours passed, I kept up a good pace, my body warmed by the adrenaline still pumping through my system from the walk through the crime scene. I turned Regan's words over and over in my mind.

When Sam died, everything that he could have been died with him.

…everything that he could have been…

Regan thought he was going to teach me something. Help me to find the real Harry buried deep inside, the thing he'd seen in Sam that he'd never had a chance to bring out. Regan thought I was a monster like him, and that by killing my case victims, undoing my good work, he was going to help me embrace what I truly was.

I was sure he didn't know it, but Regan was right on the money.

I'd always wondered if, deep down inside, there was a different me waiting to come out. A Harry that relished causing pain to others. I did get a kick out of hurting people sometimes. I'd only ever turned my violence on the rapists and molesters and abusers I encountered in my work…

But no, even that wasn't exactly true, was it? I had, in my time, hurt innocent people. I'd punched Nigel Spader a couple of times, just because he pissed me off. And now and then when a witness connected to a case stood in my way, I got rough before I put in the time and the effort to get what I wanted gently and professionally. I was known for it.

I felt a terror creeping over me as I trudged through the wet, windy night. If Regan did scratch deep enough below my surface, what would he find?

CHAPTER 39

WHEN I FINALLY reached the highway again, I was exhausted. I rested on the roadside barrier beneath the huge concrete base of a streetlight and tried to focus. Whether or not I was evil was a question that could be answered later. For now, there were lives in my hands. I stood and pulled the papers I'd printed at Bonnie Risdale's house out of my backpack and held them in the light.

I had no addresses or telephone numbers, but I did have names and case-file numbers, beginning and concluding dates of investigations. To get any more would have risked staying logged in to the police database too long. I looked helplessly at the hundreds of names, memories rising here and there. A teenager groped by a man in a darkened cinema. A young boy abused by his uncle. A middle-aged woman assaulted at work after-hours. Rain was falling on the paper in my hands. Losing hope, I was about to pack the pages back into my bag when I stopped at the sight of a name.

Melina Tredwell.

That had been a bad one. She had been confronted by her attacker in a public toilet in a park on a rainy night just like the one swirling around me now. I'd thought she'd been mad to go into the cold, isolated building at all, but she'd been driving home from Sydney and had a long journey ahead of her. Melina had lived in Narooma, another two hours south of Nowra.

Melina had been brunette, a striking beauty. I remembered complaining to Pops about the three- or four-hour drives I'd had to make down to Narooma to interview her. The incident had happened in my jurisdiction, and I'd not wanted to conduct probably trauma-inducing interviews with Melina over the phone.

Regan wanted my victims. And for some reason, he'd chosen Bonnie Risdale, two hours south of Sydney. The highways between Sydney and Nowra would be littered with roadblocks now, looking for the tall, broad-shouldered killer. Would he risk doubling back to the city, or would Regan continue south? Was Melina his next victim?

I started jogging down the shadowy grass strip along the side of the highway, ducking into the dark every time a car rushed by, trying to convince myself I was on the right path. For all I knew, there were dozens of my old victims in the area, and I had no guarantee that after all this time, Melina still lived in Narooma.

I had no firm idea of where Regan would strike next. But I had to try to find him before he killed again.

CHAPTER 40

POPS STOOD AT the side of the briefing room, barely listening to Deputy Commissioner Woods's pep talk to the command-center team about the Bonnie Risdale murder. Detective Nigel Spader sat in the front row of the briefing, nodding thoughtfully at Woods's points. While Woods entertained the gathered officers, Pops was discreetly sending a text on a mobile he had borrowed from the communications office. He directed his one and only text to Edward Whittacker.

Chief Morris here. Old number is now operational under DC Woods. Give this one to Harry if she calls.

Whitt came back almost instantly.

She called last night. Will give it to her if I hear again.

Woods had pictures of the Risdale house on the projector in front of a captivated crew, walking them through the scene like he'd been there himself.

"So now we'll get protection on all Harry's past Sex Crimes victims," Pops broke in, just as Woods was wrapping up. "We'll send out a call to every woman on her case list and warn them."

Woods dropped the hand that had been gesturing to the screen and looked at the chief.

"No, we won't," Woods said with an icy smile. "We'll instead direct the substantial manpower that rather naive course of action would take toward bringing in Harriet Blue. If Blue is indeed Regan's target, then having her in custody will draw the killer to us."

"Wherever we direct our physical resources, we will at least warn the people on the list," Pops said. "A phone call. *Anything.*"

The officers in the room were looking worriedly from one superior to another. Nigel Spader looked incensed.

Woods sighed. "No, we won't," he said again. "Warning past victims of crime that they might be in danger will only cause mass panic. Harriet Blue's connection to Bonnie Risdale will come out in the media in time. It'll leak. It always does. Harry's past case victims can get the information from there. I will not be held responsible for traumatizing possibly hundreds of—"

"An excellent initiative." Pops gave an exaggerated nod. "Let the media keep everyone calm. They're good at that."

The Deputy Commissioner's neck was turning purple.

A couple of the officers nearby sniggered. The big man turned his burning gaze on them, then stormed through the door beside Pops. The chief followed as expected, letting the glass door swing shut behind him.

"I've allowed you to remain as second-in-charge on the Banks case," Woods began through clenched teeth. "I've even resisted reporting you on clear breaches of protocol that I've observed in your past handling of this investigation. Don't make me put you on a suspension."

"You couldn't put me on suspension if you tried," Pops said. "You'd send the paperwork over to admin and they'd think it was a joke and bin it."

"If you don't agree with my approach to this case, the professional thing to do would be to stand aside, Morris, not to put up roadblocks. But you're not going to do that, are you? Because you know I'll have Banks in custody by the end of the week."

"What, with your ingenious honeypot scheme?" Pops snorted. He'd glanced over Woods's notes while he stood waiting for the briefing to begin. Woods planned to have Harriet's mother, Julia, give a public appeal for her daughter to make contact with police. During the televised appeal, carefully scripted by the police, Julia would "accidentally" make it clear exactly where she was staying. Woods obviously hoped that if Regan was going after the people Harriet loved, he wouldn't be able to resist the bait of her only remaining family member.

"This is why you won't solve this case, Joe," Pops said. "If you knew Harriet at all, you'd know using her mother as bait isn't going to work. You're not interested in the people involved here. You're only interested in yourself."

"I'm taking you off this case completely, Morris." Woods straightened. "I'll send an officer to let you know what your reassignment is."

"Call it what you want." Pops shrugged. "Consulting.

Observing. Reassigned. Active or suspended—I'm not leaving the building and I'm not giving up my hold on this case, not while my best detectives are still out there."

Woods scoffed.

"You need to warn all the victims by phone, and put physical protection on every victim Harry's dealt with from Nowra to Melbourne," Pops said. "There's a reason Banks went so far south. He's out in the wilds now. He won't double back to the city to go after Harry's mother, who everyone knows means very little to her. If we can find out where Regan's going, we can—"

"I don't have time for this." Woods held his hands up. "You're rogue, mate. Your 'best detectives' are rogue, and you've joined them. This will be the case that ends your career."

"My career is the last thing I'm thinking about, you power-hungry prick."

It was rare that Trevor Morris lost his cool. But he was losing it now. He drew a deep breath, glanced through the windows of the briefing room, where a dozen or more officers were pretending not to watch.

"You won't find Regan Banks before Harry does," Morris said. "You're too blind. Too stupid. I just hope she finds him before he strikes again." He turned to leave.

"You've just expressed your support for the intentions of an officer who's going to commit premeditated murder," Woods began to shout as Pops walked away. "I'm suspending you, and I'm putting that in the report!"

Put this in the report, Pops thought as he raised his middle finger and headed for the elevators.

CHAPTER 41

I HITCHHIKED A whole bunch as a teenager. It was often the fastest way to get out of town if I had decided to leave a foster home to go find my brother. I realized pretty quickly that the first place my foster family would look for me was at the local bus and train stations. They figured I wasn't stupid enough to get in a car with a stranger. I was plenty stupid enough.

A couple of cars passed me in the first five minutes after I rejoined the highway heading south. It was still raining and had been all night while I tried to sleep, fighting off memories of Bonnie Risdale's house. Not wanting to risk showing my face at a hotel in the area, I'd lain down in the loading dock behind a closed service station, using my backpack as a pillow. I'd awakened with the expected aches and pains, renewed sensation in the bumps and scrapes I'd acquired jumping from the train.

I wasn't sure the passing vehicles could see me in the deluge, but I pressed on along the highway with my thumb out for a couple of kilometers. When a big truck put on his brakes after I'd spent fifteen minutes in the rain, I felt my whole body swell with relief and gratitude. I climbed up into the warm, dark cabin and threw my backpack on the floor.

"You must be nuts, walkin' around in this," the driver said. He was a typical trucker. Potbellied, weary eyes under a dusty cap. I took the offered towel and wiped my face and neck as he started the vehicle back up.

"As close as you can get to Narooma, if you don't mind," I said.

He merely shrugged. Ten minutes passed in which I watched the trucker's face out of the corner of my eye to see if he was taking any interest in my body or belongings. I casually passed my backpack into the tiny room behind our seat that held cupboards and a small camp bed for the long haul, and took a quick glance around the darkened space for knives, rope, guns, anything threatening. There was nothing but chip packets, empty pie trays, beer cans and water bottles, piles of clothes reeking of sweat, and a change of boots. On the floor, I spied a map of Alice Springs. If this guy had come from as far away as Alice, maybe he was out of the loop with the search for Regan and me. In any case, I kept my cap low and my profile to the man in the driver's seat.

I thought about Regan. He'd said he'd always been bad, that the "layers" he'd built up over his life had just been hiding something evil lurking at his core. Had he been born bad, or had whatever his parents did to him when he was seven years old broken him? Changed the very essence of his being? Turned him dark? After Regan had entered the foster-care system, a judge had decided that the public should never know what had happened to him and had sealed the file. It was a move I'd heard of before. A report that detailed my friend Tox Barnes's involvement in the accidental killing of a mother and child had been sealed to protect him from ever suffering persecution in his adult life over the incident. I knew that some of the worst child-abuse cases were sealed so that the victims would never have to fear a friend or loved one discovering what had happened to them. They could begin anew, leave their secret traumas locked safely away. If Regan's parents had made him the monster that he really was, whatever they had done must have been horrendous.

In time, I tried to shut Regan out of my mind. When the trucker failed to offer any attempt at conversation, I fell asleep.

It was a big mistake.

CHAPTER 42

MY SLEEP WAS DEEP, enveloping, an almost choking fog of fatigue. I came out of it slowly, struggling to recall where I was. The truck. The grinding of the engine and the clunking of gears as the driver slowed. I sat up and rubbed my face, panic prickling up my legs and into my stomach.

"What is it? Why are we stopping?"

"Dunno," the driver said, shrugging. "Accident, maybe."

I looked out the windows. Two rows of cars slowly creeping forward toward blue and red flashing lights. Patrol cars. A roadblock. Across the highway, the opposite lanes were halted as well, two officers wandering from car to car, flashing torches in on the occupants.

"Oh, shit." I scrambled up in my seat. "Oh, *shit!*"

"What?"

"This isn't good." I searched the roadside. Nothing but rock walls on either side of us, a section of the highway cut into a hill. "I've got to get out of here." I had thought I was well out of the search zone, but the roadblocks seemed to have been extended farther than I'd guessed.

"What's the matter? It's just an accident or somethin'."

"It's not an accident; it's a fucking roadblock." I tried to soften my tone. "I . . . It's for me."

"The police are looking for *you*?" He examined me, squinting. "Why the hell would they be doin' that?"

"My husband is a local cop," I stammered. "The chief of police. We've been having problems. It's been getting worse. He hit me a couple of times. Choked me once. I . . . I got scared. I ran. He said he was going to kill me."

The truck driver looked out the windows at the headlights on the highway, the patrol cars flashing. The gap between us and the car in front had widened. A car horn sounded from behind as the queue failed to move. There were only three cars ahead of us. A cop in a rain jacket waving. While the truck driver weighed my story, I glimpsed the name embroidered on his fluorescent shirt.

"Stan," I pleaded, "don't send me back to him. Please. I just need some time to get to my mother's place in Narooma. From there I'll reassess things. Maybe try to get him some counseling."

"Jesus." Stan took off his cap, ran a hand over his bald head. "This ain't right."

"Please help me," I begged. "Just . . . Just . . ."

Stan watched a big officer in a peaked cap wandering

between the cars, heading toward us. My fictional abusive husband, the chief? I watched Stan struggle with his loyalties. He sighed and gave in.

"Get back there." He turned and pointed. "They'll probably search the cabin, but there's a panel in the floor. I don't know if you'll even fit."

I leaped over the seat and ripped up the carpet where he pointed, spying a stainless-steel hatch. Beneath the hatch was a low shelf where a person could lean while they toyed with the engine parts. The noise of the engine was deafening from here. I squeezed into the space on my knees and doubled over, pulling my head down with my hands. The panel slid over me, and I waited in the noise and heat.

The truck clunked as the passenger door above me was opened. I breathed into the gap between my knees, squeezed my eyes shut. It seemed an eternity before the truck seemed to be moving again, asphalt whizzing by. I pushed up with my back and slipped awkwardly out of the compartment, shoving away the stiff carpet flap and breathing the warm air of the cabin. It looked like the cops had indeed searched the sleeping cabin. The tiny closet door was open, and the camp-bed cover had been tossed over.

"Thank you." I crawled into my seat. "Thank you so much, Stan. I can't—"

"Cut the thank-yous," Stan snapped. "I'm not in the business of hiding runaways from the cops. I don't care who your husband is or what he's done—I need this job."

"I understand." I nodded.

"I'll drop you at the next exit. From there, you're on your own, lady."

"I got it." I grabbed my bag. "No problem."

I settled deep into my seat, hugging the bag to my chest. My limbs were throbbing. I tried to tell myself I had overcome the riskiest part of my journey. I'd had a run of bad luck, but the real danger would come when I found Regan. It would be smooth sailing for a while, surely, if I just kept my head down and carried on.

I was wrong.

CHAPTER 43

THEY STOPPED ON the slope of the highway leading down to the bridge, a long row of red lights before them in the steadily easing rain. Whitt had tried to sleep in the cramped, cigarette-scented motel room in Nowra but found the Dexies had drowned out all fatigue. He'd considered waking Vada at 3 a.m. to discuss possible theories about Regan's whereabouts, but through the curtain he could see her sleeping form in the bed, the gentle curve of her hip, her eyes closed softly in perfect slumber. It had seemed a shame to wake her. Sitting in the car beside her now, he found himself thinking of that image, remembering the envy he'd felt at her calm.

At each end of the long bridge was a two-man team of patrol officers searching vehicles, waving the occasional car past after looking through the windows and searching in the boot. Across the region, several roadblocks shut down highways and major roads, making it almost impossible to get in or out of Nowra by car without being searched. Vada and Whitt spoke to the two officers closest to them. Young men, a couple of beat cops probably brought in for overtime to cover the roadblocks. The officers seemed to resent Whitt and Vada checking up on them, sniffing and looking Whitt over as he stood by them.

"We're Boyraville jurisdiction," one of them said. Whitt read his name badge: Christopher Dunner. "Boss has already been in to check on us." Their gaze was skeptical. Whitt wondered if they could tell he was high.

"Command wants things tightened up at the roadblocks," Whitt said. "Regan Banks somehow managed to get through every roadblock on the way into Nowra and back out again. That includes blocks on side roads."

"The guy's a fucking ghost." The other officer, Constable John Swartout, spat on the asphalt. "He must have a police radio. He's listening to the channels, hearing about the setup."

"Or someone just wasn't vigilant enough and he got through." Whitt shrugged. "It's cold out here. It's boring. One lazy check is all it takes."

The two officers glared at him. He walked to the edge of the bridge and looked over at the river rushing beneath, the vertigo giving him a cold rush. When he was sure that Vada wasn't watching, he popped two Dexedrines. His partner had begun walking toward the other end of the bridge to see the officers stopping cars traveling in the opposite direction.

When Whitt's phone rang, it was Chief Morris again.

Heat flooded his face, as though the man was calling because he could somehow see what he had just done.

"Whitt," Pops said, "we're going to have to go a bit off-reservation here." Chief Morris explained the confrontation with Deputy Commissioner Woods, the planned trap for Regan using Harriet's mother as bait. "His priorities are all wrong," Pops said. "He's interested in making a spectacle of this case rather than actually solving it. I've got a small team of officers here working on the side for me. Can I count on you?"

"Of course," Whitt said. "What's your plan?"

"I'm trying to figure out how Regan got into the records room," Pops said. "I'm worried he's got eyes in here. I don't know how he knew where the records room was or that it was a soft spot in the security. I've got officers going back through CCTV in the months prior to the shooting to see if Regan was ever in the building."

"Surely he never entered the building himself," Whitt said. "He must have hacked the CCTV and looked around, found a route in. Maybe he bribed an ex-officer."

"I don't know." Pops sighed. "Thousands of people come through this building every day. Perps. Witnesses. Security. Lawyers. Specialists. He might have stolen a swipe card. Worn a disguise. If he came in, we will find the footage. I'm also going to start cold-calling all the victims Harry has ever dealt with and warning them."

"Oh, Jesus," Whitt exhaled. "Really?"

"It'll panic them. Sure," Pops said gravely. "But if Regan can't get ahold of one victim because she panicked and went to stay at a hotel for a few days, it'll be worth it."

"They'll take your badge if you go too far," Whitt warned.

"I hope they try," Pops said.

Whitt watched the dark outline of some creature approach the riverbank below him, a slithering shadow.

"Do we need to be worried about Tox?" Whitt asked. "He's a sitting target in that hospital. Regan might have said he's going after Harry's past victims, but we can't trust his word. He could mix things up at any time. He'd want to finish Tox off, wouldn't he? The man tried to kill him."

"I asked for police protection for his hospital room and didn't get any, of course," Pops said. "I'm calling in a guy I know, an ex-cop. He works in private security now. He'll watch the room. You take care of yourself. It's public knowledge you and Harry worked together."

Whitt watched as a car approached the two officers patrolling the end of the bridge nearest to him. His head felt hot and heavy, his temples throbbing. Whitt rubbed his face, tried to get a grip. He'd taken too much Dex. He was on edge.

"Regan told Harry he's planning to meet her somewhere," Whitt said, trying to focus. "Somewhere that she'll be able to see the real him. That must be why he came out of the city." He explained Harry's call, trying to keep his voice even, resisting the urge to spew his words out in a jittering stream. He told Pops about Regan's claim that Sam was responsible for his incarceration.

"But where would Regan go?" Pops wondered aloud. "Where do you get to see the real Regan Banks? And when is this meeting supposed to take place?"

"I suppose when he's finished unraveling her. When she sees what he wants her to see."

"The guy's a nutjob," Pops said. "We need to look closer at him. Figure out where he'll be and when."

Whitt didn't answer. He forgot all about the call when he heard the shouting at the roadblock behind him.

CHAPTER 44

THE OFFICER STUMBLED back in shock from the window of the car, a young woman in a tight red dress exiting the vehicle on pretty velvet heels.

"He's just a friend, Christopher!" she said.

"You said you were going to church!" said Officer Dunner, incredulous. "That's how you dress for church? Who is that guy? Hey, you! Get out of the car!"

Whitt felt his heartbeat double and then double again. A strange desire prickled in him, a taste for violence. His world was shaking with the impact of his steps. The two officers were approaching the car as the male driver exited, his hands up in surrender.

"We're just friends." The young man's voice was high-pitched with panic. "We just went to lunch, that's all."

"Who the fuck are you?" Dunner was crowding the

young driver, his partner Swartout coming along for the ride, blocking the man up against the vehicle. "That's my girlfriend, mate. That's my car! What are you doing in *my* car with *my* girlfriend?"

Whitt watched as the girlfriend grabbed at Dunner's uniform, trying to stop him barging the driver with his chest as the other officer came around him, hindering his escape.

"Tommy, Tommy, get back in the car," the girl cried. "Christopher, leave him alone!"

Before Whitt could intervene, the two officers had taken hold of the driver and were shoving him into the hood of the car.

"Hey! Hey! Hey!" Whitt pulled out his badge. "What happened? You two officers, stand down!"

"I didn't do anything!" the young driver protested. "I didn't know she had a boyfriend! Ow! Shit! Let go of me! This is assault!"

"We got this under control, Detective." Swartout came toward Whitt, a hand up, trying to back him off. "It's just a lovers' tiff. Nothing serious. Why don't you go check the roadblock at end of the bridge? We can handle this."

"Officer, I told you to stand down." Whitt stepped around Swartout. The young woman was still trying to drag Christopher off the driver, until he shoved her, almost knocking her to the ground.

"Let him go!" Whitt snarled.

The blow was sudden. Even Whitt didn't see it coming. As he balled his fist, his arm seemed to move of its own volition, as though a trigger had been pulled. He swung up and punched Officer Dunner in the side of the face, a direct hit in the right temple, splitting the flesh. Whitt hadn't punched anyone in more than a decade. It seemed to be over before it began, the shock reverberating through his arm, shoulder, chest. The officer flopped onto the concrete, releasing the young man he'd pinned to the bonnet of the car.

Whitt's head spun. He staggered back, blinking. There had been no decision to hit the officer, no warning from inside his brain. He'd just done it, like a muscle reflex.

He saw Vada running toward him from the end of the bridge. His heart was hammering. Officer Swartout was coming forward. Vada got between them.

The young couple from the car were clutching each other, staring in horror at the collapsed officer on the ground.

Vada had Whitt's arm and was leading him toward their vehicle, throwing apologies and excuses over her shoulder.

"You're shaking," she said to Whitt. "Edward, what happened? Are you okay?"

He couldn't answer. Didn't have an explanation to offer her. The officer he'd slugged was slowly waking, trying to stand with the help of his partner. Whitt slid into the passenger seat and covered his face with his hands.

"I've messed up," he said. "I've messed up bad."

"I know," Vada said.

"I'm . . ." He looked at her. Didn't have the strength to say it. "I'm . . ."

"I know," she said again. He was off his head, had

been for days. She knew it. Of course she knew it. She shut the door on him, and Whitt grabbed for his leather satchel that was lying on the back seat. He needed to even out. He was scaring himself.

He pulled a hip flask from the front pocket of the bag.

CHAPTER 45

STAN THE TRUCK DRIVER dropped me at a roadside bar and walked inside, giving me a dirty look and saying nothing as he pushed through the doors. The rain was easing. It would be up to me to find another ride, but my confidence faltered at the sight of the bar's crowded interior. There were many people here, men and women dressed alike in high-vis outfits, grabbing lunch, some cracking balls on pool tables at the back of the room. Some people were in suits, tucked into booths, and there were rowdy groups of road workers who'd had their workday canceled by the rain. There was one waitress letting empty schooner glasses stack up on the end of the counter while she talked to a fat man sagging over the edge of his stool.

I went to the bar, cagey about showing the small stack of money tucked into the pocket of my jeans, making sure I didn't meet eyes with the bartender from under my cap.

"Bourbon, neat."

"House is fine?" he asked.

"Anything's fine."

One drink, just to warm up and calm my nerves after the close call at the roadblock. I sat at the bar and listened to the coverage of Bonnie Risdale's murder on the round-the-clock news channel on the television in the distant corner of the room, hardly able to hear it over Cold Chisel playing from the jukebox and the chorus of men at the front of the bar singing along. I thought I heard Whitt's voice, but by the time I looked up, he was off the screen again.

"You been out walking?" the bartender asked as he handed me my drink. I realized I was still wet from trekking along beside the highway. The bottoms of my jeans were splattered with mud. I shrugged, didn't offer an answer.

"Is that Old Stan you came in with?"

"Leave her alone, Brian," someone said. "She's clearly had a rough morning."

I hadn't even noticed the women at my side. The one who had come to my defense and her partner were much alike in fashion sense, though one was tall and lanky and the other a short, dumpy version hunched over a phone screen. The lanky one was wearing a denim jacket long ago torn at the shoulder and sleeve, revealing an arm full of tattoos that went with the studs in her bottom lip. She was pierced all up her ears. Her partner was, too. Aging biker chicks.

"Thanks," I mumbled as the bartender retreated. The woman's fingers were ringed with big stainless-steel ornaments, a wolf head and a skull vomiting another skull. Tattoos on her right knuckles read KAZZ.

"These bartenders," Kazz said. "They get bored. Same people every day in this place. They see a new person come in, they get all nosy."

"Uh-huh." I nodded.

Her friend still hadn't looked up from her phone screen. I knew women like this from the job. These ladies had probably been the busty, dangerous, trash-mouthed girlfriends of drug-dealing bikers back in the day. Now they were old, traded out for younger, fresher models after a few decades of loyal service. Exchanged for women who didn't know so much about their partner's crimes.

The women's food arrived, two chicken schnitzels with mashed potato and peas. I watched out of the corner of my eye as Kazz poured gravy all over her food. My stomach growled. But I didn't have time to hang around, stuffing my face. I needed a ride out of here, needed get to Narooma and Melina as fast as I could. I glanced around the bar for a potential ride.

"Help yourself, honey," Kazz said, shoving a bowl of chips toward me. "Gammy and me, we always order too much."

I hesitated, and Kazz nudged Gammy, who nodded enthusiastically and licked her lips in response. I saw that she'd had her tongue surgically forked, and recently, too. The tips were red and swollen, the procedure probably done by a backyard body modifier.

"Thanks," I said again, and relented, thinking I'd have a couple of chips and no more. Soon I was shoving handfuls into my mouth. I couldn't recall the last time I'd had hot food. My whole body seemed tensed with hunger, my fingers trembling as I grabbed at the food.

"Jeez, you're like the stray puppy come in from the rain." Kazz laughed, pouring gravy on the chips for me. "Eat up, girl. There's plenty to go around." I hardly noticed how closely Kazz and Gammy were watching me eat. I was checking the back of the bar, where Stan was talking to his friends. He seemed to be describing where and how he had found me. I had to get a ride and get out of here. The guys by the door looked friendly. I turned and drained my drink, balking as the bartender placed another one in front of me.

"On me." Kazz grinned, making a smiley-face tattoo on her cheekbone wink. "You look like you need it."

"Thanks, really." I drained the drink in one gulp. "I've got to get going, though. I don't suppose either of you are heading Narooma way?"

"We could be, we could be." Kazz nodded, thinking. "What do you think, Gam? Should help the pretty puppy get where she's going?"

I looked to Gam for an answer, but I couldn't see her face through a gray haze floating thickly through the bar. I shook my head, blinked, but the gray cloud was creeping in at the corners of my vision now, making a tunnel. Kazz and Gam had started talking in sounds rather than words, bumbling tones like a soft trumpet playing with a pillow crammed in its end. I gripped the bar as the fog cleared momentarily, everything zapping back into perfect clarity. I gulped a breath before I could sink back under the influence of the cloud.

"Oh, shit," I managed to say. "Oh...No..."

I got off my stool, hanging on to the bar for support, and turned toward the men near the door. My eyelids were heavy. The fog was creeping back. When I tried to speak, my mind screamed the words *I've been drugged!*

Not a sound made it past my lips.

CHAPTER 46

I'D HEARD THIS story a hundred times.

I was having a good time. We hadn't been at the bar very long. Everything seemed fine. I was talking to some friendly guy. Suddenly my friends were gone. I realized I couldn't speak.

I couldn't walk.

I couldn't ask for help.

I hadn't been targeted by a serial rapist in a nightclub, like the girls I'd taken statements from across my career in Sex Crimes. But the terror in my chest was just the same as my body and brain failed on me. A room full of people, and I couldn't make a single person realize I was in trouble. Kazz put her arm around me, steadying me. Gammy slipped off her stool and walked ahead of us. This was all routine for her, I realized. I had no choice but to let Kazz guide me, or I'd fall flat on my face. I tried to grab at one of the men in the group by the door as we passed, but my fingers were numb. Looking back for Stan or the bartender sent my head spinning, the gray cloud swallowing my vision.

I tried to scream as they half walked, half carried me toward the door.

Help me. Help me.

I tried to stop walking, fell into someone. But Kazz was stronger than she looked. Her fingers bit into my arm.

"Herrrrr," I managed, slapping uselessly at a man's chest. "Herrrr!"

"Is she all right?"

"She's a real lightweight." Kazz yanked me away, an arm encircling my waist. "Don't worry about her. We'll get her home."

It had stopped raining, but a harsh wind howled. I knew no one would hear me, even if I finally managed to scream. They walked me around the side of the bar and down a wide, barren roadway. I tried to fall to my knees out of their grip, but Gammy slipped under my other arm, her shoulder jutting into my ribs. My toes dragged in the mud. Ahead, I glimpsed a large shed, its corrugated iron door lit by golden lamps from inside.

CHAPTER 47

THE FRANTIC SCREAMING in my mind stopped as I was dumped on the hard wooden floor of the shed, my breath leaving my chest in a harsh yelp. I needed to think, assess my situation. I knew about date-rape drugs. I'd studied their various forms and uses. There were clues about what I had been given, and so far those clues were telling me good things.

First, I wasn't hallucinating. Though my vision was blurred and my body useless, I still had a firm grip on reality and wasn't spinning off into psychedelic dreams. When my vision cleared, I could make out the benches around me cluttered with greasy tools and machines, the jars of screws and bolts. I was still conscious, and that was good. The fact that I wasn't out, and that Gammy was taping my wrists in front of me, told me the drug probably started to work fast but wore off quickly. I was probably going to be back in full working order soon. It was a drug designed to stun and incapacitate, rather than have me out for long periods of time. I'd seen men and women slipped this type of drug, then dragged into an alleyway and robbed, the assailant fleeing before the victim could recover. These drugs were low-risk, cheap. The victim wasn't going to stop breathing on them and die for the contents of their wallet.

Gammy taped my wrists and mouth before emptying my pockets, seizing the cash with a cheer. I lay watching the ceiling ticking slowly around in a circle and listened to them going through my backpack.

"There's nothing else here but papers," Kazz was muttering. "What is all this stuff? It's like criminal records or something."

"There's a phone," Gammy slurred. I heard the phone tumble to the ground. "Cheap."

"Jesus fuck!" Kazz laughed. I heard her action my gun. "Check this out!"

I rolled onto my front, tried to lift my head. My legs felt like lead. There was a pause while the two women tried to piece the situation together. The cash. The gun. The papers. I heard them get quickly to their feet.

"She's a . . ." Gammy whispered.

A cop. I was a cop. Kazz rummaged through the bag and grabbed my wallet. My badge.

"Detective Harriet Blue," Kazz read.

"Oh, shit." Gammy laughed. "We sure know how to pick 'em."

They weren't worried. Most cops would never report being tricked and robbed in such a basic scam out of sheer pride, and if they were concerned that I'd come back with my colleagues and bust them for their hustle, all they had to do was move their game up the road into another jurisdiction. As long as they didn't figure out who I was, I would be fine.

I breathed, dragged my legs into a kneeling position. The spinning in my head was slowing, but I wasn't going to let them know my strength was returning. I knelt, bent double, my hands beneath me on the dirt, my eyes closed. I silently willed them to simply take the cash and run for their miserable, thieving lives. *You robbed a cop*, I thought. *Big deal. Run now and gloat, and don't think about it any further.*

I wasn't so lucky.

"Harriet *Blue*," Gammy said. "Isn't that...?"

I could feel them staring at me. I squeezed my eyes shut, prayed to the universe that they would not say the words. Anything but those terrible words.

"There's a reward out for this chick," Kazz said.

CHAPTER 48

THEY CAME FOR ME. The duct tape had been a quick, ill-planned, temporary restraint. Now they had to get me bound up properly and out of sight. I couldn't hide that I was recovering any longer. As Gammy came over the top of me, I rolled and kicked upward with both feet. I'd aimed for her chest, hoping to propel her backward, but I was still dizzy. One foot glanced off her side, the other sinking into her fleshy stomach. She gave a breathy groan and doubled over, Kazz backing off in shock.

I rolled away, tried to stagger to my feet, but I wasn't completely in control yet. Balancing on one knee, I ripped the duct tape off my mouth. I thought about screaming for help but doubted anyone in the bar would hear me. The music had been pretty loud, and Kazz and Gammy's familiarity with the shed suggested they brought their victims here regularly. The bartender might have been in on it. Even if I thought I'd have a chance of being heard, I wasn't going to cry for help in front of these bitches. Half a fight is bluffing, looking like you know what you're doing. They had to know I was prepared to defend myself, that I didn't appreciate being lured and captured like an animal.

"I'll let one of you run," I offered. "There's no need for both of you to get hurt." I didn't expect them to take the bait, but it was worth a try—getting down to one opponent might have equalized things in my incapacitated state.

The two women reassessed the situation, Gammy clutching her stomach, eyes watering. Three breathless adversaries, already twitching with adrenaline. If I could convince either of them, it seemed likely to be Gammy. She was younger, simple-looking, the sidekick hanging around the tougher, stronger Kazz. Gammy was dumb, but she could see I knew how to fight.

"It's only money," I told Gammy. "Whoever stays is going to leave here in an ambulance."

"It's a hundred fucking grand," Kazz sneered. "Don't let her mess with your head, Gam. We got this."

"Be smart, Gammy," I warned. "You can leave here and continue your miserable, parasitic life hustling small change out of unsuspecting drifters. Or you can roll the dice for some hard cash and end up eating your next meal through a tube."

While they calculated their chances, I tried not to look at my gun lying on my backpack just a few meters away. The women appeared to have forgotten it. But if I leaped for it, I knew I'd remind them and they'd get to the weapon before me. The room was still slowly turning, blurring. I didn't have the time to unbind my wrists. I reached for the nearest weapon—a good-sized wrench sitting on a set of shelves.

Kazz came first. Her eyes were on the wrench, so I faked, knowing she'd duck, and swung at the side of her head. My movements were exaggerated by the drugs, off-balance. The heavy wrench had been a bad choice. In a downward chopping motion, I missed her head completely. She sank her fist into my stomach. I fell into the shelves, sending glass jars falling, smashing, spraying screws and bolts. Gammy rushed in, emboldened by Kazz's success, and grabbed a handful of my hair. I dropped the wrench and reached up, sank my nails into her hands, raked down as hard as I could.

They were both on me, a tangle of arms. I reached out, grabbed an iron clamp that had fallen off the table and swung wildly. With a lucky shot I got Kazz right on her collarbone. I heard the dull *thunk* of the iron hitting the bone through the denim of her jacket and through her skin. She wailed in pain, struggled away, and I swung again, holding the clamp like brass knuckles, hitting Gammy with a half-strength blow in the side.

They backed off once more, but not for long. I was proving a nuisance, but I hadn't scared either of them yet. I needed to draw blood. Break bones.

In the seconds before they came again, I ripped at the duct tape on my wrists with my teeth, slashing through the sticky plastic. I pulled, and my wrists parted reluctantly. The clamp wasn't enough. I needed something long-range. I ditched the clamp and fumbled over the glass and screws and metal on the bench behind me, never taking my eyes off my opponents. There wasn't time to choose carefully. I lifted something.

A claw hammer. We all looked at the tool. I turned it in my hand so that the claws faced forward. I was feeling pretty good about myself until Kazz reached for a weapon on the bench beside her and pulled up a shiny new hatchet.

CHAPTER 49

"THAT IS NOT a good idea," I said, trying to keep my voice strong. Kazz examined the hatchet. Gammy, looking as confident as I did about her partner's choice, stood trembling nearby.

"If we kill her, she's not worth nothing," Gammy mumbled. The hatchet was so new, it still had a price sticker on it and a plastic guard over the blade. Kazz peeled the guard off and smiled. I could see the handle of my gun beyond them, poking out from beneath some of the papers they'd discovered in my bag.

Kazz hefted the hatchet in her hand, gave it an experimental swing. "Get on the fucking ground," she ordered, pointing to the floor with her free hand. Big mistake. The pointing caused her pain. She winced. I realized I had indeed done some significant damage to her collarbone, maybe cracked or dislocated it. Weak spot. I sidestepped along the bench, the hammer feeling like a lead weight in my fist.

"I'm leaving here," I told the women. I looked at Gammy, whose commitment to the fight seemed to be waning. "I'm leaving alone, and of my own free will. That's a fact, ladies. You just have to decide how much blood you'd like to donate to the floorboards before I walk out that door."

"You got a lot of fucking nerve." Kazz shook her head. "You're losing. Look at you." I felt a dribble on my lip and realized my nose was bleeding. I must have caught a stray hand or elbow in the scuffle, and the drugs had been masking my pain. There was blood running down my ankle. My breath was coming in hoarse growls, like my ribs were crushed. I sidestepped a little more, making my way toward the gun.

They followed, keeping their distance.

Without so much as a glance at each other, they came again. I watched the hatchet swing before me, threw myself backward into the shelves. She swung too hard. Before Kazz could swing upward again, I lunged at her, going for that injured collarbone, punching the hammer forward like a sword. I hit paydirt. She screamed but didn't back off, using her weight to shove me into the shelves. Something sharp pierced my back, not deep. I twisted away, lifted the hammer and brought it down hard. The two claws embedded themselves in the soft meat of her shoulder.

She didn't have the strength to draw breath, to scream again in pain. While she was stunned, I grabbed for the hand that held the hatchet but missed. The hatchet blade swished past me and *thunked* into Gammy's upper arm as she tried to join the fray, slicing right through her jacket into bone. Gammy's howl made my eardrums throb.

The hatchet fell, Kazz letting go of it in horror. I grabbed it and threw it away, used the distraction to make a break for my gun. Gammy was sitting on the floor, clutching her upper arm, blood running in dark rivulets from between her fingers. She was stunned, out of the fight. Kazz was crawling after me, her white shirt quickly becoming red where I'd stabbed her with the hammer, her teeth bared. I grabbed my gun and rolled, lying on my back, pointing the barrel at her. She stopped her advance in an instant. Her face tightened, grimaced with the realization of her defeat. I smiled and couldn't resist telling the older woman what she plainly already knew.

"I never lose," I said.

CHAPTER 50

WHITT CRASHED. Like a plane slowly pointing downward, sailing toward the ground, rushing faster and faster as gravity pulled him. He let Vada drive him to the dingy motel by the side of the highway that had been commandeered as a base of operations. She guided him between the groups of officers waiting there, just barely getting him through the door before he saw the bed and fell onto it, landing just short of the pillow, his arms and legs limp before they hit the coverlet. In the hours he slept, he recalled snippets of movement. Vada taking off his shoes, turning off the lights, plugging his phone into the charger.

As he struggled to wake, Whitt seemed to recall Vada doing some other things, too. Things he couldn't understand. He'd thought she was setting an alarm on his phone, but she seemed to handle the phone for a long time, swiping and selecting things. Had he heard the sound of her unzipping his bag? His belongings shifting about? Whitt was sure there was an explanation for these things. She'd cared for him like a girlfriend, a wife. When he opened his eyes, she was there at the bedside, a chilled bottle of water on the nightstand, which she took and placed in his hand.

"Oh, Jesus." Whitt put a hand to his head, followed the line of searing pain from his forehead to the back of his skull. "Jesus."

"You can't pray your way out of this hangover," Vada said. "Drink the water."

He sipped, felt his stomach lurch. He wondered if he could make it into the bathroom before he was sick. That would be his rock bottom, surely, throwing up on the carpet of a motel room in front of his new partner.

Vada was freshly dressed, her red hair pulled taut into a high, neat bun.

Her eyes were sympathetic under her bangs, an understanding smile playing on her lips.

"I have a problem," Whitt said. He struggled to find the words that had been so available to him last time he said them, sitting in a gathering in a dusty Scouts hall, part of a circle of seated men. He tried to drink the water again and failed. "I'm an addict. I was recovering, but I...I lost control. I let Regan go, and it's because of me that...that..."

Whitt squeezed his eyes shut, pinched the bridge of his nose. He wasn't going to cry in front of this woman. That would be a level even deeper than throwing up in front of her. Punching a cop in front of her. Passing out drunk in front of her. Whitt wondered how deep the layers went, when he would bottom out. He needed to pull out of the case before he went much lower.

"I knew there was something wrong before we left Sydney," Vada said. "It's not as obvious as you think. You hold yourself well."

Whitt burned with shame, his face in his hands.

"I smoothed over the fight on the bridge," Vada said. "Those Boyraville cops don't want us to support the young driver's claim that he was assaulted. That's if he makes a claim at all. When I put you in the car, I went back and it seemed like the boy just got caught up in a love triangle he never knew he was a part of."

Whitt nodded, trying to breathe through the sickness.

"What are you on?" she asked.

"Dexedrine," he admitted.

"Wow."

"What?"

"They use Dexedrine to treat patients with narcolepsy," she said. "Too much of it and you'll give yourself a heart attack."

"That wasn't my main concern at the time," Whitt said. "I just needed to bounce back. I needed something to keep me going."

Whitt reached reflexively for his heart. His chest felt tight, but that might have been from sleeping on his front, something he never did. "I'll bin the rest of them."

"Don't," Vada said. He frowned at her. "You shouldn't go off them too quickly, not if you've been popping them like candies. Give them to me, and I'll dole them out to you."

"It's okay. They can give me something to come down on in rehab."

"You can't go to rehab," Vada said. She seemed about to say more, but her words failed. She sat on the bed beside him, slid the tie out of her hair and ran a hand through it, sighing as she shook out the burnt-orange curls.

"You can't go. I want you here," she said.

Whitt was surprised by one of her hands in his, the other on his chest. How had he missed this? All the time he had been focusing too hard on trying to stay even, trying to get through the minutes and hours on the chase for Regan, he'd never noticed her watching him, wanting him. He couldn't remember even a hint of it, a smile held too long or a conversation wandering into intimate territory. But then, she was moving toward him now, and the sudden awakening of a furious hunger in him made it hard to breathe. Vada was in his arms, and her lips were against his, and he was pulling her and turning her and stripping her clothes off without a spare thought for any of the horror of the night just beyond their door.

More easily than it seemed possible, she was all that mattered.

CHAPTER 51

I THOUGHT ABOUT shooting Kazz and Gammy in the legs, just to teach them a lesson about robbing people. Just a single bullet each in the calf, not a deadly serious injury, just a little reminder for the rest of their miserable lives that crime doesn't, or at least shouldn't, pay. I stood holding my gun, considering my options.

I bound both women with the duct tape and wrapped Gammy's badly bleeding arm with some cloth I found in a tub on the bench. Kazz's wounds weren't so bad—I'd punctured her in the right side of the chest, but no deeper than a couple of centimeters. It was the broken collarbone that had her seething. I dug into Gammy's pockets and retrieved my money, then stuffed my papers back into my backpack.

"I've decided I'm not going to hurt you further," I told them. "But you might consider making an honest living before the next no-hoper you try to scam puts you in the ground. Gammy, you're probably just smart enough to sort plastic cutlery in a factory. Kazz, they're always looking for people to put the bolt in the cows' brains at the abattoir. I think you'd enjoy that."

"We know who you are." Gammy tried to sound tough, but she was holding back tears. "We'll find you!"

I went into the pockets of Kazz's jacket and found a set of keys.

"This is your bike, huh?" I jangled the keys in her face.

"Fuck you," she snarled.

I leaned in close so she could feel my breath on her face. "When I get where I'm going," I told her, "I'm going to torch it."

Kazz screamed a stream of abuse at me, the colorful language of old-school bikie chicks. I left the women there and walked out of the shed.

I found the bikes, a couple of ancient Harleys meticulously restored and gleaming, parked behind the bar. Kazz's had a big, flaming *K* airbrushed into the fuel tank. I wheeled the bike around to the side of the shed and threw my leg over it, revved it a few times so that the women would hear, before I rode out into the fading light.

CHAPTER 52

CHIEF TREVOR MORRIS entered the small house with his hat in his hand, the way he had done many times in his career, bringing news of a loved one's death to frightened, wide-eyed relatives. But the elderly woman who walked ahead of him now had already heard that news many years ago. He imagined that night, the patrol officers who had come into the neat dining room and sat at the table with the Howeses, the way they'd tried to avoid looking into the eyes of the couple in case they should accidentally, somehow, worsen their experience. Death notifications were, in a strange way, ceremonial. There was a script. A right and a wrong way to hold one's facial expression. Pops was sure that none of it helped.

Only Diane, Rachel's mother, was here tonight. She'd told Pops on the phone that Rachel's father couldn't handle talking about their daughter's murder by Regan Banks more than fifteen years earlier. He had gone out for the evening while Pops visited. Pops hadn't been assigned the case at the time, but he'd seen pictures of what Regan had done to the pretty veterinarian in the clinic on that awful night. He put a notebook on the dining-room table and refused coffee. Diane Howes was a picture of her daughter at an age she would never reach. Elegant, slender, the strong hands and short nails of a woman accustomed to wrangling animals. Pops spied a pair of enormous Great Dane hounds staring at him through the windows to the patio, taking quiet but intense interest in his presence.

"I know you've already been interviewed by police as recently as a week ago about Regan," Pops said gently, finally allowing his eyes to rest on Diane's. "But I'll just make sure by asking what I'm sure you've been asked—Regan has made no contact with you, has he? You've received no strange calls or visits?"

"No, nothing," Diane Howes said. "Honestly, Regan Banks has been responsible for so much horror, I'm sure he doesn't even remember Rachel or the effect he's had on our lives. I saw her picture in the newspaper the other day. A single photograph as big as a stamp in a collection of others, distinguished only by being his first victim."

She glanced at a folded newspaper at the end of the table. Pops wrung his hands in his lap.

"Regan was seventeen at the time." Pops tried to take refuge in his notebook. "You got to see him in court."

"He was a ratty-looking child." Diane nodded. "Lean, lanky. Hollow-cheeked. He'd been out that night stalking around the neighborhood, trying to get into trouble. Rachel shouldn't have been working so late, but they'd had a particularly difficult surgery that day. A young dog that had been hit by a car. She would often stay late with the very sick ones."

"Was there ever any suggestion, as far as you're aware, that Regan might have had company that night?" Pops felt the muscles beneath his eyes twitch as he braced for an answer he wasn't sure he wanted to hear. "The reason I ask is that I've come into some information that might explain the connection between Regan and Samuel Jacob Blue."

"The Georges River Killer," Diane said. "Or so they say."

"Yes."

"It's his sister who's missing now, isn't it?" Diane looked at the newspaper again. "They think Regan's after her. Or that she might be after him."

"That's her," Pops admitted.

"I don't believe anyone but Regan was responsible for my daughter's death," Diane Howes said. "I looked into that boy's face, and he stared right back at me, and I could almost see in his eyes what he had done to my child. As a mother, you can feel these things, and I felt a cold wave of emptiness coming off that boy that could cut you right to the bone."

Pops nodded.

"In court they played a recording of a phone call," Diane said. "It was made at the same time that Rachel was being attacked, some streets away. The anonymous caller contacted Crime Stoppers and posed as someone who was watching the break-in at the clinic happening, but of course that wasn't possible from such a distance. So it was someone who had seen Regan go into the clinic, but someone who hadn't hung around to see what occurred. Police theorized it was a young woman who'd perhaps driven by and stopped at the phone box and then continued on her way."

"I see." Pops nodded as he wrote.

"But when I heard the call, I thought that the voice wasn't a woman, but a boy." Diane squinted as she remembered. "The voice was high. Young. I thought he sounded uncertain. Almost guilty."

"Guilty because he'd helped with the break-in?"

"Maybe," Diane said. "But I've always felt it sounded more like he was dobbing in a friend. I don't know how to describe it. He almost sounded disappointed."

Pops pursed his lips. It made sense. Regan had told Harry that Sam had been responsible for his going to prison. An anonymous call to police during the attack on Rachel Howes would have made Regan a sitting duck.

"Did Regan ever say anything to you at all during the trial?" Pops asked.

"Oh, no." Diane spread a hand on the lace tablecloth, stared at it, remembering. "He pleaded guilty. Didn't offer an explanation or an apology for the sentencing part. Something that's always confused me was that the prosecution wanted to bring in a report from Regan's childhood to aid their argument during sentencing, but the judge wouldn't allow it."

"The *prosecution*?" Pops said.

"Yes." Diane nodded. "Whatever it was, the report

would have aided the case *against* Regan. It spoke of his inherent danger as an individual."

"There are plenty of reports of him being violent during his childhood years in care," Pops said.

"And we heard all of those." Diane said. "But this one was something different. I believe it was about what happened to get Regan into care in the first place."

Pops felt the hair on the back of his neck rise.

"Did the judge say why he wouldn't allow the report?"

"No. I don't think so." Diane shrugged. "But I remember only a few things from those days, because I was so weighed down by my grief all the time. Walking through fog, you know."

Pops folded closed his notebook, signaling that Diane could end their meeting then if she would like. He had imposed on her enough, and the heaviness of the grief she spoke of was plain in her face. He expected her to rise from her chair, but instead she spoke.

"I remember the psychologist saying something that ended up being struck from the record," Diane said. "That always stayed with me. It confirmed an idea that I already had about Regan."

"What was it?" Pops asked.

"He said Regan gave him the impression of someone who knew how to kill." Diane lifted her eyes to his. "Because he'd done it more than once."

CHAPTER 53

I APPROACHED MELINA'S house from the rear, having walked the motorbike from the end of a narrow alleyway behind the property. I remembered parking at the front of the house years earlier, in what felt like such a carefree time in my life—the hard-nosed cop striding up to the house in the daylight, folders of perp photographs clasped against my chest. The properties here were wide and sprawling, divided by an asphalt lane where kids had left their tricycles and footballs, and a small fort constructed in a bottlebrush tree in the neighbor's yard. There wasn't the thick forest cover I'd had behind Bonnie Risdale's house, so I left the bike by a fence and walked forward on my own, settling by a low stone wall.

The sun was sinking on the horizon. All was still. A strange calm settled over me, as though simply by being here I was protecting Melina from Regan. He wasn't going to touch her. If I had to, I would give my life to make sure of it.

An hour passed. I knelt in the wet grass, a loyal sentry, watching the house. Doubt drifted through my mind, a haze that descended and rose unpredictably. I didn't know for sure that Melina was Regan's next target. I didn't know where he was leading me, or when he would decide it was time for us to face each other. Was he planning to torture me until he became bored, or was there some special date he was waiting for, a day selected in his sick diary on which he would mark our union? Our first date. The first steps after our journey of getting to know each other. When was that day? There were so many important moments in Regan's life he might choose. The day he killed Rachel Howes. His first day in prison. The day he met Sam. The day Sam died.

I had perused Regan's file and knew none of those dates were soon. It was only weeks since my brother had been laid to rest. I brought my knees up to my chest and stared at Melina's house and tried to think.

I could see down the left side of the building from my vantage point, right to the empty front yard and the street beyond. But the right side of the house was a mystery to me.

So I had no warning when, from that direction, he appeared.

CHAPTER 54

POPS PERCHED ON the edge of the pool table and looked at the whiteboard before him. Deputy Commissioner Woods had commandeered his office and banished the chief from the bullpen where the Robbery, Homicide, and Sex Crimes divisions were based. He had entered paperwork for Pops's suspension, but the old man hadn't bothered to hang around to wait for it to be issued to him. His new center of operations had been easy to find. He'd spent many years here on the first floor of the command building in a small, dingy room off the car park. The night patrol's rec room.

It didn't have the glamour of his office upstairs. To one side stood a row of wooden bunks, four of the six beds neatly made and unoccupied, two sporting lumps beneath the blankets where tired patrol officers slept between shifts. On the walls, nude *Playboy* centerfolds that had been ignored by the female officers for years had become faded and cracked, some enhanced with speech bubbles or crude bodily appendages. The pool table, vending machine, and couches were the originals from Pops's time as a recruit.

No one seemed overly curious about the senior officer using their rec room as a command center. As the shifts changed and the officers came and went, some glanced his way and whispered, or greeted him respectfully, but they otherwise let him be.

On the board before him, Pops had pasted the composite sketch of Regan Banks given by Bonnie Risdale's neighbor, and the photograph of the man from his time in prison. Stretching out from the photographs, following his lines of inquiry with connecting arrows, were notes about possible means of finding Regan, some of them reaching outward from the center before being abruptly cut off after only a few stages.

One of the short arms of the investigation was the "Resources" route. Most fugitives, Pops knew, went straight to their network of resources for funding or shelter when they were being pursued by police. But Regan had no living relatives, and no one at the apartment building where he had lived after his release had been able to recall seeing a single other person in the man's company. He had no social-media accounts, no email, no registered phone. No waitresses, bartenders, bus drivers, or shopkeepers near his home recalled him when shown pictures and questioned. He was a shadow man. In the time he had been free from prison, Pops couldn't account for Regan doing anything other than setting upon his plan to frame Sam Blue, and for that he had scarce evidence.

Regan is alone, Pops thought, looking at the photograph, at the black, empty eyes hardly reflecting the camera's light. *But does he avoid people, or do people avoid him?*

A longer arm of the diagram read "Past," but there were no leads there, either. No foster parents or siblings had seen or heard from Regan since his childhood. There had been no unexpected visits, calls, threats, or pleas, and the parents and families of his victims, like Diane Howes, had heard nothing.

Thinking of Diane led Pops's attention to the last arm of the diagram, the one that read "First Kill." Pops's eyes wandered over the Georges River Killer's victims. They had all been so like Doctor Howes. Regan had a type. Ambitious, beautiful brunettes. Wide-eyed, happy women, thriving, full of potential.

Was Rachel Howes indeed where it all started for Regan? Would he return to that place, the way it seemed he had with the Georges River, trying to connect to a moment lost or undo a terrible decision made? Killing Rachel Howes had been a pivotal moment for Regan, after all. It seemed that she had been the one to inspire his type.

Pops tapped his lip with a stubby finger, ignoring a group of young officers bashing the vending machine, trying to free a trapped can of Coke.

The "First Kill" arm of the diagram was right next to the "Family" section, which lay empty.

Pops looked at the two lines and took his phone out of his pocket.

CHAPTER 55

THE RECOGNITION WAS immediate. The tall, broad-shouldered ghoul from my nightmares, the hooded face that stalked my every move, leaving a trail of victims behind him. *Rachel Howes,* his first victim. *Marissa Haydon, Elle Ramone, Rosetta Poelar,* the Georges River girls. I was too late. Melina Tredwell would be Regan's next kill. I ducked behind the low wall and watched as Regan paused at the corner of the house, seeming to look right at me through the dim blue light of impending night. He patted his pockets, as though he had forgotten something, and turned back the way he had come.

For the first time, I had to force myself to move. Terror had immobilized me. It would be so easy to stay where I was, call the police, let someone else rush into the danger. But in a moment I was up and following, my gun at my side.

I lifted the barrel and pointed it at the man as he reached for an open window at the side of the house. My thumb had already raked back the hammer of the pistol as the words spewed forth from my lips.

"Don't. Fucking. Move."

My voice struck him like electricity. He jolted at each one, head bent, hands frozen in the air.

Even with him paused there before me, his broad back only centimeters away, my thoughts were racing. What was I doing? I'd come here to kill him, not arrest him.

I realized the hand that held my weapon was shaking. I drew a deep breath and put the barrel of the gun against the back of his skull.

CHAPTER 56

"HARRY?" SOMEONE CALLED.

Her voice barely penetrated the ringing in my ears. The boy in front of me was cowering, turned as much toward me as he would dare, one wide eye peering over his shoulder at my gun. I was aware suddenly of movement beyond the teenage boy under my gun, toward the front of the house. Melina Tredwell, older than I remembered, hugging a coat around her. The teenage boy bent and sank to the ground. I realized the ringing sound was his pitiful whimpering, along with the panicked screaming of a teenage girl just inside the window to my left.

"Harry!" Melina had been running toward me, and now she slowed, her palms out flat. "Harry, please put the gun down."

"She's gonna kill me." The boy I'd thought was Regan Banks crouched against the side of the house, trying to make himself as small as possible. "She's gonna kill me!"

I dropped the aim of my gun. My legs felt numb. I staggered, wiped at the sweat on my brow. My jaws were locked together so tightly, it took a concerted effort to part them.

"Harry, it's me." Melina took my arms carefully, her touch gentle, fearful. "It's Melina."

"I almost shot that boy," I said. My voice was flat. Cold. "I thought he was Regan. I almost killed him."

"You're shaking," Melina said. "Come inside."

She turned to the boy on the ground. The kid's enormous, weightlifter-style frame was in stark contrast to his smooth, hairless face and big, innocent eyes. He couldn't have been older than sixteen. He appeared to have left the house by the window beside me, forgotten something, and was heading back in. In the house, a teenage girl, maybe fifteen, was tugging a robe around herself, eyes fearful, locked on me.

"You." Melina pointed a finger at the boy on the ground, all her softness suddenly gone. "Both of you. In the kitchen, *right now*."

CHAPTER 57

I WAS LED into the kitchen, the boy trailing guiltily behind us. I was surprised to see it was 11 p.m. on the
clock above the fridge. Pots and pans were drying on the
draining board from their dinner. Suburban bliss. Melina
took the gun carefully from my stiff hand. She carried it
to the table pinched between two fingers, as if squeezing
it too hard might set it off. I sank into a kitchen chair.
The teenagers crept to the corner of the kitchen farthest
from me, both with their eyes on the gun.

"Winley"—Melina shook her head ruefully at the
boy—"your mother is going to lose her goddamn mind
when I tell her I caught you around here in Janna's room
again."

"You—" Janna began.

"Not a word!" Melina roared, pointing at the girl. "You

are in *so much* trouble right now, girl, you better shut your mouth and pray I don't slap you senseless."

The family fell into silence. I had no strength left. All I could do was watch and listen.

"Who is she?" Winley gestured to me.

"She's no one," Melina said. "In fact, I want both your mobile phones. Give them to me right now. Neither of you idiots are going to go Snapchatting about this."

The teens handed over their phones. Melina snatched them and put them in a drawer, muttering angrily to herself as she bustled about the kitchen, "...through the bedroom window like a fucking tomcat..."

The teens watched me. I watched them back.

"Your nose is broken," the girl said.

"Is that a real gun?" the boy said.

Melina handed me a glass of water. I drank greedily. She sat down across the little table from me, the gun between us.

"I saw the news last night about Bonnie Risdale," Melina said. "They're saying she was one of your old cases. That's why you're here. You thought he might come for me."

I could only nod. The teenagers were whispering to each other, stuck standing against the wall like prisoners caught in a watchtower spotlight. They were putting it together. Bonnie Risdale. I heard the boy mention Regan's name. The girl's eyes widened, and she reached for his hand. Melina seemed to be thinking, her eyes wandering over my bruised face.

"Mrs. Tredwell, can I please go home?" Winley asked.

"No," Melina snapped. "You come sneaking around

here, you should be prepared to stay. Neither of you is going anywhere until Harry's safely on the road, with a reasonable head start."

The girl scoffed. "What the hell? We get in trouble for sneaking around, and you're going to help out a wanted criminal?" Janna pointed at me. "Mum, the police are looking for her! Isn't what you're doing *breaking the law*?"

"I'll break *something* in a minute," Melina murmured.

The girl fell back into line, pouting. I wasn't sure, but I thought I heard her whisper that this whole situation was bullshit. Melina ignored the child, turning back to me.

"Let's get you fixed up," she said. "You've got a killer to catch."

CHAPTER 58

REGAN WAITED ON the doorstep of the Jansen house, just beyond the reach of the glow coming from the stained-glass panel in the thick wooden door. As usual after a killing, he'd left Bonnie Risdale's house with more than a few nicks and scratches, most notably a claw mark down the side of his neck that he was now trying to hide with the collar of his shirt. He remembered her doing it, a desperate swipe as he squeezed her throat, catching him just as he twisted out of reach. He knew there'd be no fighting tonight. This was going to be a gentle, warm, drawn-out evening. He was smiling to himself as he heard a pair of feet slowly shuffling toward the other side of the door.

She was everything he had envisioned. Small, bent-backed, peering at him through reading glasses that gave her large and bewildered eyes. She turned on a stern frown as he had expected she would, clutching her fluffy dressing gown around her.

"Yes?" was all she offered. An old woman mildly peeved at having to answer the door at such an hour.

"I'm so sorry to bother you," Regan said. "My name is Sean Geyser. I'm with the Australian Electric Company."

"We're quite happy with our service." Eloise Jansen took the door in hand. "And what an inconvenient hour to be—"

"I'm not selling anything." Regan put his hands up. "I'm here because your neighbors across the street have been experiencing some unexpected power surges. I wondered if I could come in and check your system. We just want to make sure everyone is safe."

"Power surges?" Mrs. Jansen glanced into the hallway behind her, hands fluttering with tension. "Oh, dear. Of course. Come in. Are we in danger? Should we turn the power off?"

"Oh, no, no, you're perfectly safe," Regan lied. He crossed the threshold and closed and locked the door behind him.

In the living room, collapsed into an ancient recliner covered with a crocheted afghan, sat an old man, his hands on the armrests. Regan stood in the doorway, looking around the room as Mrs. Jansen went to the old man and poked him, which only resulted in louder snores.

"Gary? Gary? It's the power man. The power man's here."

Regan rather liked thinking of himself as "the power man." He strolled to the wall beside the huge, pine-veneer television set and looked at a collection of photographs hanging there. About fifty frames of different sizes and shapes had been arranged in a sort of cloud shape, each perfectly positioned at the same distance from the next, a smattering of faces in every conceivable circumstance. There were small, cheery-cheeked toddlers feeding ducks at sunlit ponds and early school-age girls lounging on a rug, playing with dolls, whispering in one another's ears. Childhood secrets. There were teenagers reluctantly posing for their photographs, holding certificates awkwardly by their corners. Gary, finally roused from his living-room slumber, had shuffled to Regan's side, a pair of thick glasses almost identical to his wife's now perched on his nose.

"What is it? The electrics?"

Regan nodded, hardly willing to go much further with the ruse. The power man was in the house now. He dropped all pretense, pointed to the picture wall while the elderly couple stood waiting for instructions.

"Tell me about this," he said.

"We haven't got time for chatter," Gary grumbled, gesturing to the clock, which read 11 p.m. "It's the middle of the bloody night!"

"Those are the lovely children we've taken into our home over the years." Eloise stepped forward, embarrassed by her husband's gruffness in the face of an official visitor. "We could never have children of our own, so we fostered. That was many years ago." She gave a small chuckle. "We're too old now, aren't we, Gary?"

Gary shuffled off to the kitchen, muttering to himself. Regan perused the pictures until he found the one he was looking for. He'd almost missed her, she looked so much like an angry teenage boy. Harriet was sitting on a brick wall, her arms crossed, glaring up at the camera as though she'd only just noticed she was being snapped and was about to launch into a tirade of protest. Red flannelette shirt, wild, short-cropped black hair. Regan took the photograph off the wall and held it in the dim light. A plain black plastic frame, no frills. Perfect. Eloise Jansen was frowning at his having removed the picture, and her frown deepened when he spoke.

"Tell me about this girl, Mrs. Jansen," Regan said.

"I don't mean to be impolite," Eloise said, "but it is rather late for a visitor. Should we perhaps get on to the business of the electrics? My husband gets rather tired in the evenings. He's eighty-four, you know."

She tried to take the picture frame from him. Regan held on, and when she insisted, he tugged the picture out of her hand.

Eloise took a step back, surprised.

Regan advanced on her slowly, backing her into the corner of the neat living room. The old woman looked like she wanted to scream, but from her lips came only a tiny whimper.

"I said"—Regan held the photo close to the woman's face—"tell me about this girl."

CHAPTER 59

I SHOWERED, THE hot water running down my muddy arms, over the grazes and cuts on my knuckles, dirt swirling on the tiles beneath my bare feet. I was given a towel and clothes, and dressed in a cluttered bedroom while the girl, Janna, argued with her mother about having to provide me with her best pair of jeans. The black top, grabbed hastily from a shelf by Melina, read "Gucci" in white block letters. I waited on the couch for instructions, staring at the clock as it struck midnight, my mind too torn by what I had done to provide any guidance.

I'd almost killed a child.

How far was I going to take this?

My phone on the coffee table before me buzzed with a call from an unidentified number. Regan. I didn't answer. I wouldn't let him into this house, even if it was only by phone. While the girl and her mother argued, Melina searching the kitchen cupboards for food to stock my backpack with, the tall young boy wandered the house awkwardly, trying to get a proper glimpse of me, not brave enough to offer conversation.

I fell asleep. The sensation was like being punched out, a sudden warm darkness, sounds slowly receding.

I was lying on the couch. The windows were lit pink when I dared to open my eyes. The teens were on the second couch, curled together, eyes glued to a huge television set, fingers dancing over black plastic gaming controllers, bowls of cereal uneaten before them. I tried to make myself get up, but the fatigue was too heavy.

Janna's voice drew me out of sleep again. "Don't touch it."

"I could just hold it for a second," the boy said. "You snap a picture. Two seconds. She'll never know. It'll go viral on Insty. Can you imagine?"

"My mum will kill you."

"Two seconds! I've never held a gun before. It's probably not even loaded."

"It is loaded," I said, sitting up. The teens paused the game and looked at me. I took my gun from the coffee table where it had been lying in plain sight, probably placed there by Melina so that the kids couldn't sneak off with it without her knowing. I ejected the clip and the chamber bullet, let the slide shunt forward and slammed the clip back in. The boy's eyes were wild with intrigue. I'd given him a show, at least. The kids lifted their eyes from the gun to me, two attentive kittens, bewitched.

"Are you really gonna kill that guy when you find him?" Janna asked.

"That's the plan," I said.

"Won't that make you, like, a murderer?" she asked. She glanced at the boy for courage. "Won't it sort of... bring you down to his level?"

Melina appeared behind my couch, giving the young ones a warning look as she put a hand on my shoulder. The kids went reluctantly back to their game as I took up my gun and phone. I wanted to give the kid an answer, but I didn't have one.

CHAPTER 60

IN THE KITCHEN, my backpack sat fat and zipped up on the counter.

"There's plenty of food," she said. "And I put in an extra jacket and a rain poncho. I put the cash you had in your jeans in there, your wallet...I charged your phone while you were asleep."

"Thank you. I can't tell you how much I appreciate this."

"Well, it's not every day you get to harbor a wanted woman," Melina said. "I'll see you off, and then I'm taking Janna and heading for a hotel. I got a call from one of your colleagues."

I warmed slightly at the knowledge that someone was warning victims from my past cases that Regan was interested in them. I grabbed the bag and prepared to leave, but before I could, Melina hugged me. I held on, not realizing how much I'd needed the physical contact until that moment. Melina was leaner and stronger now than she had been when I first met her, sitting with a couple of family members in the station interview room. I remembered her elbows and knees had been grazed from being thrown on the floor of the public toilet where she was attacked. She'd been a good witness, strong and practical. She'd come to the interview with a notepad, scribbled with notes of everything she could remember about her attacker. Now here she was, aiding and abetting a dangerous vigilante, packing my bag for me like a mother sending her kid off to camp.

"I've gotta go," I said when she broke away from me.

"One more thing," she said, handing me her phone. "This has been running all morning." Another press conference, this one with a very familiar face sitting wedged between a decidedly smug-looking Detective Nigel Spader and Deputy Commissioner Joe Woods. My mother had dolled herself up for the interview, but she was dressed inappropriately as always in a denim miniskirt and low-cut singlet top that showed off her upper-chest tattoos.

"I'm asking you, Harriet, to please make contact with the police," Julia was saying. She was reading from a prepared statement, her finger moving slowly across the page. "I am concerned about your welfare, as are your...coll..."

Woods leaned in and whispered in her ear.

"Colleagues," Julia said.

As the press conference ended, Julia picked up an orange-and-white coffee cup that had been sitting by her microphone and held it at chest height. Nigel and Woods boxed her in as the cameras flashed around them, talking over her shoulder. She was captured on the screen for a good five or six seconds, simply standing there holding the coffee cup. I recognized the distinct orange-and-white pattern from the Bristol Gardens hotel chain, the big letter "B" on the side of the cup confirming it as the trio eventually moved off the screen. The old honeypot ruse. Woods and Nigel would have put Julia up at the Bristol Gardens Hotel in the CBD and jammed the place up with undercover police, hoping Regan would see the press conference, take the bait, and make an appearance. It wasn't a bad move, but my faith in the plan was slight.

"Do you think your mother's in danger?" Melina asked.

"No." I handed back the phone. "He knows me better than that. Regan hates my mother, and he expects me to as well. He'll go after people who mean something to me."

"That's why you thought he'd come here," Melina said. "Because of us. My case."

I struggled to find the words. "Melina, being there for you...for people like you in my job...It's the only thing I've ever really been proud of. I'm a cop. That's all I am. There's nothing else to me. I don't have a life outside this, I..."

This was pathetic. I straightened, took my cap from the counter beside me, where it had been sitting, freshly washed and dried. I tried to move away, but Melina had my arm.

"You know that's bullshit, right?" Melina said. "Harry, you should be proud of so many things in your life. You're a good woman. I can tell."

I didn't look at Melina as she spoke. She didn't know what was inside me. She didn't know the furious hatred that burned there, the vengeful fantasies, the dark memories of what I had endured in my childhood.

She couldn't be so sure of what I was.

Even I didn't know.

As I retrieved the bike from the bushes behind the house, the boy I'd almost killed appeared, head down, hands in his pockets, making like he'd been freed from the house and just happened to have decided to go the back way only seconds after I'd left Melina and her daughter. I swung my leg over the bike and waited for him to tell me whatever he wanted to tell me, but he just stood there admiring the Harley, nodding appreciatively.

"I really, um..." the boy said, staring off at the suburban horizon, his chest filled with air but his teenage brain empty of words. I sighed, dragged my pistol out of my back pocket, ejected the clip and the chamber round, and handed it to him.

"Oh, man," he whispered, weighing the gun in his hand. He pointed it at a nearby tree, looked down the sight, pulled the trigger a couple of times, listening to its impotent click. "Oh, this is fucking sweet."

"*You're* fucking sweet." I laughed, taking the weapon back.

I tightened the straps of my bag and prepared to go. I glanced at my phone as it buzzed.

A single word. *Bombala.* A town an hour and a half south.

CHAPTER 61

POPS EXITED THE elevators on the third floor of the command building, jangling his car keys in his hand as he moved between the desks. It was uncharacteristically quiet on the floor. Usually almost every desk would be manned by detectives, heads down, phones to ears, chasing up leads or tapping away at computers. Instead, many of the officers were hanging around the central conference room, where a series of screens showed live streamed footage from the Bristol Gardens Hotel.

Detective Nigel Spader was seated at a bank of computers, his attention fixed on the screens. It was just like Woods to be at the hotel somewhere standing by, ready to jump in front of the cameras if Regan was captured, leading the killer to a car and posing just outside the door. Pops had seen such a photograph in Woods's office once, framed, the demoralized suspect staring bewildered into the camera's flash.

Nigel Spader looked right at home manning the command side of the operation, coffee at his elbow and a healthy audience of enraptured junior detectives at his back. On the screens, Pops could see the grand hotel hallways and the sprawling barroom were stocked with undercover officers talking, laughing, pretending to drink. A select crew of very nervous hotel staff appeared on screens showing a view over the concierge desk.

"No sign of the quarry?" Pops asked as he approached. Nigel turned toward him, his face inked with contempt.

"Chief Morris." Detective Spader smiled without warmth. "This is a surprise. I thought you were taking leave, sir."

"Oh, believe me"—Pops held his hands up—"I want nothing to do with such an egregious waste of police time and resources."

"What do you want, then?" Nigel bristled.

"Banks's Care Initiation Report, the file from the Department of Community Services detailing why he was taken into foster care as a child. It was sealed back when Regan was seven and the state took custody of him. Did Deputy Commissioner Woods apply to have that information unsealed?"

"He did."

Pops waited. Spader watched the screens, his thick arms folded.

"I'm sure you, as Woods's acting 2IC, would have been privy to the contents of that report?" Pops stifled an irritated sigh.

"As a matter of fact, I was."

"And what did it tell you about Banks's parents?"

"That they're deceased."

Pops drew and released a slow breath.

"And the circumstances under which Banks was taken into care?"

"Chief Morris." Nigel Spader's eyes wandered back to the chief's, exhausted. "With all due respect, we're trying to catch a very dangerous fugitive here. We're not researching him for an episode of *This Is Your Life*."

Someone from the group of officers nearby snorted a laugh.

"Was there anything at all relevant in the file?" Pops asked.

"Like what, exactly?"

"Any important locations or dates?" Pops said. "Anything emotionally meaningful to Banks? We know that fugitives are very family-focused when they're under the pressure of pursuit."

"His parents are dead," Nigel said. "His family home, the one they owned when he was born, is a factory site now." Pops noted Nigel's contemptuous tone had softened. Behind his eyes, Pops could almost see wheels turning.

"Maybe there was somewhere else," Pops offered. "Somewhere farther south. We know Regan went out of the city for a reason."

"He went out of the city to target one of Harriet Blue's past victims," Nigel said. "We believe it's likely he chose somewhere nonmetropolitan because he could access Bonnie Risdale easily. She lived alone. Her property was in a rural location. We've now provided Regan with a plum target here in Harriet's mother. He's going to double back to the city, and we're going to catch him."

Pops didn't answer. Detective Spader cleared his throat and spoke louder, as though Pops couldn't hear him.

"We're taking a two-pronged approach. One of the mothers of the Georges River victims has agreed to speak publicly, addressing Harriet, asking her to come in. That was *my* initiative. Harriet can't possibly justify her vigilante mission if the mother of one of the victims doesn't support her. She has to understand she's not the only person grieving for someone Regan killed, and not all of the other victims' families want to see Regan dead. Some of them want him to languish behind bars. It's not her choice alone to make. When Blue hears the message and turns up, Regan will follow, if we haven't already got him in custody from the hotel sting. Deputy Commissioner Woods and I are very confident in our plan."

Pops chewed the inside of his lip. The detective's eyes were following an officer across the hotel lobby on the screen. Pops hadn't wanted to be put into the position he was in now, having to ask a junior officer in front of all the officers present something he already knew the answer to. But he was left with no other choice.

"You sound like you have everything under control," Pops said. "My viewing of the Banks file shouldn't disrupt your plans."

Spader didn't even look at him.

"You may not view the file," Spader said after a long, humiliating moment of silence.

"Detective Spader," Pops managed, "do I need to remind

you of the rank structure in the New South Wales Police Force?"

"Apologies." Spader looked at the chief. "You may not view the file, *sir*. Deputy Commissioner Woods has it with him. He considers the information in it of the utmost confidentiality."

Pops glanced around the audience of officers near them.

"Detective Spader," he said carefully, "have you ever heard the expression 'switching horses midstream'?"

"Of course," Nigel said, a little too fast. Pops waited, but Nigel gave no indication of knowing why Pops had mentioned the old proverb. The chief turned on his heel, giving Nigel a look that he hoped communicated a promise that he would not forget the exchange they'd just shared.

The old man jangled his keys to the rhythm of his steps as he made his way down to the reception area of the command-center office and over to the front desk, where a young woman in a patrol officer's uniform was waiting for him.

"I couldn't get a phone number, but here's the address," the young officer said, handing Pops a folded slip of paper. "Judge Edgar Boscke."

CHAPTER 62

THE PHONE IN my pocket buzzed. Regan. He had called a dozen times while I slept at Melina's house, and twice more since I hit the road. I could almost feel his rage through the phone, a pulsing heat that seemed to make the phone hot to the touch. I took a breath and waited for the ringing to stop.

Before me, the dense bushland bordering the Bombala River, wet grass leading to reeds at the edge of the water.

I had pulled the bike over and entered the park after miles of fast, dangerous riding, the highways clear now of roadblocks looking for us. My face and neck were spattered with cold rain, and my socks were damp. Maybe by bringing the bike to death-defying speeds, taking corners at suicidal angles, I had been trying to tempt God, or fate, or whatever the hell was in control, to shut down my pursuit of Regan. If I was taken out of the game in an accident, I wouldn't have to face that terrible act, the one I knew was coming. The moment I would cross over and deliberately, with coldhearted planning, end a life.

I don't know what made me finally give in. But I picked up the phone as it started buzzing again and pushed the answer button.

"When I call, you answer," he said. His voice was smooth, quiet. But the danger was there. He sounded tired, slightly puffed, as though being unable to contact me had drained his physical strength.

"Or what?" I laughed. "You don't have any leverage over me left. You don't get to make demands when you're killing off the people who mean something to me. I don't have to participate in your bullshit."

"You could have made it easier on some people by co-operating," he said.

I crouched by the bike as my knees became weak. Who were these people, and what had Regan done to them? Or was he talking about something he was about to do, a plan now set in place that I could have talked him out of if I'd answered my phone? Across the river, a couple were taking a lunchtime stroll along the river-bank. I took my gun from my bag and actioned it, hardly daring to look in case I saw the inevitable shape of him appearing from the tree line, heading toward them. There would be nothing I could do but scream for help, fire aimlessly, hoping to scare him off. My breath caught in my chest even as I tried to sound calm.

"I'm outside the Bombala Town Hall," I lied. "Come get me."

"No, not yet, Harry."

"When, motherfucker?" I snapped. "How long do you think I'm going to keep playing this game? What if I just stop answering? What if I hand myself in?"

"You won't."

"You really sure about that?"

"I know you, Harry."

"You don't know jack shit. You're a disease. You only know how to infect and consume things."

"I know you're frustrated. But the time is coming. This is all a process. You need to just let go." He gave a small laugh, casual, like a man trying to convince a friend to try a new type of dessert. "It was easy for me. I had no choice. I went to prison. There were bars and cuffs and big walls to teach me who was in control. Harry, I'm in control of you. I'll give you your gift when it's time."

I said nothing. The couple across the river strolled safely out of sight.

"I'm going to send you another address," Regan said.

CHAPTER 63

THIS WAS BAD. Whitt was putting everyone in danger now, his colleagues, members of the public, Vada in the car beside him. She was in command, and had been all day, feeding him the pills seemingly whenever he asked for them, and sometimes when she said she thought he looked strung out. She was giving him more than he needed, but he didn't say anything. It wasn't her job to know the dose. And the boost he got when he tucked the pill into the space between his lips and gums, not just chemical but emotional, had become essential to his life. Three days high, and he was already a slave again.

Whitt was sure no one had noticed yet, but there were signs. He kept checking the safety on his weapon. Over and over, pushing that already pushed-down switch harder, until the grooves bit into his thumb. He kept hearing his phone ring, but it wasn't ringing. Kept spacing out when Vada was talking to him. And now he was climbing out of the car in a heady rush, the street blocked by patrol cars, the blue lights painful and blinding. Locked and loaded. Whitt pulled his weapon just as everyone else did, ready to go in, a walking time bomb unable to defuse himself.

An anonymous tip to the Bombala police station fifteen minutes earlier had brought much-needed energy to a mindless day of checking roadblocks, coordinating air searches, responding to possible sightings, the most recent in Bega, south of Nowra. Whitt and Vada were going to be there with the first responders. He was trembling with tension. Was it Regan again? They had an address. They were on.

Whitt followed the responders to the front door now, trying to be just a face in the crowd. He half-listened to the commands coming from the men in front of him.

"Who is it?" he asked Vada, who was there at his shoulder. Zinging memories of her body on top of his every time he looked at her, making his stomach clench. "Do we have any intel?"

"An old couple," Vada said. "That's all I know."

Whitt and Vada followed two huge men in tactical gear leading the charge. The door went down in a thump. All of a sudden he was inside, on his own, turning left and sweeping his torch and gun over darkened rooms. He could almost feel himself accidentally shooting someone. The gun bucking in his hands, an old woman falling as his bullet tore through her.

The front rooms were empty, painfully neat. Books on shelves, hand-stitched pillows sitting on antique furniture. Through the lace curtains, Whitt could see / officers running down the sides of the house, doing a sweep of the perimeter. He backed out of the front rooms and called out the clearance, heard a heavy gasp toward the back of the house.

The victims were in the dining room. Whitt caught a glimpse of two people sitting in ornate wooden chairs before one of the tactical officers pushed past him, heading for the front door, a gloved hand up against his mouth.

CHAPTER 64

RED. BRIGHT, ALMOST luminescent, a halo of it on the wall above their heads, blood sprayed as the killer worked. Their bodies were both drenched in it, sitting tied in the chairs back-to-back, his woolen slippers soaked in blood. Their deaths had been a drawn-out affair, maybe hours long. There were already flies, and a glass of water sat on the circular table, fingerprinted with pink, the killer having become thirsty midway through his task. Her robe was in a pile on the floor, boot-printed. She had been the focus of the attack. The old man was slumped forward, a necklace of dark blood running from a neat slit in his throat. Whitt couldn't see much of her from where he stood, but he knew she'd been worked on. Her angles weren't right. The foot nearest him was turned outward, the bare toes curled.

Whitt was following Vada through the tidy kitchen

and out the back of the house, the only sound in his ears the rushing of his own breath. He knew he was gasping, panting loudly, but couldn't stop the sound. Images he wasn't sure he'd even really seen were flashing before his eyes, as detailed and colorful as photographs.

Matted hair. Strips of wet duct tape. A handprint on a wall.

A group of three men in tactical suits rushed up to them in the lush garden.

"Detective, I've got men north, west, and east," an officer said. "I'll send this team south."

"No, send these men west," Vada said. "I've just heard a callout on the command line that Regan's been sighted near the end of the street."

The officer nodded and the men fled. Whitt found he was grabbing Vada's arm, something to hold on to as terror rushed through him in waves.

"I didn't hear any callout." He tugged at the radio on his belt. "Are we on the same frequency?"

"Don't worry about it." Vada peeled his hand from her arm. "Stay here. Take charge of the crime scene. I'll do a quick sweep south and be back in a flash."

Before he could answer, she was gone, her absence leaving him cold, shaken. He caught a glimpse of her, gun drawn, as she disappeared through the gate and into the forest at the southern end of the property.

CHAPTER 65

IT WAS TIME TO RUN.

I'd stayed as long as I could, crouched behind Eloise and Gary Jansen's house, watching the patrol-car lights on the trees. I'd called the local police as soon as Regan gave me the address, not knowing if there was a chance the couple might still be alive. I'd arrived just minutes before the first officers, hoping to catch Regan, but finding only my dead foster parents. As crews of tactical officers headed toward me, blind to my presence, I turned and ran through the yard, through the gate.

I imagined myself running from what I had seen, but as I pushed on, the tears forced their way up from my chest, into my throat. I sobbed once, giving myself just a second to surrender to the pain. Then the fury came, hot and comforting as it always was, rushing like fire through my veins. I glanced up and saw a helicopter tracking west. Curtains were twitching and front doors were opening. A neighborhood responding to Regan's horror.

Eloise and Gary had fostered me when I was a teenager. I had almost no memory of my time there, meaning I'd probably been in their care only a couple of months. The address hadn't rung a bell, but the extensive garden, full of wet flowers and flat, sprawling trees, had. I remembered Eloise had put the most effort into trying to crack my armor. She'd started predictably, with baked treats. Invitations to have "girl" chats. New clothes. The couple had been fostering a pair of toddlers at the time they had me. I had spent much of my time in the garden, brooding in the shade of one of the trees, a book in my lap that I only lifted as a shield when Eloise approached me.

I ran through the forest now and turned left down a wide dirt track cutting through the trees. I was breathless, unable to stop a furious growling coming from between my teeth, tears streaming down my face. The blood rushing through my head was pounding so hard that when I slowed and searched my pockets for the keys to the bike, I didn't even hear her approaching. I went to the bike, hidden behind a huge eucalypt trunk, and brought the keys out of my pocket.

"Harry."

I jumped at the voice, turned, and saw a red-haired woman standing at the roadside, seemingly as puffed as I was. I'd seen the woman through the back windows of the house, sweeping the crime scene with her gun. Whitt's new partner. She must have spotted me as I turned and ran off into the woods.

She didn't say another word. As I turned to flee, she raised the gun and fired.

CHAPTER 66

THE FIRST SHOT whizzed over my shoulder, the muzzle flash lighting up the trees around us. She was not experienced with the weapon. The gun had kicked and she had to adjust her grip on it, her fingers sliding, probably with sweat from the run. I turned and saw she was aiming right at my chest. I fell, scrambled, the keys falling from my hand. I got up and ran. The second shot knocked my right leg out from under me. I sprawled on the soil, then rose and staggered away from the trail and into the trees.

I'd been shot before, so I recognized the sensation. A biting, burning pain in my calf, creeping up to fever pitch, making the whole limb shake as I powered along. I told myself I wasn't going to stop, though every ounce of my body begged me to.

The forest floor fell away suddenly, a steep embankment. I rolled and slid, pushing myself off a thick tree trunk, using the momentum to keep my pace toward the river.

CHAPTER 67

WHITT COULD BARELY comprehend what he had
seen. He walked stiff-legged down onto the track where
Vada was standing. She was panting with adrenaline, trying to unjam the pistol's slide and eject the round stuck
in the chamber. When Whitt's foot snapped a twig lying
across the road, Vada turned on him, her eyes wild.

"You shot her," Whitt breathed, hardly believing the
words as they came out of his mouth. "You shot Harry."

"She pulled a gun on me," Vada said, handing the
weapon to Whitt. Whitt unjammed the pistol as though
in a dream, picking the round up from the mud with
shaking fingers. Vada held her hand out for the weapon,
but Whitt found that his own hands were clamped on
the gun so tightly, he didn't seem to be able to give it
back. His mind was screaming for him not to hand it
over.

Again and again, he saw Vada's arm rise as she pointed the gun at the shadowy figure of Harry.

Harry's back had been turned.

Hadn't it?

"Harry's now a dangerous fugitive," Vada said. "She pointed a gun at an officer. You saw it. You saw her try to fire on me, didn't you?"

Whitt stood trembling, looking at Vada's open palm.

"Whitt," Vada said, "give me the gun."

He didn't resist as she pried the weapon from him. She tucked it into her holster, her eyes imploring him. When her hands came to his shoulders, he almost sank into her arms.

"I need you to back me, Whitt," she said. "The way I've been backing you. Remember those officers on the bridge? No one needs to know about this."

"She was turned away."

"You're buzzed out of your mind. You don't know what you saw. Harry's your friend. She made a mistake. We'll find her before she hurts herself or anyone else."

He said nothing. She gave his hand a squeeze, then went ahead up the narrow animal trail toward the crime scene. While her back was turned, Whitt considered his plan.

CHAPTER 68

THE OLD ADAGE was that crime didn't pay. Pops thought that even though that probably wasn't true, there was something to be said for maintaining the illusion. He parked the patrol car a block down from Judge Boscke's enormous house in Kirribilli, thinking that while he was saving the judge the embarrassment of being seen to be hosting a police officer in the early evening, he was probably loading that same embarrassment on some politician or actress or another. As he switched off the ignition, a reminder pinged on his phone. Pops opened his internet app and found the live feed of the press conference without trouble. A dark-haired woman was on the screen, reading from a piece of paper at a lectern. Cameras flashed in front of her. The paper in her hand was shaking, as was her voice.

"My name is Annie Parish. Doctor Samantha Parish was my sister," the woman said. "She was a warm, clever, funny person. She was a gifted medical professional, and a good mother to my beautiful niece Isobel, who was also taken. I've lost two members of my family to Regan Banks."

Pops turned the sound up on his phone, glancing outside the car.

"It is my understanding," the woman continued, wiping at a tear with a trembling hand, "that there is a police officer, Detective Harriet Blue, who is missing out there somewhere. A reward is being offered for information on her whereabouts. I would like to speak directly to Harriet Blue, if she is listening."

Pops winced, realizing he had chewed his thumbnail down to the tender flesh beneath. The woman on the screen looked at the cameras, letting the hand that held her written speech settle on the lectern's surface.

"Detective Blue," Ms. Parish said, "I encourage you to find that son of a bitch Regan Banks, and kill him."

Pops's mouth fell open, as did those of the men and women at the edges of the screen, standing behind Ms. Parish. Someone strode forward, a family member maybe, and put a hand on Ms. Parish's shoulders. Tears were streaming down the woman's face.

"Make him suffer," she said, her blazing eyes looking right down the camera. "Make him suffer the way my sister and my niece suffered."

The crowd of reporters burst into questions, yelling, microphones rising out of the gathering below the stage. Pops watched as the news program cut back to the anchors, and then he shut his phone.

So much for the two-pronged plan.

CHAPTER 69

POPS WALKED TOWARD the judge's house, caught glimpses of the sparkling harbor between the mansions, the golden bridge yawning across the shores. After he was admitted through the gates of the Boscke residence, Pops stood watching a marble water feature bubbling by the front door for an inordinate amount of time. Judge Boscke answered the door himself, wearing black slacks and a T-shirt pulled down over a belly rounded by wealth.

The library was on the second floor. It wasn't often that Pops felt young these days, but he did following the judge up the stairs, pausing to give him a better lead every three steps or so. They sat in leather armchairs, and no drink was offered, though there was an elaborate drinks table by the windows. It was a bad sign.

"Joe Woods's father was a great man," Boscke said by way of beginning. "I spoke at his funeral."

Pops felt the air leave his lungs heavily, pressed out by a new, great weight.

"I'm not trying to make waves here." Pops put his hands up in surrender. "Obviously, Joe and I have our differences. We're not on the same page about running this investigation, and that's fine. But disarming me so that he can go ahead and do things his way? That was wrong."

"He shouldn't have suspended you," the judge reasoned. "From what I know of Joe, he was probably just trying to be the big man in town. He's a hothead. It works for him. Sometimes you need the swift, heavy-handed players in this game and sometimes you need the slow, methodical types, like yourself. But the two types shouldn't interfere with each other."

"I'm not going to obey the suspension," Pops said.

"Nor should you," the judge said. "This Banks fellow is a runaway train and we're all his terrified passengers. We need everyone we've got on this."

Pops shifted, preparing to begin his request.

"I know why you're here," Boscke said before he could speak. "The sealed report. I can't help you with that."

Pops slumped in his chair.

"In accessing the sealed files on Banks, he's inadvertently cut you out," the judge said. "Even if I wanted to tell you what those records say, I couldn't. I don't have them here, and the approval was for Woods only. I rushed it through because I know the man. If you want to see them, you'll have to have Joe show you or you'll have to make an application to the court yourself, which will take time."

"Woods isn't going to let me see the file."

"What's your interest in it, exactly?" Boscke asked.

Pops explained his theory that something in Regan's early childhood might be calling him, that maybe he was heading south, leading Harriet toward a place that was meaningful to him.

"If there was some clue in the files, why would Joe keep that from you?"

Because he's an arsehole, Pops thought.

"Maybe he's missed something in there." Pops sighed. "He doesn't see the file's significance. He's very focused on finding Harriet. He doesn't trust her."

"I think we can both understand why that is," the judge reasoned. Pops hadn't considered it before, but perhaps part of Woods's hyper-focus on Harriet was to do with his own daughter's troubles. At seventeen years old, Tonya Woods had been in the back of a vehicle full of her less-than-reputable friends when a pair of patrol officers pulled them over in Blacktown, in Sydney's Western suburbs. The officers had made the car as identical to one described driving by a house only minutes earlier and opening fire on the front of a property. The house that was fired upon had seven people in it. A man had been killed, and a six-year-old boy had taken a bullet in the arm as he slept in the front bedroom.

The papers had loved the story. Joe Woods had been an up-and-coming Homicide star not yet faded from the national news, the head of a team who had solved a serial-rapist case a month earlier. He'd caught a whiff of celebrity, of the promotions and power that would come with being a police poster boy, and then suddenly his own daughter was on trial for murder. Tonya had escaped with good lawyers and convincing stories about not having any knowledge of what her friends had planned to do. But she had been in and out of the newspapers in the years since; drunk, high, on the periphery of violent crimes.

"Whatever daddy-daughter issues Joe has with his child, they can't come into this investigation," Pops said. "He can't punish Harry because he doesn't have the balls to rein in his kid."

"What can I say?" Judge Boscke held up his hands. "You've got an impasse, the two of you."

Pops leaned forward, clasped his hands as though in prayer.

"I know you've tried thousands of cases in the family court," he said. "And Regan was taken into state care more than thirty years ago. You couldn't possibly remember the details of every single case. But is there *anything at all* that you can remember from the Banks case? Do you remember what happened with his parents? Why you sealed the file? Did you look at the file before you approved for it to be released to Woods?"

"Morris." The judge shook his head slowly. "These days I struggle to remember my own damn phone number. I didn't look at the file when I signed the release."

Pops hung his head.

"All you could do," Boscke carried on, "is have a look at my notes from the year Banks entered the system. I always kept a journal, especially when I was in the Family Courts. Some of those hearings went on for years."

The judge stood and went to a set of shelves nearby.

He selected a red leather book from a vast collection, opened it, and leafed through the pages idly.

"I might have written about sealing the Regan Banks file. I might not. If there's anything about it, it'll be in here somewhere."

Pops found he'd risen from the chair without meaning to, his fists clenched in anticipation. He could hardly wait to launch into the books as the old man left the room. He took down the one the old man had picked out, but it was the wrong year. He fumbled through the books, sliding them out and dumping them on the little desk, flipping pages and staring at dates. The sections were uneven, the judge's handwriting almost indecipherable.

Regan had gone into care in 1982 at seven years old. But when had the state decided they would pursue full custody of Regan? Had Regan's custody automatically been handed over to the foster-care system after the incident that got him removed from his parents, or had there been a hearing? Had his parents fought to have him back? Pops needed to know exactly when the decision to seal the file had been handed down in all the proceedings after the incident, and he didn't even know exactly when the incident, whatever it was, had occurred. Pops found his head was pounding. He sat down at the desk, slightly woozy, and forced himself to advance more slowly through the yellowed, scrawled pages.

CHAPTER 70

AT FIRST, WHITT tried to get through it one second at a time. *Tick, tick, tick.* He set his features, cleared his mind, nodded, and did what he had to do, his hand on his phone in his pocket, waiting for the safest moment. All afternoon he directed the techs as the bodies were removed and the evidence and photographs taken, standing beside Vada as she took reports from the teams searching for Regan in the local area. As evening descended, senior officers arrived from Bombala and surrounds and took over some of the required duties, cordoning off the street and keeping the neighbors and press who gathered on the nearby lawns at bay. When he was convinced it was safe, Whitt walked in the dark toward his car. With apprehension sitting sharp and heavy like a rock in his stomach, he glanced back toward the house, where he had left Vada supervising the crime scene, and dialed.

Pops answered on the second ring.

"I was just going to call you," Pops said before Whitt could speak. "I'm chasing down what I can on the Regan Banks CIR file. I feel like we need to take a different angle on this. The answers are right here. I just need to find them."

Whitt drew a deep breath, tried to keep his voice steady. He couldn't think how to respond to Pops's comments about the files, had hardly heard them. He closed his eyes and let the words come.

"Harry's been shot at," Whitt said.

There was a pause. Whitt heard the older officer's strained intake of breath.

"She's been shot?"

"Shot *at*," Whitt corrected. "I don't think she was hit. She ran off. We've got a new crime scene here in Bombala. It's Regan. Harry showed up. Regan must have told her where to go. My partner discovered her, and she shot at her, and I don't know where Harry is now."

Pops was speaking, but Whitt's head was pounding so hard, he couldn't focus. He held the car for support, felt adrenaline rush through him, the Dexedrine responding to his terror.

"I think Vada should be called back to Sydney," Whitt said. "She's a good officer. But I think she's in the wrong frame of mind about Harry, and—"

"Vada who?" Pops thundered. "Who the fuck is this person?"

Whitt felt his skin grow cold.

"Vada Reskit," Whitt said. "She's from North Sydney metro. Woods assigned her."

More silence. Whitt's jaw was clenched so tight, his teeth clicked.

"She said you'd approved the assignment," he offered.

"I've never heard of her," Pops said. "I didn't approve the assignment of any new officers to this case. What did you say her name was again?"

Whitt was about to answer when the phone was taken from his hand. He turned and watched Vada end the call, her features sharp and pale in the light of the screen. He would have reached out to stop her, snatch the phone back, but the gun in her hand was pointed right at his belly.

She lifted her eyes to him, and they were the tired, sad eyes of someone well-versed in betrayal.

"Get in the car, Whitt," Vada said.

CHAPTER 71

THE FOREST WAS ALIVE.

As I'd run from the crime scene, there had been no time to consider what Whitt's partner shooting at me had meant. I'd simply fled.

I didn't know how far I'd come. The land beneath me sloped downward and then flattened, the thick bush receding suddenly at the edge of a pine plantation. I lay down beneath a tree and waited, panting, for the inevitable return of the pain in my calf, the sensation kept at bay by the adrenaline surging through my veins.

"Shit," I seethed, dragging the shuddering limb toward me, tentatively pulling up the blood-soaked leg of my jeans. I wiped away handfuls of blood. "Shit. Shit. Shit."

It was a graze, but a deep one. The bullet had entered the back of my calf, heading diagonally through the flesh, tearing away a hole in the meat the size of my pinkie finger. I pulled my jacket off, sweat pouring down my chest and ribs, thinking I'd have to remove a sleeve for a bandage. The air was misting in front of my mouth as I breathed. I unzipped and emptied the backpack on a whim, hoping I wouldn't have to sacrifice my much-needed warmth to patch the wound.

There, at the bottom of the bag, a Ziploc first-aid kit with a roll of cotton bandages.

"Melina," I moaned. "Melina, you fucking champion."

I rolled the bandage around the wound tightly, making soft, whiny sounds at the pain. The limb felt hot and numb now, the nerves shocked or dead. More pain would come later, I knew. When I had fixed the wound, I lay on the damp ground and looked at the sky between the black spears of branches above me.

I slept. When I woke, it was dark. I lay trying to decide where I was, how tight I still held my grip on reality.

Like clockwork, my phone rang, startling something big and wild hiding in the forest nearby that had probably drawn forward by the smell of my blood and the sound of my whining. I answered the phone, packing my bag again, the precious body heat I'd gained in the run now gone and my limbs starting to shake.

"Harry," Regan said.

"I've made a decision," I told him.

CHAPTER 72

HE WAS SMILING. I could hear it in his voice.

"What's your decision?" he asked.

"When I find you," I said, "I'm going to shoot you in the leg. You deserve to have all the pain you've caused to others inflicted back on you. I'm going to start there, and I'm going to continue shooting until you're just a pile of broken bones and bloodied flesh."

"You have a very graphic mind," he said. "I enjoy hearing your little violent fantasies. I really do. I have my own ones. You've been able to see some of them."

"Lucky me," I said, curling on the ground, holding the phone to my ear.

"You sound cold," he said. "I spent a lot of my time in prison feeling cold. I know you're out there in the wind and rain hunting me. With every layer I strip from you, you're going to feel that icy chill. Brand-new skin exposed to the air. It's kind of exhilarating, isn't it? Those people, Eloise and Gary Jansen, they're another layer I've taken from you."

"You keep their names out of your filthy mouth," I snarled.

"Eloise told me some things about you," Regan said. Wherever he was, it was dead quiet. "She didn't take much prodding to remember you among her collection of needful children. You were her dark-hearted one. Her wild bird. She had to really work on you. You trusted no one."

I closed my eyes and listened, remembering.

"She said she could tell you'd been in the system a long time. When she tried to hug you, you backed away. You ate furiously. She caught you hoarding snacks in your room. She said you were utterly without warmth toward the smaller children they were caring for at the time. You didn't find them cute or entertaining. You'd probably been around so many of them in your life, right? What's another snotty-nosed brat who no one wants?"

He was really enjoying this. I held the phone against my ear, trying to catch my warm breath and filter it back against my face with the collar of my coat. My leg was throbbing. I remembered Eloise trying to show me how to crochet, sitting on the couch, colorful balls of yarn all around her. When she'd tried to take my fingers, reposition them on the hook, I'd dropped everything and stormed away. I wished now I'd given her more of a chance.

"Eloise Jansen told me all these things about the child Harriet Blue," Regan said. "She told me that you came around. That you eventually learned to trust them. She'd wanted to keep you longer, because she knew you had promise."

I squeezed my eyes shut, not wanting to listen but not being able to pull the phone away.

"I have those memories now. I even have a little picture of you that Eloise kept on the wall. The illusion you've held about yourself all these years is wrong, Harry. That layer is gone. The hope and the brightness and those warm moments with people like Eloise Jansen—I've taken them away."

"How long am I going to have to listen to this?" I asked. "Listening to you talk makes me want to peel off my own face and eat it like a crepe."

"You're not enjoying this?"

"Not at all."

"I am," Regan said. "This is all about you, sure. But every time I take someone meaningful from you, I get all these beautiful things in return. It's good work that I'm doing here, Harry. You'll see."

"Wonderful," I said. "I'm glad you're happy. You enjoy those things while you can. I'm going to take them back from you when I kill you. It'll be like a trip down memory lane. Me remembering, you screaming in pain."

He laughed. I wiped my running nose on my sleeve.

"The Sydney police tried to set me up," Regan said. "They used your mother as bait."

"Oh?" I said.

"They really have no idea, do they?" he said. "She was just a vessel for you. I'm not interested in her. I want to take the people who you really value, the ones you think you need."

"You really like the sound of your own voice, don't you?" I said. "You're such a versatile killer. Some people you strangle and stab. Others you bore to death."

"Our mothers were the same," Regan mused. He was almost talking to himself now. "Just empty shells."

I paused. The exhaustion was pulling away my anger. I needed to start listening. He wasn't just talking. He was trying to draw me into his mind.

"Did you love her?" I asked.

"No," he said. He sounded comfortable. Relaxed. Perhaps the kill had tired him. "I've loved in my life. You know that I have."

"My brother," I said.

"Yes," he admitted. "That was the first time. I was seventeen. I'd never felt it before. Those last few days with my mother were probably the closest I ever got. She'd walk me up to the lighthouse and we'd stand together, and I'd try to love her. So close, but . . ." He trailed off. I pressed the phone hard against my ear.

A lighthouse, I thought. *I have to remember that.*

"Where do I go next?" I asked him. "You're taking me somewhere that's important to you, aren't you? You said I'd understand you when we met. When will this end, Regan? Just tell me."

"This is about me, Harry," he said. "But it's also about you." There was an odd pause, the phone going silent, as though he'd taken it away from his mouth and I couldn't hear his breathing any longer. When he returned, his voice had gone up an octave. Excited.

"Things may be moving faster than I'd planned," he said.

CHAPTER 73

THEY DROVE. WHITT focused on the lines on the road, the wheel in his hands something to hang on to when all else seemed to be falling away. He was hyperaware of the gun in Vada's hand, still pointed at his belly. He swigged from the bottle of Jack he had kept in the car since they'd left Sydney. She didn't seem to mind him drinking. He wasn't going to crash on the back roads they took between the fields, at a carefully chosen speed she wouldn't allow him to exceed. The directions that came from her were softly spoken, the same intimate tone she'd used when she'd been in his arms in the motel bed, her lips against his ear.

She'd been so tender. So reassuring in those moments as he moved inside her. Now she was the same. Tender, but lethal. Walking him gently toward his death. They pulled over as she directed, and she took his cuffs from his belt. As she leaned in toward him, he could smell the familiar scent of her body. So strange to twitch in terror at her touch now when it had given him such pleasure only a day earlier.

"Vada," he said, breaking the heavy silence. "Vada, let's talk."

She cuffed his wrists to the car's steering wheel, took the keys from the ignition, and closed the car door behind her. Whitt watched her walk to the back of the car. She had taken out her phone. He twisted awkwardly and tried to listen through the back window, which was slightly ajar.

"But I need you to come," Vada was saying, her voice smaller, frailer than Whitt had ever heard it. "Why not? Where are you? I can't...I can't do it myself again. The first time, the cop in the records room drew his gun and I could...I could *do it* then because I needed to. I can do it again but I've been with Edward three days. Just this time. Regan, please."

There was a long pause. Whitt listened to the wind.

"He's definitely the best choice," Vada said. "He's the closest person to her now."

Whitt twisted and watched Vada's shape in the dark. Her arms were hugged around herself.

"It's almost over," she said. "You promise? After this, it's over."

CHAPTER 74

WHEN SHE GOT into the car again, her cheeks were rosy from the cold. She uncuffed him and ordered him to continue driving. After a time impossible to measure, Whitt broke through the sizzling tension.

"Karmichael and Fables," he said.

She sighed.

"You went in through the car park." Whitt shuddered. "You shot them both. You took the file, and you fled into the building rather than back out. You passed me in the dark in the hallway. I smelled the gunpowder."

"Whitt," she said gently, "stay on the road."

He steered the wandering car back toward the center of the dirt road. The headlights rolled over a group of cows resting under a tree.

"You didn't have a swipe card that next morning, the day after we met." He swigged the bourbon. "I didn't

238

even notice. I never saw your badge. No one ever questioned your presence. Everyone must have just assumed you were meant to be there. But you're not a cop. Of course you aren't. You didn't know how to unjam your pistol when you—"

"Whitt."

"That's how he's got around all the roadblocks. That's how he avoided the searches. You've been his eyes and ears on the ground."

"This isn't helpful," she said. He glanced at her. Her eyes were so dark, the whites looked pale blue.

"You must have been terrified," Whitt said. "At any moment, I could have mentioned you to Woods or Morris and it would all have been over, the whole charade."

"I was terrified," she admitted. Her face was expressionless. She said the words like she was reporting the time.

"Who are you?"

"I'm Vada Reskit." She turned to face the windscreen. Whitt thought about grabbing the gun. Was the safety off? He couldn't see. "Regan was my patient."

Whitt squeezed the steering wheel.

"The prison psychologist's reports," he whispered, almost to himself. "That's why they were missing from the file." Whitt laughed humorlessly. "I didn't even chase it up. There was so much paperwork on Regan. I assumed all it would say was that he was a psychopath. But it would have mentioned your name, so you never gave it to police."

She seemed reluctant to explain it all. Whitt drank, sucking the burning liquor down, a piece of his fractured mind desperately recording sensations, knowing these were going to be his last. The last field he would ever see, moonlit through the window before him. The last words he would ever hear.

"We were together for six years." She gave a tiny smile. "Every Tuesday, every Thursday. Regan had been in prison for a long time when he was assigned to me. He was a lot of work. He played a lot of games. Tested me. Trying to see if he could trust me." Vada gave a shuddering sigh. "He became my only real project. The only thing I cared about. It was like, the rest of the week I was on fire. As soon as he laid eyes on me, I'd feel relief."

"Regan Banks is a vicious killer," Whitt said. "He killed a child. You stood in that house back there and you looked at what he'd done to those people. You . . . you sat before me and you *looked* at the autopsy photographs of those girls . . ."

Whitt was almost shouting. When her words cut over his, her voice was thick with some hidden emotion.

"Regan is *worthy*," Vada said. "You couldn't possibly understand, because you didn't sit with him for half a decade and learn about his life, about what made him this way. You don't think what he does hurts him? He is worthy of—"

"Of what?" Whitt howled. "Of saving? *You're* going to save him? You're out of your mind! He's not a rescue dog! He's a *serial killer!*"

Whitt struggled to breathe. The car was crawling along the dirt road slowly, delaying the inevitable. She didn't seem to mind.

"He made a killer of you," Whitt said. "He brainwashed you so completely...I can't believe I didn't see this. Those five weeks. We couldn't find him. Of course we couldn't—you were harboring him."

"Turn here." Vada pointed. Whitt looked and saw a tiny turnoff, a track that died no more than two car lengths into the forest. Whitt did as he was told.

"He sent you to get close to me," Whitt said. His throat was so tight, it was hard to swallow. "To watch the investigation, and to see if killing me would hurt her the most. You asked if she was my girlfriend. You wanted to know if I was the right choice."

Vada motioned for him to get out of the car.

"You are the right choice," she said.

CHAPTER 75

DETECTIVE NIGEL SPADER found Deputy Commissioner Woods in the concrete smokers' courtyard behind the command building. The big man was hugging his coat against the wind, pacing back and forth, a small mobile phone clutched tightly to his ear.

"Tonya, I'm not asking you to go back to the facility," he growled. "I'm telling you. There will be enough money in your account to get your arse in a cab and not a cent more."

Woods canceled the call, stabbing the phone with his thumb like he was squashing a bug. When he saw Nigel watching him, he scowled.

"I've authorized the Bristol Gardens operation for another night," Nigel said. "Just because Regan hasn't turned up yet doesn't mean he won't show tonight. He might be waiting for something."

Woods patted his pockets for his cigarettes, didn't

answer. When Nigel offered his pack, the bigger man snatched them coldly from his fingers. The shadows from the courtyard lights made his eyes unreadable.

"Sir, I have another suggestion," Nigel continued.

"I'm all out of patience for helpful fucking suggestions," Woods barked, taking his phone from his pocket and silencing the call that was coming through. "Put it in an email and leave me alone."

"With all due respect, sir, it may be more time-critical than that," Nigel said. "I've been dealing with Chief Morris, who has been trying to access the Banks CIR file. He believes we may have overlooked the importance of Regan's childhood to what he's doing—"

"Detective Spader." Woods massaged his brow, squeezed his eyes shut. "If you think I want to hear theories from the genius mind of Chief Morris right now, you really do have your head planted firmly up your own arse."

"Sir"—Nigel approached his superior officer cautiously—"Chief Morris's theory might be bullshit. But he's pursuing it. And if he's right, and we're wrong, we run the risk of handing this whole case and all the due credit for solving it to the man we just ousted for his sheer incompetence."

Woods exhaled smoke, squinting through it at Detective Spader.

"He thinks Regan might be going back to where the incident occurred."

"And why the fuck would he want to revisit something like that?" Woods said. "What I read in that file makes me sick."

"That's just what this guy is," Nigel said, shrugging. "Sick."

Woods considered. "We don't know when he would go there," he said eventually.

"Better to set up a team immediately, then," Nigel said. "And every night until he shows. If he shows."

Woods licked his teeth. He dropped the cigarette and stamped it out, his decision made.

CHAPTER 76

"START WALKING," VADA said, poking him in the shoulder with the gun.

"Think about what you've done for this man," Whitt said, taking uneven steps forward in the dark. "You've killed two people. You've...you've impersonated a police officer. You're going to...you're..."

You're going to kill me.

He couldn't say the words. He swigged the bourbon.

"This isn't you," Whitt said. "You've made a mistake. Surely they told you this when you signed on to counsel convicted killers. Surely they told you how manipulative they can be, how seductive."

He stumbled, fell on his hands. The bottle sloshed into the mud. She nudged him with her boot.

"Get up."

Whitt looked around. There was nowhere to run, and

he was too drunk to attempt it. If he sprinted away now, he'd fall helplessly, bash into trees, stagger unarmed until she found him and ended him. His only chance was to keep talking. It was so cold. His jacket was back at the crime scene. He gripped the bourbon bottle so hard, his knuckles ached. They walked in silence.

"I know what you're thinking," Whitt pressed on eventually. "He's a dangerous animal. He's clever. Cunning. *Bad*. But you understand him. Only you. And that makes you special. Of course it does. You understand the real Regan. That's why you do what you do. Because you refuse to give up on them. The worst of the worst. Maybe ... maybe someone refused to give up on you, and now ..."

"Stop walking," she said. "Get on your knees."

"He's not what you think he is."

"I said kneel down!"

"There's a part of you that's not sure about this," Whitt said. "You shot at Harry. Regan would never have allowed you to do that. Maybe you thought you could kill her, end Regan's game. End it for him *and* you. Vada, there's still a chance to—"

"It's over, Whitt," she said. "Please kneel."

She clicked the hammer back on the pistol and pointed it at his face.

He knelt.

Whitt's mind raced, new frantic arguments forming, but before he could voice them, the strange automatic impulse that he'd felt when he punched the officer on the bridge overtook him. He lunged at her legs.

The gun's blast lit up the forest.

CHAPTER 77

THEY FELL TOGETHER, and Whitt heard the gun clatter to the dirt. He didn't know where the shot had gone, but he knew he wasn't hit. Whitt rolled in the dirt, managed to get on top of Vada, his hands gripping hers over the gun. He was on autopilot, watching a man who was not him grapple for the weapon, trying to force all his weight down on her. He could not focus on her face. He knew seeing her desperate eyes would confuse him, remind him of the Vada he thought he knew, distract him from what he needed to do. He let go with one hand and punched downward, a half-strength blow that glanced off her jaw. Just enough to stop her, not enough to really hurt her. She rolled, and he lost his balance, and the gun's deadly eye swung around at him again.

Another shot. This one seemed to be louder.

Whitt cowered, his hands on his head, unable to take his eyes off Vada.

She was just as surprised by the shot. The blast had not come from her gun. She swung her weapon in the direction that it had come, but through the darkness came another muzzle flash, the shot this time whizzing over both their heads.

She got up and ran. Whitt watched the space between the trees into which she'd vanished, his hands still gripping his skull. When he turned back toward where the gunshots had come from, he saw it.

It emerged, bent-backed, the shoulders slightly slanted and the head lowered, two black eyes visible through slivers of icy blond hair. A ghoul or ghost, a twisted, hellish skull mask, the cheeks hollow and the eyes sunken. As he walked, unsteady, into the moonlight, Whitt recognized the ominous line of a battered leather jacket, one dirty steel-capped boot swinging, landing, with the deadly confidence of an executioner.

Tox extended the gun in both hands as he came toward Whitt. He motioned as he passed, palm out, telling Whitt silently to stay where he was.

Then Tox disappeared.

Like a specter, his movements were smooth and soundless, leaving enormous prints behind in the mud. Whitt wasn't sure what was real now and what was a dream, brought on either by the drugs, the booze, or the threat of his own death.

He waited in the dark, standing alone, until Tox returned, the gun hanging by his side.

"She got away," Tox growled. "Worst shooting of my life. I should have thrown the fucking gun at her."

CHAPTER 78

WHITT WRAPPED HIS arms around the other man.

"Get off." Tox shoved Whitt away. "We've got to get out of here before she doubles back on us." As he pushed his friend, Tox almost toppled Whitt over. He grabbed a handful of Whitt's sweat-damp shirt and pulled him steady.

"What's wrong with you?" Tox's face was narrower than Whitt remembered, darkened by a thick brown beard. When he frowned, his features pointed, dangerously sharp. "Are you...are you *drunk*?"

"Yes," Whitt admitted. "And high."

Tox considered the man before him. Then he slapped him hard across the side of the head.

"Oh, fuck!" Whitt gripped his face. "What was that for?"

"For being drunk and high in the middle of a fucking

police investigation—what do you think?" Tox shook his head, disgusted. He grabbed Whitt by the shoulder and shoved him toward the edge of the forest. "Jesus Christ, people are gunfighting around you and you're sippin' margaritas."

"What the hell are you doing here?" Whitt stumbled forward as Tox kept shoving him.

"I got sick of being babysat in a hospital bed like a drooling invalid," Tox said. "I'd have come earlier, but Chief Morris put some goon-for-hire friend of his on my room who wouldn't let me leave. I had to take him out with a fold-up chair to the back of the head. It'll probably strain the relationship." He considered this for a moment, then shrugged. "Meh."

As the route through the forest widened, they walked side by side.

"How did you find me?"

"Didn't take a genius," Tox said. "I saw the news reports about Bombala and followed all the blue and red lights. I was walking right toward you down the road outside the crime scene when I saw some chick come up and stick a gun in your guts."

"I didn't see you," Whitt said.

"You were distracted," Tox reasoned.

"I'm so glad you're here." Whitt drew a ragged breath. "I'm so—"

"Hug me again and I'll pull your spleen out."

Whitt nodded. He observed that Tox wasn't walking right. The ghoulish appearance he'd had as he emerged from the dark was the result of weight and color lost during his coma. He had the strained look of a man who

should rightfully have been dead but hadn't quite returned to the land of the living yet, either. He walked
slightly twisted, a hand braced against his stomach
where five weeks earlier he'd been stabbed with a ten-
inch kitchen knife.

"Should you be out of bed?" Whitt asked. "You don't
look right."

"Heh! This from the fucking booze hound with
pupils like dinner plates," Tox said. As they emerged
onto the moonlit road, he pointed. A dented black vintage Monaro was parked at an odd angle against a fence.
"Get in the car. Then you can tell me all about the crazy
bitch who nearly just blew your brains out."

CHAPTER 79

THE SUNLIGHT CAME and went. In the bare, windswept farmhouse where I spent the night and most of the day sleeping, I saw no sign of it. Curled in a corner on the floor, blocked from the view of the open doorway by a table I had turned on its side, I lay and dreamed of Regan's victims, my brother in his jail cell, and for some worrying reason, Pops in the back of an ambulance. Memories, visions, premonitions, I didn't know. My leg was throbbing again. I unrolled the blood-soaked bandage, cleaned the wound with alcohol wipes from the small first-aid kit, and rewrapped it.

As I emerged into the thick twilight and looked across the field toward the mountains, I called Pops on the new number Whitt had given me.

"Jesus Christ, Harry," he breathed. "All day I've been sitting waiting for them to tell me you were dead. Were you hit?"

"Yes," I answered. "Not badly. Scratch on the leg. Who shot me?"

"Her name's Vada Reskit," Pops said.

He told me about her. In her time as a prison psychologist in Long Bay's maximum-security unit, she had gained access to some of the country's worst serial killers and rapists, and a couple of men imprisoned for their role in terrorist plots targeting Australian cities. For six years, Vada and Regan had sat together twice a week talking about the ins and outs of his twisted mind. Evidently, she had grown close to him. Learned to love him, perhaps. Pops told me that in the past twenty-four hours, while I had slept, the news media had already begun digging into what they could about Vada, had drawn out her shocked mother and brother for interviews and started spinning write-ups on her childhood.

She'd been a strange, isolated teenager. Vada had been taken out of her high school at sixteen for having an "inappropriate" relationship with her married physical education teacher. She'd been married herself at twenty-one to a poker-machine mogul who was edging into his seventies, an abusive, manipulative man who dumped her for his personal assistant when they'd been wed only three weeks.

Vada was not only a mixed-up, lonely woman, she was a gifted fraud. No one had been able to confirm exactly where she'd obtained her psychology degree or what year she'd graduated, and a raid on her house that morning had uncovered a real-estate agent's blazer and badge and dozens of folders crammed with paperwork for a mortgage company she didn't appear to work for.

Vada Reskit been known by four other names. Homicide detectives had obtained CCTV footage of her in the street one block away from the Parramatta police headquarters on the morning of the shooting in the records room, crossing the street with a bag on her hip.

I listened to Pops's tale and remembered the woman I'd glimpsed marching into the crime scene with Whitt, totally at ease pretending to be a law-enforcement official. I remembered her face above the gun, suddenly colder and devoid of life compared to the stern, determined look she'd had the first time I'd seen her. Mask on, mask off.

Vada had probably learned the art of deception from the men she drew to her. The teacher who preyed on his students. The older billionaire who burned through people like he did dollars. The dangerously attractive serial killer who, for years, bent and twisted her mind to his will. But maybe I was being too kind to Vada. Maybe she was as darkly clever as the predatory men she had partnered with over the years. Maybe all along I had been dealing with not one psychopath, but two.

Pops told me of Whitt's near miss with Vada.

"I haven't spoken to Whitt," Pops said. "He won't answer his phone. I'm getting all this information secondhand from officers in Bombala. I don't know how he got away, but he's safe, they tell me. They're searching for Vada now."

"They won't find her," I said. "She'll go to Regan now."

"Harry," Pops said carefully, "I know you won't listen to me. But I'm going to implore you anyway. Please come in. We know Regan's not alone now. He's going to lure you into a trap, and you're going to go willingly because you think it's your duty or something. Harry, I know why Regan went into foster care. I know more about this man than you do."

A chill came over me. I stood, had to steady myself in the doorway.

"He's a monster, Harry."

"Tell me what happened," I said.

Pops sighed.

"If you know *what* happened to Regan as a child, you know *where* it happened," I pressed. "Tell me."

"I'm not going to help you put your head in the lion's mouth," Pops said. "I'm not even sure he's leading you there. The house isn't there anymore. It was lost..." He paused. "Harry, please, you have to listen to me, vengeance for your brother is not—"

I hung up and grabbed my bag from inside the farmhouse, gritting my teeth through the pain. Night had fallen. If Pops wasn't going to help me, I wasn't going to waste my time trying to convince him. Regan was out there, and now I knew he had a friend, a woman who'd spent her life lying, manipulating, searching for that dark partner in crime she'd found in Regan Banks.

She was going down with him.

CHAPTER 80

AS I HEADED TOWARD the highway, my phone buzzed.

"Well, well, well," I said before Regan could speak. "Someone's got a *girlfriend*. Turns out she's a chronic fuck-up as well. Couldn't pour water out of a boot, that one. Your squeeze had me at ten paces and she couldn't hit me, and now she's let Edward Whittacker slip away."

Regan was quiet for a moment.

"She had you at ten paces?" he repeated.

"Oh, she didn't tell you she fired at me?" I laughed. "Now, that's funny. I think your little love pet might be aware that you only have eyes for me." The words had spilled out, but they trailed to a halt as I burned with a sudden pang of regret. I didn't know how complicit Vada was in Regan's plans. She might have been his victim, too, and even though she had tried to kill my friend,

I wasn't sure I wanted to be responsible for signing her death warrant with Regan just yet. I decided to lie. "You should give her a break. I fired first. She was only defending herself."

"Harry," Regan said, "we can talk about Vada later. We can talk about all of it. I really wanted to do more, you know. I think that taking away that layer, helping you to realize that your strange, small circle of friends doesn't really mean anything, might have been really powerful for you."

"You've only taught me how important my friends are to me," I said. "Your plan is failing."

"We'll see. For now, I've run out of time to carry on. We have to meet."

"Why now?" I asked.

He seemed surprised. "You really don't know?"

"No."

"This is about me and you, Harry. About my gift to you. You don't get it?"

"The day you start making sense is going to be the greatest day of my fucking life," I said.

"You'll see, in time. I have faith. I'm going to give you an address."

Those ominous words I had heard before, words that made my skin crawl.

"I think we're going to have company," he continued. "But you'll work out how we're going to be alone. You'll understand when you see the lighthouse."

CHAPTER 81

TOX SAT ON the end of the motel bed where Whitt slept, looking at his cigarette between drags, admiring the glow of the embers in the dim light. There had been no smoking in the hospital. None of life's necessities, really. For the first few days after waking from his coma, Tox had not smoked, drunk, or felt the press of a woman's naked body against his. And that was a very unusual thing. He'd lain silently like a pathetic, wounded animal, watching the pretty nurses coming in and out, giving him drugs, adjusting his sheets and pillows, starved of all joy. Then he'd heard a couple of those nurses walking by his room giggling about "Mr. Handsome in number twelve." With effort, Tox had shuffled down on the mattress, leaned forward, and grabbed his chart from where it hung near his feet. The top of the page read "Barnes, Tate John. Room 12."

Mr. Handsome? Huh.

A few careful looks, some of his rusty but serviceable romantic charm, and he'd managed to get a couple of Jim Beam minis stuffed under his pillow one day. Then, about a week later, one of the young ladies had tucked herself under his arm and helped him hobble to the fire escape, stood watching him with a nervous smile as he sucked down three cigarettes in a row. Tox thought he'd pushed his luck just about as far as it would go when, one night, a darkened shape had come creeping in and flipped the lock on the door after closing it behind her. They'd both laughed as she slid back his sheet, pushing his hospital gown up his hairy legs.

No, hospital hadn't been so bad. But that didn't mean that Tox was going to leave the score between him and Regan unsettled. He'd been selfish to try to take Regan down himself, keep the girl-killer for his own plaything when really it was Harry who deserved that prize. Tox had learned of Sam Blue's killing while in the hospital bed. He'd tried to leave then but only made it as far as the foyer before hospital security dragged him back to his room.

Tox would help Harry kill the beast. That would make things just about even, he figured.

Whitt stirred in his sleep and Tox glanced at him. It had been sunrise by the time he'd got his partner down from the twitching, nodding, buzzing state he'd found him in. Half of it was the Dexies, and half of it was probably having come within a whisker of his own execution. Tox had taken his emergency pack of naloxone from the Monaro, listening silently to Whitt's ramblings about the Reskit woman and her connection to Regan Banks. He'd shot Whitt up with the Narcan, the way he had on many occasions when friends from the darker corners of his life had needed it. Then he'd leaned, smoking, in the doorway of the motel bath-room and listened to Whitt explain all that he could about Reskit. How he had been completely duped into thinking she was a cop. How he'd fallen off the wagon. How stupid he felt about it. All while Whitt knelt at the toilet, vomiting between streams of words. When Whitt looked like he was slowing down, Tox had dragged him to the bed, dumped him on the coverlet, and sat down to think.

He'd known a few women like Reskit in his time. The cruelest and meanest pimps were the ones who had the most girls fluttering around them, trying to be the one he really loved and trusted, the one who under-stood him. Tox had been running an informant named Jasmine back in the 1990s who let her street daddy push her around, and she'd turned up to a meeting once with her own front tooth mounted on a big gold chain around her neck like she was proud he'd smacked it out of her. Tox had put the guy's hand in a sandwich press and there had been no more tooth necklaces after that, but for every Jasmine he tried to look out for, there were ten he never heard about.

Murder trials were filled with these violence-attracted girls. Rows of pretty young things in the front row of the gallery making eyes at the perp, trying to pass handwrit-ten letters to the defense team. Tox didn't get it.

Didn't matter. He didn't need to get it. He just needed to make it right when he saw it, catch the pigs and put them out to slaughter.

That's what he was going to do now.

CHAPTER 82

TOX EXHALED CIGARETTE smoke, leaned over, and picked up Whitt's phone from beside the bed.

"Whitt?" Pops said.

"Guess again," Tox said.

"Is that you, Tox?" Chief Morris said after a shocked pause.

"None other."

"Well, for fuck's sake," Pops said. It sounded like he was driving. Tox could hear a blinker clicking. "I wish someone would tell me what is going on."

"I left the hospital."

"Yes, that's one thing that I *do* know," Pops said. "You gave my guy a concussion."

"He was in a hospital. Good place if you're gonna get one."

"What are you doing on Whitt's phone?"

"Nobody paid my phone bill while I was down for the count."

"Where's Whitt?"

"He's sick." Tox glanced at the sleeping detective. "Cold. Headache. I dunno. Could be Spanish flu."

"It didn't sound like a fucking cold when I spoke to him," Pops said.

"Your hearing goes when you get old."

"Tox," Pops said, "I need you to take Whitt back to Sydney."

"No deal," Tox said. "Once he's had his beauty sleep, we're getting on the road. You just gotta tell us where we're heading. Whitt told me you might have dug up something on Banks."

"You're not heading anywhere," Pops said. "Deputy Commissioner Woods has deliberately denied me access to the Banks file and tried to convince me there wasn't anything in it that might be a significant location to Banks. Well, that's not true. Yes, I've found details about his childhood another way. And yes, I believe I know where he's going. If Woods ever sees sense, he's probably going to set up a trap for Regan and Harry at that location."

"Sounds plausible." Tox stubbed his cigarette out on the edge of the bed and flicked the butt into the corner of the room.

"Harry wanted to know, and I'm not telling her because Woods is convinced she's dangerous. He'll approve his officers for use of all necessary force. I know he will. She'll get herself killed on this stupid revenge mission."

"Wouldn't be a bad way to go," Tox mused. "You don't want to tell her, fine. Tell us. We'll keep your secret."

"Yeah, bullshit," Pops said. "Take Whitt back to Sydney right now and report to the hospital. That's a direct order."

"Didn't I hear you were suspended from this case?" Tox said. "Aren't I working for Woods now?"

"You're not working for *anyone*!" Pops growled. "You're on medical leave!"

"I'm confused. You just gave me a direct order."

Tox heard a harsh exhalation on the end of the line. He smiled and hung up the phone. The next number he called he knew by heart. It was like that for many of his contacts—having a list of numbers saved in a phone seemed like asking for trouble. Al Cerullo answered with a grunt.

"Oh, great." The parole officer sighed when Tox greeted him. "What have I done now?"

"I wonder if it's ironic that you work in a prison and you're the guiltiest man I know," Tox said. "I'm calling about the Reskit woman."

Tox could hear the fat, thick-throated man shift in his worn leather desk chair, picture him in his little green box in the heart of Long Bay Correctional Complex. Last time Tox had come calling, he'd noticed that the parole officer's workspace was just a converted old concrete cell, the small slit of a window still covered with clouded plexiglass. Depressing.

"Every man and his dog has been calling about her," Al said. "All day the phones all over the complex have been jammed up by press from every corner of the goddamn country. I just spoke to some guy from Kimba. Where the fuck is Kimba?"

"South Australia," Tox said. "They've got the Big Galah there."

"I could have told you this was going to happen. All shrinks are nutjobs themselves, and you put them in with the psycho killers and they get converted. I've also been saying for decades they shouldn't let women work in here," Al said. "They get the crims all antsy. I remember when it was an all-male crew. Place was like a yoga camp."

"Sure. Except for that riot in '81, of course," Tox said. "And the one in '87. And the cell block fire in 1990. And—"

"You know what I mean, arsehole."

"I need you to get me access to Vada Reskit's work email."

"Forget it. I've gotta tell you what I've been telling people all day: No comment. We've all been instructed not to cooperate with anyone on Reskit. The warden's working with the police. If people call, we're supposed to hang up."

"Why didn't you hang up on me?" Tox asked.

"Because . . . I like you?"

"Really? Huh!" Tox said. "I thought maybe it was because you're still scared of me after I slammed your head in the door of your own Camry. You remember that? It was just after I found out you were texting nudie pictures back and forth with that seventeen-year-old."

Al made an uncomfortable noise.

"How is the divorce going, by the way?"

"It's fine," Al murmured.

"You're going to get me into that email account, aren't you?" Tox said.

"Yes, I am," Al said.

"I thought you would." Tox lit another cigarette.

CHAPTER 83

DARKNESS DESCENDED.

I walked, my leg now worryingly numb, slowly working through the snacks Melina had put in the bag for me. Regan's message came, and with it the place of our meeting. I still didn't know when I would be able to find Regan there. He'd said I would realize soon enough. Was he leading me somewhere to wait hopelessly for him while he picked off more of the people I loved? When I thought about his attempt to target Whitt, my whole body burned. Edward Whittacker had given up his entire life on the other side of the country to help me try to save my brother. With Vada's help, Regan had searched through my world to find someone who I held as evidence that I was not all bad. If someone as sweet and as wholesome as Whitt could accept me, I had hope. Regan wanted to strip away that layer of me. The rage rattled in my bones at the thought of what I had almost lost.

At the corners of my mind, Regan's plan was creeping, a shadow falling slowly. I considered that if he'd been successful in taking Whitt from me, Regan would have snuffed out a flame I'd tried to protect. Some people liked me. But take away those few deeply flawed individuals, and what was I left with? Only badness. A selfishness, callousness, aloofness that was inherent in my character, that was undeniably bad.

Take away the few good moments from my childhood, and what was left there?

Badness.

Take away the work I did for the women who came to me in my job, battered and bruised and looking for justice, and . . .

No.

I wasn't going to do this to myself. I wasn't going to let Regan get into my head.

I crossed the empty damp plains of Nungatta, the southward highway a gray streak in the distance to my left. Herds of goats lifted their heads as I approached, eyes luminescent in the dark, skittering away when I came near. My sneakers became clotted with mud and grass, which I shook off as the land became drier.

I thought about Regan's parents. The mother he had felt no love for, the "empty shell" she had been to him. I'd heard a lot of terrible stories in my time in foster care, both the sudden violent incidents that saw children confiscated from their parents and the long, slow, drawn-out situations that did the same. I'd seen kids pockmarked with circular scars, spotted like leopards from parents who thought getting high and putting out their cigarette butts on their kids was a lark. I'd listened to the tales of kids left alone with an abusive grandparent, their parents returning to find their child completely changed, terrified, and bruised, the grandparent denying everything. I'd known kids who'd watched one parent murder the other; had listened to their whispers from across the dorm-room aisle in group homes.

Whatever had happened to Regan, it was so bad that a judge had decided it should never be known to the public, lest Regan have to suffer the humiliation of the event being revealed in his adult life. I walked and wondered what a person could possibly to do a seven-year-old that warranted that. I had some ideas, and just considering them made me sick.

I wondered if what happened to Regan had made him the monster he was deep down inside. Was he born bad, or was he taking me to the place where he had been made that way?

I had turned back toward the highway, half formulating a plan to catch a ride to the nearest town with a car-trouble story, when I spied the stone building on the edge of the next paddock. An old house with darkened windows, a car parked, still shimmering with rain. My ride to the meeting that I knew would end a life.

Regan's or mine.

CHAPTER 84

THE FIRST INDICATION that they were in the right place might have been missed by a careless onlooker. Tox hadn't been entirely sure he was on the right track but had set out with Whitt on a half-theory, unable to stand the motel room any longer.

Al Cerullo had been more helpful than he'd anticipated. Instead of simply giving Tox the password to Vada's email account, Al had unlocked her whole work profile for him, giving him the woman's login to the prison's intranet. There wasn't much in the email account to drive Tox's search, but he had discovered that the prison recorded each employee's Google search history to ensure staff didn't get up to any unsavory online behavior during work hours. There, between searches for academic articles on antisocial personality disorder and the relative benefits of Clozaril as an antipsychotic medication, he'd spotted a Google Maps search. The land was in a place called Bellbird Valley.

Now as Tox slowed the Monaro before the row of roadworks signs, he felt his curiosity piquing at the apparently ordinary scene before him. A dusty yellow digger had been parked by the side of the highway, three men standing around it, not doing much of anything, their high-vis vests painfully bright in the light of the lamps rigged around the roadblock. Tox was behind two other cars. He eased off the brake and let the car roll as he was directed west by a large "detour" sign and another man with flashing handheld pointers.

"This is it," he told Whitt.

Whitt shuffled upward in his seat, having been resting against the window.

"How do you know?" he asked, squinting into the dark.

"They're not using that crawler excavator to pull up the road," Tox said as they drove away from the roadblock. "It's built for muddy earth. Probably borrowed it from a local farm for show. Those three goons standing leaning on their shovels didn't look like they'd ever done a day's manual labor in their lives, and they've got bulges under their jackets which I'd hazard are too big for radios. They'll be undercovers making sure a couple of country bumpkins on their way home from the local rodeo don't drive through the middle of the country's biggest manhunt."

Tox parked the car not far from the detour and got out. He walked to the back, popped the boot. Whitt marveled at the array of weaponry that was lit by the flickering red interior bulb. A pile of guns, haphazardly dumped in the trunk, barrels and stocks poking at odd angles, shoulder straps tangled across magazines. Tox took a hunting blade the size of his forearm from the edge of the pile and attached it to his belt. He handed Whitt a similar knife and then put a foot on the bumper, extracted a sawed-off shotgun from the collection, and started fitting it with shells.

"Is this overkill?" Whitt asked, picking up a huge magnum revolver from the pile of guns heaped on the carpet before him.

"The Kalashnikov would probably be overkill," Tox said. Whitt hadn't even noticed the huge semiautomatic rifle lying at the bottom of the pile until he spotted its camouflaged stock. Tox took the revolver from Whitt's hand and tossed it back into the pile, handing him a Glock instead. "Take this. You don't want to be fumbling around in the dark with a cylinder."

They shut the trunk, and Tox snapped the shotgun closed. Without so much as a glance at each other, the two men turned and started walking back toward the detour on the highway. They came within a hundred meters of the men pretending to be road workers, then turned and walked into the darkened bush.

"Try not to shoot me," Tox warned his partner. "I've had enough of hospitals for one year."

CHAPTER 85

THE HELICOPTER WARNED ME.

I spotted the chopper tracking along the mountain range in the distance, a tiny moving star among a thousand others, drifting slowly east toward the coast. The chopper might have represented anything—the coast guard surveying the beaches for signs of trouble, a pair of pilots taking a night ride, a traffic crew scanning the general area for their evening report. But as I walked toward Bellbird Valley, having hidden my stolen car in the bush off the side of the highway, I saw the chopper stop and track back the way it had come. It was a police chopper, holding off until it was called. I stood on the side of the road and watched it pass between the tops of two trees.

They were waiting.

I pressed my palm against my forehead and groaned.

Pops. He must have been right, that Regan had decided

to take me to the place where whatever had happened to him as a kid had occurred. *This is about me,* Regan had said. He wanted me to know what had happened to him.

My body heavy with fatigue and disappointment, I paused and tried to decide what I would do. With the state's best specialist officers lying in wait for Regan, there was no way he would come tonight. No way I would be able to take him down on my own, even if he did. I sank onto the ground at the roadside and tried to draw some remaining strength from deep inside my body.

We were nowhere near a lighthouse. A quick scan of Bellbird Valley on the car's GPS had told me I was miles from the sea.

I thought about walking into the forest, making myself known, letting the team pounce on me and drag me into custody. I needed medical attention, and fast. I hadn't felt any sensation in the toes of my wounded leg for an hour. I was dehydrated, exhausted, and covered in the various cuts and scrapes that come with living rough. I was hungry, dangerously on edge. Here was the perfect opportunity for me to surrender before I crossed the line I'd been steadily approaching over the past weeks, the one that would change my life.

But I didn't.

Regan had said he thought we might have "company" in the valley. He was right. But I knew there was a chance this was the night he had chosen for me, and that he wouldn't spot the trap waiting for him. That he would come, and they would pounce, and someone I cared for, maybe Whitt, maybe Pops, might be hurt. And I also knew there was a chance I could get to him before my colleagues put cuffs on the monster in their midst and wrapped him safely in the protective arms of the justice system. I had come too far to give up all hope now.

I kept walking, using the land beneath me as a guide. I knew I was adjacent to a narrow, deep valley. I turned off the road and walked quietly into the bush, fitting my feet carefully between large branches and sticks, trying to be as silent as I could.

The forest stretched around me, ringing with quiet. It was so dark, I brushed against huge tree trunks I didn't know were around me, my hands out and wandering in blackness. Tall ghost gums marked my way, smooth and cold as I passed, silent sentries watching my progress. In time, I noticed a flicker of red light to my left and froze.

Through the trees, a long army truck emerged in my vision, its square outline barely discernible in the blackness. They had draped the mobile-command center in camouflage netting and nestled it at the base of a small incline. The red flicker I had seen was the night-vision torch of a man heading toward the door of the truck. As he pushed through the black flaps on the doorway, I glimpsed the crimson-lit interior, crammed with people.

The operation was bigger than I had anticipated. The tactical vehicle was one I recognized from a tour I'd taken as a teenager, when I'd flirted with the idea of joining the army rather than the police. It was the kind that housed submachine guns and racks of rifles, night-vision gear and sniper scopes the size of baseball bats. They'd pulled out all the stops to find Regan, and it didn't look like they were going to make his capture a priority. They were going to shoot to kill.

This was not Pops's style. My chief was not a "blast them out of the water" type but the kind of man who favored small, smart teams and maximum safety for all officers involved. Knowing that I was out here looking for Regan, Pops would never have authorized a crew of special-ops guys running around in the dark shooting at anything that moved. It was probably Deputy Commissioner Joe Woods in charge, and he'd no doubt authorized necessary-force protocols for both Regan and me.

Okay. New tactic. I crouched in the dark and thought. The only way I was going to get to Regan and avoid capture by the specialist team was to be on an even playing field with them. I needed the same equipment they had. And there was only one way to obtain that.

By force.

CHAPTER 86

TOX WASN'T FEELING GOOD. Every muscle in his body had been completely inactive during his two-week coma, the carefully built tissue slowly draining away, not helped by the three weeks he had then spent lying around after he had woken. He figured he'd worked those muscles to their limit just getting to where he was now, creeping through the darkened woods. He'd probably also torn or stretched something in the pit of his guts, which had barely been given time to heal after being severed by a kitchen knife. And yet it was Whitt who was lagging behind him, stopping every fifty meters and leaning against a tree. Tox went back to his partner. The two stood in the dark until Whitt had caught his breath.

"I'm all right." Whitt straightened. "I can go on."

He swayed a little. Tox put a hand on the man's shoulder, inhaled deeply.

"Why do you smell like hooch?" he asked.

He'd taken all the Dexes from Whitt and flushed them, poured the contents of the bottles in the motel minibar down the drain. Yet he could distinctly smell whiskey. A pungent odor he knew well.

Tox's eyes widened as he remembered.

"Is that the Blue Label from the back seat of my car?"

Whitt didn't answer. He hung his head and drew the narrow, half-empty bottle from the pocket of his coat.

"Do you know how expensive that shit is? Do you know how long I've been saving that?" Tox raised a hand to smack his friend in the head again but softened at the last minute.

"You really have taken up right where you left off, haven't you?" he said.

"I'm okay." Whitt's eyes moved to him in the dark. "I just needed to take the edge off."

"You're not okay." Tox took the gun from Whitt's other pocket.

"I have to keep going," Whitt said. "Harry's probably out there. She needs all the help she can get. If I'd seen what Vada was doing, I could have—"

"If!" Tox spat. "If, if, if. You know how many miserable fucking losers have driven themselves into the ground trying to chase down ifs?"

Whitt shook his head.

"Let me tell you something, Whitt," Tox said. "You can hunt your fantasies about what should or shouldn't have happened in your life all the way back to your daddy knocking your mama up with a future rehab regular. But you know what? I've done you a favor. I've gone down that road already, and I can tell you there's nothing at the end of it."

Whitt straightened slightly.

"We've all made mistakes trying to catch this murdering arsehole, Regan Banks," Tox said. "But sitting around crying about it isn't going to make it happen."

Whitt straightened completely. His partner's words seemed to fill him with vitality. He looked at the whiskey bottle in his hand and seemed to make a decision. He threw the bottle down, shattering it against a lump of sandstone sitting nearby.

Tox stared at the glass shards in the dirt.

"You could have just—" He sighed. "Never mind."

"Give me back my gun." Whitt put his hand out. "You're right. We've wasted enough time already."

"No chance, mate." Tox shoved him down against the base of a nearby tree. He wrenched the knife from Whitt's belt and forced it into his hands. "You're gonna be the standing sentry. Sit here and wait. If anything comes within five feet of you, close your eyes and start stabbing."

"But—"

"You're the one who's got your heart set on the blame game," Tox said. "It's not gonna be my fault you got yourself killed because you can't handle your spirits."

He patted Whitt on the shoulder, turned, and left him alone in the dark.

CHAPTER 87

TWO OFFICERS ESCORTED Pops to the tactical truck, rifles up. He was led into the red-lit interior, where Woods was sitting at a foldout table surrounded by maps and laptop screens, a group of men around him. He didn't even look up when Pops entered. The crew inside the mobile unit appeared to be watching footage fed from a drone fitted with a heat-seeking camera.

"Deputy Commissioner Woods," Pops said, drawing the uncomfortable attention of all of the men before him except the man he addressed. "I'm here to officially request that this operation be aborted for the safety of my officer, Detective Inspector Harriet Blue."

Woods said nothing, still refused to look up from the screen that was casting a green light on his face. The officers behind him glanced at one another. Nigel Spader was standing in the corner, a headset clamped to his ears, looking at a sheet of numbers. When he spotted Pops, he raked the headset off.

"Chief Morris," Nigel said as he advanced toward him, "I can help you with any inquiries you have. Let me escort you to the roadblock."

When Nigel grabbed his arm, Pops shoved the junior officer in his narrow chest.

"Back off, you brownnosing, coattail-riding worm," Pops sneered. "You're only here because I clued you in to Banks's plan."

Woods was ignoring the entire exchange unfolding at the edge of his table, as though it wasn't happening at all.

"Jeez, the picture quality isn't great," he said to one of the officers nearby, pointing at the screen before him. "What's that? Is that a person or an animal?"

"The drone camera is brand-new tech," a young officer said, clearing his throat. "The one on the chopper's better, obviously, but we don't want to spook the targets by doing flyovers."

"The *targets*," Pops said, putting his hands on the table. "Woods, have you briefed these men about the possible appearance of my officer? Is she considered a target? Because if she is, I'd like to know on what authority you—"

Woods glanced up at Pops and sighed. "Chief Morris, you're a suspended officer interfering in an active police operation at this very minute. Can you say whatever it is that you need to say and then leave?"

"Have you authorized the men out there for use of necessary force against Blue?" Pops asked.

"I have."

"You can't do that without an arrest warrant!"

"Just watch me." Woods smiled.

Pops looked around the room. "You all heard that, didn't you? Harriet Blue has not been formally charged with a crime. Even if you did try to get a warrant now, all you'd have is resisting arrest at best, which doesn't justify force. Harry's wounded. Did he tell you that?"

The men shifted, looked away.

"This man is endangering her life by setting up a sting for an innocent officer of the law."

"Harriet Blue is a dangerous individual." Woods stood, his barrel chest expanding. "While we have not set up this sting to catch her specifically, I anticipate that she'll come wandering in, making a hysterical show of herself, just the way you have, Morris. And I intend on taking her into custody for her own safety and the safety of the man she's come here to kill. We can apply any relevant charges later. For now, Blue is a danger to herself and a danger to others."

"This is bullshit." Pops rubbed at his chest, where a familiar ache was beginning. "If she does turn up, and she gets killed because of your mistrust of her—"

"Keep your voice down. You're—"

"I'll be right there at the inquiry, Joe," Pops snarled, pointing a finger in the bigger man's face. "I'll be right there to tell everyone how you handled this."

"It's a date," Woods said.

Pops felt a spike of pain run up his ribs. He tried to catch his breath, but the air moved through his lips in short, strangled gasps.

"Give me time to go out there," Pops said. "I'll find her. I'll call her in."

Woods looked at one of the men over Pops's shoulder and jutted his chin, a signal. Pops tried to turn but found his arm seized and twisted behind his back.

"You can't—" he gasped.

"You're a suspended officer," Woods repeated. He waved at the men behind Pops. "Put him somewhere he can't cause any trouble."

Pops didn't struggle as they dragged him away. He was too focused on the straight, tight band of pain spreading across his upper chest.

CHAPTER 88

I HADN'T SET many traps for offenders during my career in Sex Crimes. Rapists are cowards and tend to want to fight their way out of trouble in the courtroom rather than in the street the way drug dealers and thrill killers do. But when I was in basic training, and in my time as a beat cop, there had been plenty of capture-and-chase scenarios.

The first step was to establish the most likely route of entry. The only way to get to the bottom of the valley by vehicle was along the badly disused road running west to east, which had long grown over with towering wild grass and had become misshapen by mudslides over the years. Woods's team would probably assume Regan would walk or drive in along this road, if he didn't spot the trap set for him, as I had. There would be a vehicle hidden in the bush off the side of this road that would drive forward and block his exit once he arrived. That meant that there would likely be two men at the road, and eight or so positioned in a semicircle around the back of the property in the east. The men waiting in the east for Regan's capture would be within earshot of one another, as would be the men manning the block truck.

That left one man alone. The scout. In training, we'd always put the smallest or least experienced man in the scout position, because all he was required to do was wait outside the danger zone, watching, alerting the team to the target's arrival. The scout would be high up in the valley, close enough to the road that he could see exactly who was coming in, so that he didn't command the whole team to attack an innocent bystander. I turned and headed silently through the forest toward the road.

The moon rose. Through the trees as I walked around the curve of the valley, I could see on the valley floor a space cleared of trees where tall grass grew around the charred remains of a house. Pops had been right. The house had been lost. It had been small, a cottage maybe, the foundations thick blocks of sandstone. Whatever this place was, it had not been Regan's childhood home, or the home of any relative of his. He'd never been fostered by a family who lived here, and yet this was the place where something so terrible had happened to Regan, his parents had instantly lost custody of him. They'd never regained it, and it had been all but erased from history.

Regan wanted me to know what had happened here.

He'd wanted me to discover this place, to arrive stripped of the layers of myself, so that when I stood in the charred remains of the house, I was the real me.

The bad Harry. Murderous, vengeful. Just like him.

But when would Regan meet me here? And what did he plan to do when we finally looked each other in the eyes? For all I knew, Regan had already come, been intimidated by the police presence, and left. He'd said that he was running out of time. How much time did I have left?

In the darkness ahead of me, I heard a sound. The soft, unmistakable crackle of a radio.

CHAPTER 89

THE YOUNG MAN was crouched at the edge of a rock ledge, looking down at the road, his rifle leaning against his thigh. I stood in the dark and watched him for a long while, trying to get a feel for my opponent. He was big, but young and inexperienced. Though I could only see the outline of his face as he turned in the moonlight, I saw pudgy, hairless cheeks and big lashes. He wasn't the best lookout I'd ever observed. The heavy tactical gear was annoying him. He kept adjusting something near his crotch, and the cold was making his nose run. He sniffed, wiped his nose on the back of his wrist, took his eyes completely off the roadway for a full ten seconds. I pulled my gun from the back of my jeans and walked toward him, rolling my feet slowly on the dirt so that I didn't make a sound. I reached down and twisted the power off on his radio. He heard the click in his earpiece, but by that time I had the gun pressed firmly against the back of his neck.

"Stand up slowly," I said.

He didn't stand up slowly. Young blood, full of testosterone and the call of the crime-fighting hero. He swiveled in a flash and smacked the gun away. I wasn't ready for it, lost the weapon, and stumbled backward as he launched himself at me. He connected, knocking the wind out of me, both of us scrabbling in the dirt for the gun at his hip. I brought my knee up and hit only buckles, hard plastic, the scratchy surface of Kevlar. The big hand that mashed my face, pinning my head against the dirt, was strong as a steel claw. I fumbled in the dirt for something, a rock or a stick to lash out at him with, but he rolled me before I could find a weapon and tried to draw my arm up behind my back.

"I got you," he said, his voice almost breaking with laughter. "I got—"

I bucked wildly, taking advantage of the mistake he'd made leaning down to talk to me. I felt the impact of the back of my head against his mouth, not hard, but hard enough to shock him. His hands loosened. I slithered from beneath him and grabbed my gun just as he grabbed his.

"Don't," I said, flicking the safety off with an audible snap.

His face fell.

CHAPTER 90

HE LAY ON THE ground and breathed shallowly as I put his own cuffs on him. Even in the low light, I could see how disappointed he was with his predicament. He was limp and silent as I took his tactical knife and both his pistols and unhooked his radio, dragging the cord from inside his bulletproof vest.

"How does a baby like you get on a team like this?" I asked as I tucked the guns into my backpack.

"I'm twenty-two," he growled.

"The question stands."

He sighed, resigned. "My dad's a chief super. I'm third-generation."

"Well, if I was you, I'd tell Daddy to let you sharpen your teeth on the streets a bit longer before you start trying to hunt serial killers."

The officer said nothing.

"How many in your team?" I asked. Again, no answer. I nudged the young man with my gun. "Hey, rookie. Lesson one: someone's got a gun in your ear, you answer their fucking questions."

"Twelve."

"They're across the other side, huh?" I said. "Two on a block truck down on the road?"

He turned his head slightly and frowned at me, bewildered. I took that as a sign that I was right.

"I'm going to give you two choices," I said. "When I leave here, you can kick and holler and scream and try to get the rest of your team to come over to this side of the valley. If that's your plan, I'll leave you cuffed. You'll look like an idiot, and you'll blow the whole operation, which is probably why you haven't tried that already."

He lay silent, his face in the dirt.

"Or"—I pointed into the dark—"if you stay quiet, I'll leave your rifle leaning against a tree two hundred meters that way. I'll hook the handcuff key on the front sight. You can uncuff yourself and walk back to the mobile-command unit with some dignity."

The young officer didn't answer. He was giving me the silent treatment.

I nudged him in the side. "Hey."

"Option two," he grumbled.

"Good choice." I patted him on the shoulder and walked off into the dark.

When I was a good distance away, the rifle and key left for the young man I'd subdued on the ridgeline as promised, I hooked his radio onto the waist of my jeans and fed the earpiece into my ear. As I made my way through the dark, moving quickly down the slope toward the bottom of the valley, the speaker in my ear burst into life.

"Command to ground units, unit one has been compromised."

There was silence, and then a flurry of male voices.

"Command, can we have more information?"

"Command, this is unit five. Is there a casualty report?"

I heard fear in the voices ringing over the radio. I didn't know if that fear was directed at me or Regan. No one had asked who had taken out the scout. For the first time, I felt a chill rush through me at the thought that the men out there in the dark might be afraid of me, might be assuming that I had hurt or killed one of their number. I knew I had a violent reputation among my colleagues, but just how dangerous did these men think I was? If they found me, what degree of force had they been authorized to use? Would they kill me to take me down?

I stopped and pushed the button on the radio.

"Come in, tactical units," I said. "This is Harry Blue speaking."

CHAPTER 91

THE RADIO WAS silent for a good twenty seconds. I guessed suddenly hearing the voice of one of their quarry might have stunned them into speechlessness. When no one spoke, I clicked my radio open, hardly knowing myself what I wanted to say. The bush around me was unnaturally silent and still.

"I just took down one of your men," I said. "I didn't hurt him. I'm not here to hurt any of you."

No answer. I crept slowly farther down the slope toward the clearing where the house was situated.

"I came here to stop Regan Banks," I said. "Regan is a merciless killer. I've seen his handiwork. I've seen it, because it was meant for me. This is my fault. If anyone's at risk trying to stop this man, it should be me. If he has as much trouble taking one of you down as I just did, you're all in real danger right now."

There was a small crackle on the radio, two of the men out there speaking to each other.

"Unit seven, are you hearing this?"

"Yeah, two."

The men's voices were shocked, high with tension. Still, no one answered me directly. I clicked the mic again.

"I'm asking you not to consider me a target," I said. "And I'm asking you to leave now, while you still can."

The radio cracked to life again. A voice heavy with anger, clipped with the certainty of someone in command.

"All tactical units, this is Command. Switch radio frequencies, and disregard rogue transmissions," the voice said.

My radio fell silent. I tore it from my ears and dropped it in the dirt. I'd never find the secondary tactical frequency, even if I scanned the airwaves all night. All I could hope was that the men had heard my plea, and that they would at least pair up so that if Regan came, he would have two men in each position to contend with.

I also hoped that if I ran into any of them, they'd remember what I'd said and not shoot me.

CHAPTER 92

POPS COULD HEAR the voices but had lost all sense of where they were coming from. It seemed to him that Harry was in the mobile-command center with them, but through the hazy red light he couldn't see her. Woods had instructed two of his officers to escort Pops to the farthest end of the truck, where they sat him on a fold-up chair and cuffed his wrists behind his back. The pain across his chest, the one he had been experiencing for days, was not receding the way it usually did. If anything, it was becoming more specific, a sensation like a belt tightening endlessly around his chest, pulling inward at his sides. It felt to Pops as though his rib cage wanted to collapse in on itself.

Pops could just make out the broad figure of Woods at the other end of the truck, Nigel Spader standing restlessly beside him, watching the screens on the desk.

"He's not coming," Woods grunted. "The bastard's not coming tonight."

Nigel didn't answer.

"Any minute now, we're going to get our first press van up at the roadblock," Woods complained. "These country hicks are smarter than you think. Some local yokel will see through the road-crew charade. Half the population out here works on road crews. Before you know it, our failure to trap Banks will be on the national news."

"None of the press spotted the Bristol Gardens sting," Nigel reasoned.

"If this whole thing comes to nothing, Spader, I'm pinning it on you," Woods snapped.

Pops listened to the argument, trying to keep his breathing even. One of the officers guarding him bent and looked closely at his face, and when Pops tried to return the gaze, he saw the man's features were clouded with green-and-yellow bursts of light.

"Deputy Commissioner Woods, sir," the man said, "Chief Morris ain't lookin' so good over here."

"He's fine," a voice said from the other end of the narrow red room.

"Should we at least loosen the cuffs, sir?" the officer persisted.

"I said he's fine."

Pops panted as the two young men sat again on either side of him, their rifles leaning between their uniformed knees.

"If ole mate here drops dead on us," Pops heard one of them murmur, "I know who's getting the blame. Take the cuffs off."

"You reckon?" the other whispered.

"I reckon. He's not gonna cause any trouble. Chief Morris? We're gonna take the cuffs off. But you just sit there and take it easy, all right?"

"Yeah," the other officer whispered in Pops's ear as he leaned back in his chair, discreetly pulling the old man's wrists toward him. "And don't go croaking on us, boss."

CHAPTER 93

THEY WAITED IN the dark, lying on their bellies, each with an eye pressed to the infrared scope of their rifle. Stephen was glad that when the order had come through from command for the tactical officers to team up, it had been Shona who had made her way through the dark toward him. He knew from their academy training that she had the ears of a rabbit, and she could take the bullseye out of a paper target at a kilometer's distance.

He'd never admit it, but Stephen was a little nervous. He'd been on special operations before, but the danger had always been clear and present. Once, he'd laid sniper cover for a hostage situation for three hours outside a bank in the CBD, the back of his neck searing in the sun as he watched the negotiator pacing behind a truck at the front of the glass building, trying to talk the man down. Stephen had known exactly where his target was, had eighteen other sets of eyes anticipating his every move and reporting it through the radio. *Target is heading north, approaching doors. Target is retreating from doors, heading south.*

He ached for the same kind of certainty, any certainty at all, in fact. Their stationary position, waiting for the approach of the killer, meant the animals and birds in the blackness around them had relaxed in their presence, and every twitch of a branch gave him the shivers. Stephen knew from talk within the crew that target Blue was just a psycho bitch running loose, trying to stick her nose into a manhunt where it wasn't appreciated. His only fear was that she might punch him out, as she was apparently wont to do. That wouldn't go down well with the boys. It was Banks that Stephen was really scared of. No one really knew what the guy looked like. Some of the boys had sent around photos from the crime scenes on their phones, and it looked to Stephen like the work of an animal. There were reports Banks was working with a woman.

"Hey, Steve," Shona murmured, and he took his eye from his scope to look at her. "You think if we catch Blue we still get the reward?"

"You don't get a police reward for doing your job," Stephen said.

"It's not a police reward; it's private."

"Then maybe."

"I see Blue and Banks out there, I know who I'm gonna run for," she said, pushing her cap up so that the peak didn't rest on the rifle scope. "Hundred grand? Worth a shot."

An animal moved in the bush near them. Both officers lifted their heads, listened. Stephen felt every muscle in his body tense. After thirty seconds, when no sound came, they went back to their rifle scopes.

"I gotta piss," Stephen said.

"Real snipers piss in their pants."

"You'd love that, wouldn't you?" He nudged her as he got to his feet. "Everybody thinking I pissed myself, scared of the dark out here."

He walked a few meters, within sight of his partner lying prone like a black log in the moonlight, and unzipped his fly.

At first he thought he'd walked into a low-hanging branch, grabbing at the sharp, sideways tug across his throat. But when his fingers pressed to the flesh, they came away wet. Very wet.

Stephen stopped in his tracks and clutched at the wound, just as a shadow passed before his vision, blocking his path back to Shona.

It all happened in absolute silence. A hand gripped his hair, slashed again at the base of his throat. He didn't even have time to grab at the knife on his belt, or the pistol tucked into the holster on his ankle.

As he hit the ground, he heard his partner's voice. The rustle of her clothes as she got to her feet.

"Steve?" she asked. Her voice was small.

CHAPTER 94

THIS WASN'T RIGHT. I sat on the edge of an embankment, watching the charred house at the bottom of the valley in the moonlight, seeing nothing. I watched the moon cross the sky and guessed a couple of hours had passed since I first walked off the road toward the valley. The tension in my chest was tightening, a hard ball of pain pushing up toward my throat. Regan had said to look for a lighthouse. The only house here was a blackened pile of sticks and sandstone.

I rubbed my eyes, trying to avoid the temptation to sleep. The helicopter on the horizon was still tracking back and forth. As it crossed the slope of the highest point of the valley wall, I felt a ripple of electricity in my body.

There was a rock formation on the eastern side of the valley, a sharp slope of sandstone just visible beyond the trees. The rock sloped down almost at a forty-five degree angle, then jutted in and went straight down. The shape was unmistakable; the sloping roof and side wall of a house made from stone. As the chopper doubled back, it disappeared for an instant behind the rock, and then its light flashed for no more than a second as it passed across a hole in the house-shaped silhouette.

A house. A light. *A lighthouse.*

I shot to my feet and started making my way through the dark.

CHAPTER 95

AN HOUR MIGHT have passed as I crept through the bush around the rim of the valley. As I approached the jagged sandstone ledge jutting out from the hillside where the house formation stood, I drew my weapon, pausing, not wanting to confront Regan while wheezing and struggling my way up the incline. My whole body had begun to tremble lightly with terror. I walked with aching care toward the rock and swept my gun across and above it, my heart twisting as the shapes of trees and rocks and branches became the ominous figure of a broad-shouldered man. The lighthouse formation was narrow, punctured by ancient winds right through the middle, the rock hole forming a window through which I'd seen the helicopter's light. In time, my pulse slowed, and I stood in the wind, waiting for what would happen next.

Nothing happened. Another hour. I crouched in the bush, cold sweat pouring down my sides. As my mind wandered, the shape of the sandstone house wavering in my exhausted vision, I ached with regret about the young tactical guy I had subdued and probably humiliated.

Twenty-two years old. Jesus. They were really scraping the bottom of the barrel for—

My breath caught in my chest. I rose to my feet, the realization rocketing through me. I gripped my hair as I frantically counted off the days.

Tomorrow was my birthday.

I understood.

This is about me and you, Harry. About my gift to you.

Regan wanted to strip me down, show me myself, facilitate my sick rebirth into what he'd hoped I was always going to be, my potential fulfilled. In the weeks since my brother's death, I'd forgotten all about my birthday. It wasn't something I celebrated even when I remembered it. My childhood had been full of forgotten birthdays. He would have known that from my files. The story about my mother showing up high on my fourteenth birthday—he'd relived that terrible incident with me over the phone.

Regan wasn't going to turn up tonight. He was going to turn up on my birthday. But did that mean midnight, when the date rolled over? Or the following evening, under the cover of darkness? I had no way of telling the time without lighting the screen on my phone and potentially giving away my position. I stared up at the moon, followed its pale blue glow into the woods.

And then I saw it. Another flicker of light. Not in the valley in which the charred house stood, but to the east, where the land dipped away again, thick forest receding to flat moonlit fields. A wider valley, right next to the one Regan had been leading me to. In a clearing below me, someone was walking, shining a red torch to light their way through the tall grass.

I headed down the other side of the ridge.

CHAPTER 96

ON THE VALLEY FLOOR, approaching through the blackness with my gun drawn, I realized the torch carrier was another tactical team member, probably assigned to the valley adjacent to the one where the trap had been set. I looked up the incline behind me toward the stone house, wondering if I should return there so that I could see the activity in both valleys at the same time. But the radio the figure was carrying would likely have access to the tactical channel, and hearing what the police team was up to would be advantageous to me.

The figure had the shape and movement of a woman. I thought I could see a bun poking out from the back of her ball cap. She had walked to an ancient sandstone structure in the middle of the field and now sat heavily on the stones, wiping her brow and setting her rifle on the surface beside her. As I crept forward, low enough that my silhouette wouldn't be visible across the top of the grass, I saw that the structure she was resting on was the remnants of an old well.

She was peeling off her black gloves as I emerged from the grass.

"Freeze," I said.

She gave a little yelp of surprise and threw her hands up, one palm gloved, the other bare.

"Oh, shit!"

"Turn around and put your hands on the well. Reach for the gun and I'll slug you."

"Oh, fuck." Her voice was tinged with the same shame I'd heard from the young officer I'd put down in the other valley. "I can't believe this."

She acquiesced with my commands reluctantly, slumping forward with her hands on the well. I took the cuffs off her belt and tucked my pistol into the back of my jeans.

"Don't feel too bad—" I began. But before I could continue, she'd twisted back around, and I could feel the press of a sharp point in the soft flesh of my throat.

"Oh." Vada smiled in the dark. "I don't feel bad at all."

CHAPTER 97

BREATHE, I TOLD MYSELF. *Just keep breathing. Don't panic. This isn't over yet.*

The mental pep talk didn't work. I was so surprised by Vada's presence, so shocked at my sudden loss of the upper hand, that I stumbled, my weak leg giving out, almost pitching me forward into the well. She had both my guns and my knife before I could even comprehend how she had taken them. I dropped the cuffs, and they were lost in the shadows, too risky for Vada to crouch down and try to find. She shoved me down onto the sandstone, ratcheting my hand behind my back.

So stupid. So thoughtless. I'd been so caught up in my realization about Regan's plan that I'd completely forgotten his partner.

This is about me. But it is also about you.

It was also about Vada. At least for now.

The knife that she put on the stones beside my face was bloodied. This woman had already killed tonight, and she was handling me so roughly that her fingernails dug into my wrists as she bound my hands with cable ties. She yanked me upward. Unnecessary force. This was personal for her. I could feel the hate coming off her in toxic waves.

I let her shove me into a walk through the grass toward the edge of the forest. My leg hurt, but now I limped badly, wanting her to believe I was less mobile than I really was. Make your opponent think you're weak. Make them underestimate you until you can form a plan. I feigned a stumble over some rocks, and her fingers bit harder into my arm.

"None of your bullshit, Harry," she snapped. "Try anything funny and I'll put another bullet in you."

I walked, one of her hands clasping my wrists, the other pressing the knife into my shoulder blade. My brain was in full panic mode, frazzled and frantic. I saw flashes of Pops. Not surprising that the old man would come to me now, the closest thing to a parent I'd ever had. The sensation of his breath on my face as we danced around the boxing ring together, his padded hands taking furious punches until I was shivering and sick with exhaustion.

"*Come on, Blue. You're stronger than this!*" he'd growl.

He was right. I *was* stronger than this.

Wherever she had got the tactical uniform from, she had not taken the officer's utility belt, probably thinking it would weigh her down. She'd bound my hands with cable ties from the breast pocket of the bulletproof vest.

Cable ties I could work with. All was not lost, but I would have to think and act carefully.

I couldn't fight right now. But I could talk. Reason was my only available weapon.

"So you're Vada," I said. "Regan's next victim."

She gave a baffled, tense laugh.

"What? You don't think he's going to kill you once you've fulfilled your purpose?" I asked.

"Just walk," she ordered.

"I'm walking. I'm having a great time. What a beautiful night. Better enjoy this little stroll we're taking through the moonlight, because you're about to die, bitch," I said.

"You think so, huh?" She dug her nails into my wrist.

"I know so," I said. "This whole mission is about me, not you. If you take me to Regan, he'll have no further use for you. You think he'll do it quick, like that little girl and her mother, the doctor? Or will he do it slow like that helpless old couple? Which one means he loves you more, in your fucked-up brain?"

She shoved me forward into the edge of the woods. As my eyes adjusted to the new darkness beyond the reach of the moon, I picked out the shape of a barn. There was a dim light inside the structure.

"You killed two cops for him," I said. "I assume there were more tonight. That's where you got the uniform. You took out one of the tactical—"

"Shut up, Harriet."

"He must have encouraged you to kill," I said. "He probably prepared you for it mentally when you were forming your plan together. I bet he told you it would make you feel powerful. You've probably never felt powerful in your life. You've spent your whole life following men around, men who wanted to care for you. But Regan treated you like an equal."

"Don't try to psychoanalyze me, Harry," Vada snapped. "You don't have the training for it."

"I might not have your training, Vada, but I have something you don't."

"Oh, yeah? What's that?"

"Foresight."

"Please." She sighed. "Spare me."

My stomach plunged as she pushed me forward. I dug my heels in and turned, wanting to look her in the face.

"You can stop this now," I said. "Or we can go in there, and I can watch him kill you."

"You really do think this is all about you, don't you, Harry?" Her knife was pointed at my sternum, only an inch from the surface of my jacket. "I'm surprised someone like you, who's started your life over so many times, can't see what this is. You spent your whole childhood going from house to house, family to family, dozens and dozens of fresh starts."

"Don't pretend you know me," I said.

"I don't know you. But I know Regan. He wants to start over," Vada said. "And he's worthy of that. He's a great man. He has incredible potential. But before he can start again, he has to be finished with his old life."

She tapped the knife against my chest.

"He has to be finished with *you*."

CHAPTER 98

HE WAS THERE in the barn, perched on the edge of a stack of dusty pallets, a gun resting on his thigh.

Vada pushed me into the room, where the air was thick with the smell of mold and decay and the unmistakable reek of rodents. The barn was divided into two sections: a wide space with a foldout table, and a section for horses. Two of the walls dividing the stables were collapsed in and splintered. On the walls around me, I could see the outlines of tools that had once hung on angled nails. Wind whistled through the corrugated iron roof, gently swaying a single dim bulb that must have been powered by the generator I could hear humming somewhere.

Vada led me to a thick beam supporting the heavy trusses above us and cut the cable tie from my wrists, yanking me into position with my arms behind me around the beam. She slipped another tie around my wrists.

I watched Regan as Vada secured me. He was leaner than I had anticipated, his body probably worn from the chase and his injury in the Georges River. His hair was longer. Even with a face that had been windswept and hardened, his eyes were a little too big, too blank, like those of a man reminiscing and not really focusing. I thought of those cold eyes gazing over Eloise Jansen as he worked on her, or staring down the hallway at little Isobel Parish as she ran desperately from him.

Regan didn't look at Vada as she stepped away from me. Those dead eyes were only for me.

"Did she give you any trouble?" he asked.

"No," Vada said. "She was fine."

"He was talking to me, you idiot," I snapped at Vada. Anything I could do to undermine her confidence in him. To try to warn her about what was coming. I turned back to Regan. "No, *she* was fine. Now let her go. Let her turn herself in. She might be able to convince a prosecutor that you brainwashed her, threatened her, maybe. Stockholm syndrome. I'm sure you could come up with something, Vada. You're a shrink. You could get parole in fifty years if you play your cards right."

"She's convinced you're going to kill me." Vada gave a little laugh, coming to Regan's side.

He put an arm out, and she slipped under it, curling against him.

"I tried to explain to her that you need me for what comes next. Your new life. Our new life. But I'm not sure she understands."

Vada looked me up and down, and there was a flicker of pity in her eyes. But the light was soon gone, and her eyes were taking on a blankness now that was almost as complete as his. She was dehumanizing me in her mind, the way he'd taught her to. Detaching herself from the idea that I didn't deserve what I was about to get.

She sneered. "She said that now I've done my job, I'm no good to you."

"You have done a very good job, Vada," Regan said gently. He gave her a squeeze and let her go, taking a step away from her.

Suddenly free of his embrace, she looked impossibly small. Childlike. Her features were twitching with sudden confusion. She could see in his eyes the same thing I had seen in her—detachment forming. The false warmth dissipating.

I opened my mouth to tell Vada to run, but I knew it was hopeless.

Her eyes flicked to me. We could both feel it. The change in him. The switch flipped. The mask fallen away.

She didn't even have time to voice her surprise. Her heartache.

Regan lifted the arm that held the gun and shot her point blank in the face.

CHAPTER 99

I WATCHED VADA RESKIT jolt as though shocked with electricity, her head snapping back. She staggered once and then crumpled to the floor, her head hitting the ground hard. Regan's gun was small and silenced. He looked at Vada's body, her head and shoulders lying in the shadow of the rickety old work table, and then turned to me like her death had been of only passing interest.

"She thought you loved her," I said. "What did you tell her? That you were going to run away together? Assume new identities? Two broken, misunderstood souls finally united?"

"I didn't have to tell her much," Regan said, refusing to look at her. "Vada had plenty of experience piecing together fantasies. I just told her that if she did what I said, I'd give her everything she wanted. Isn't that what all women want to hear?"

"Not me," I said. "I want to hear the noise you make when I feed you into a woodchipper."

The words were coming, but I wasn't paying attention to them. I was focused on the cable tie around my wrist. Vada had pulled it tight, but I was sweating, so there was some lubrication. I tried to shift the thick plastic locking mechanism sideways from the back of my right hand to the gap between my wrists. The edges of the plastic were cutting, scratching my flesh.

Regan was approaching me. Moving cautiously, as though trying to corner a bird he planned to pounce on. As he came nearer, I found myself pressing against the beam, trying with all my might to shift the taut plastic.

"Vada was very different from you," Regan said. "Some people, they need someone to save. The more damaged and unwanted, the better they feel. I'm sure you saw it a thousand times as a child, the way I did."

"Don't come near me," I warned. The locking mechanism was between my wrists now. I gripped the loose end of the tie and started tightening the band, pulling as hard as I could. My fingers and hands were numb almost instantly. I yanked hard on the tie, cutting the plastic into my flesh.

"You don't need to feel sorry for Vada, Harry. I gave her what she wanted. She thought she was helping me, and that made her happy."

"Come any closer to me and I'll fucking kick you," I snapped.

He kept approaching, and with his every step, my body hardened, shook with rage and fear.

"I will bite your fingers off, I swear to God."

He was pressed against me suddenly, my jaw in his hard, warm hand.

We both knew I wasn't going to kick him. I was having enough trouble standing upright. His breath was on my face. I bared my teeth, prepared to bite him if he tried to kiss me. A smile fluttered at the corners of his mouth.

"You wouldn't really hurt me, would you, Harry?" he asked.

"You wanna make a bet?" I thought about spitting at him, but my mouth was too dry. He squeezed my face so that my cheekbones ached, seemed to want to give in to his desire to hurt me. But this wasn't the time. He'd brought me to this place, at this time, for a reason. He would play this out slowly, so that he could enjoy it. He had been waiting a long time for this. In a dark, awful way, I had too.

"You need to understand what happened here," Regan said.

CHAPTER 100

THEY WERE ALL fresh starts for her. Fantastic adventures. Regan saw his mother's face change with every new house they entered, as though she was actually taking on the features of the people who lived there. Heather Banks found the house-sitting jobs in the newspapers and arrived at the city apartment or country estate or isolated cabin ready to enjoy a little escape from reality. For a weekend, a couple of weeks, a few months, she would adventure through the lives of the people who owned the homes, caring for their pets and rearranging their bookshelves, while her husband, Ron, worked out in the fields or walked the streets, preferring to admire the different landscapes alone. Little Regan had been to every corner of the country, minding the houses of strangers he almost never met. Heather told other adults it was good for Regan to travel. He'd not fit in, the first time they'd enrolled him in school.

"He's very intelligent," she explained. "He gets bored."

Regan was indeed always bored, but he was also aware that removing him from school and taking him on the road was his mother's way of trying to make him a "good boy." There were no other little boys and girls to bite and scratch and tug at here, no one to hear his screaming, squealing, convulsing tantrums that sometimes carried on for hours. They would arrive at a cheery farm and unpack their bags at the homestead, and she would turn him by the shoulders toward the fields and give him an encouraging shove, saying, "Now, be a good boy." Would this be the place that brought out the goodness in him? Or would they have to keep searching? Highway by highway and house by house they searched, Regan curled in the back seat of the car sleeping as eucalypts rolled by the windows.

Bellbird Valley was no different. Regan had wandered the bushland around the house, determined to find a way to be a good boy. And he had found nothing but miles of tangled bush and animals that were afraid of him, birds that took flight before he could line them up in his slingshot and kangaroos that bounced away at the sound of his footsteps. He assumed that goodness was something he would feel, something that would make him smile the way his father smiled at his mother sometimes. Regan would watch the two of them as his father put his arm around her waist, and he'd hear him say, "Gee, you're a good woman."

The day that it happened, Heather had taken Regan

out on the porch and sat with him, as she had every morning. They would watch the sun rise through the hole in the little stone formation on the top of the valley, making for a moment the shape of a warm little dwelling with a lit window. Heather had discovered the lighthouse the first morning they'd been there, sitting on the cane lounge with a steaming coffee in her hand. "We should go up there," she'd suggested, and they had, Regan following her begrudgingly up the slope, whipping bushes with a stick. They'd stood at the rock and she'd smoothed the slope with her hand, and then sat, giggling, in the wind-worn hole like a girl on a swing.

Regan had looked at her that morning and tried to feel the goodness. Tried to think of her as a good woman, and him as a good boy. But there was nothing in him. No goodness. Just a hollow cage in his chest, a place waiting to be filled with life.

His father had crossed the valley to the adjacent stretch of land where the owners had a well and a barn for horses. From where they stood, Regan and his mother could see the sun gleaming on the animals' coats as they lingered in the clearing. A thick rope was tied around the tree nearest the well, disappearing into the blackness of the stone structure.

"What's he doing down there?" Regan had asked.

"The owners think the well might be leaking. They've asked Daddy to take a look," she had said, curling a finger in the hair at the back of his head. "Regan, I want to talk to you about something. I've got some special news to tell you. I think it's going to make you very happy."

She explained about the baby, her hand now withdrawn

from his hair and unconsciously smoothing the gentle curve of her belly. Regan watched the horses and listened.

"Having a little brother or sister is going to be great, isn't it?" She smiled, rubbing his shoulder encouragingly when he didn't answer. "Isn't it, love?"

"Let's go see Daddy," he said, and started walking down the incline.

Heather followed her son down the hill, not knowing she was heading toward the place where she would die.

CHAPTER 101

THEY ARRIVED AT the well, Regan and his mother and the baby inside her that was not only good but great. Regan stood on his father's toolbox and leaned over the edge of the well and looked down. Twenty meters below him he could see the top of Ron Banks's head as he stacked heavy stones on one side of the empty well.

"Hello, Daddy!" Regan called down, and his father looked up, squinting in the light, a gloved hand held against the sun.

"We've come to see how you're doing down there." Heather leaned over the edge of the well, too, and cast a shadow on her husband. "Can you see the trouble?"

"I think so," Ron said, brushing off his muddy gloves. He explained to Heather about the crack in the concrete casing, the clay at the bottom of the well. Regan watched his mother leaning over the stone ledge, her skirt fluttering gently in the wind.

She had only a moment to scream when he grabbed her leg and lifted it. No time to twist or clutch at the wall under her hands. Regan was so fast, so perfect in his aim, that he counterbalanced her before she could steady herself and pitched her into the well.

There was a thump, the sound of screams. Regan jumped back onto the toolbox and looked down into the well, where his parents were collapsed together in the mud. His mother's head and mouth were bleeding. It was funny, the two of them writhing together, trying to untangle themselves. A pair of pigs in mud. His father was groaning, gasping, trying to grip the wall to pull himself up.

Regan laughed down at them.

"Are you okay? Are you okay? How did you fall?"

"I didn't fall! He...he..."

She couldn't say it. There was blood pouring down her face from a deep gash in her forehead. The two of them looked up at the grinning boy, dumbfounded.

Regan wondered if the great baby was inside her looking up at him, too.

"Re—Regan?" Heather stammered. "Honey, why did you—"

He stepped down from the toolbox and flipped open the lid. He could hear their voices still, bouncing off the stone walls of the deep well.

"Try to stay still. You've hurt your head badly."

"Why would he...Why would he...?"

"Jesus, I think my arm is broken."

Regan took the box cutter from the top shelf of the toolbox and pushed the blade out with a series of clicks. He went to the rope hanging over the side of the well.

"Heather, you might have to try to climb up. I can't use my arm. Honey? Honey, are you okay?"

Regan set the blade to the rope and started sawing.

"What's that sound?" Heather's voice was thin and high. "Ron? *What's that sound?*"

CHAPTER 102

REGAN SAT WHERE he had been sitting when I arrived, like a man lounging with a beer in his hand rather than a gun. He was watching me as his tale unfolded, those empty eyes examining my reaction.

"I went back a lot," Regan said. "I kept checking on them, seeing what they were up to. They had all these plans to get out, to scream, to signal for help. They would try to talk me into helping them. Promise me the whole world. And then they'd be screaming up at me viciously, promising punishments. I'd never experienced such awesome power before."

He looked at his hands spread open before him, as though he were holding the power itself.

"The sound of the begging and pleading and bargaining. It was addictive."

I said nothing. There were no words. I braced my body against the beam and listened.

"It couldn't last forever, of course. I got bored of the games and left them for a day. When I went back, they were begging for water. My father went first," Regan said. "A combination of things, probably. Septic shock from the broken arm. Dehydration. Exhaustion. It was an unusually hot summer. On the third morning, I went to check on them and he was dead. She tried to climb out a few times, I think, but every time she fell back in, it took a lot of the strength out of her. It was the seventh or maybe the eighth day, I went back and she was lying there making strange noises. So I got a few big rocks from the forest and came back and just kept dropping them in until I got her."

I breathed evenly, trying to control the sickness that had been rising in me while he told his story.

"People started calling the house," Regan said. "I didn't answer. The day before the owners were due to come back, I found a packet of matches and lit a curtain on fire. Bored again, I guess." He smirked. "That brought an end to it all."

"You're evil," I said. "Your file wasn't sealed because of what your parents did to you. It was because of what *you* did to *them*. You're just . . . You're just . . . "

Regan looked at me. "I'm bad," he said. He put his gun on the pallet beside him and came toward me. "I was born bad. My parents were great people. They never did anything to me to make me behave the way I did. It was just in my nature."

I shook my head.

"She kept asking me while she was in the hole," Regan said. "She kept saying, 'Don't you love me?' and I kept saying no. I was just telling the truth. That's what this is all about, Harry. Bringing you here, showing you who I really am. Throughout my life, I've been taught to try to hide that badness. Layer upon layer, covering myself up. They tried to help me in the system. Cover up the badness with friends, with activities, with pretend families."

He tried to touch the side of my face, but I twisted away from him. The movement sent a spark of rage through his features, just a flash that was gone before I could really be sure it was there. His big hand took my jaw again and pinned my head against the beam.

"I've stripped layer upon layer away from you," he said. "Just like I was doing with Sam. I took away your silly ideas about being a good cop, a good kid, a good friend. I'm showing you the truth here. Giving you a gift. You probably think there's going to be a good little Harry inside there, when I finally get done with you."

He took hold of the zipper tab on the front of my jacket and started pulling it down.

"But you're bad, Harry," he said. "You're just like me."

"What are you doing?" I flattened against the beam, tried to twist away from his hands.

"What's the last thing I could take away from you, Harry?"

He ripped the zipper down.

CHAPTER 103

I STOOD SHIVERING as Regan took a knife from the back pocket of his jeans, shoved my jacket open and cut my shirt right up the middle, stripping the cloth off in a furious tug. He returned the knife to his pocket and leaned in, grabbing my breast hard. I needed to let him forget himself. To sink deep into his fantasy, the one he'd been playing and replaying in his head since my brother's death. The one in which he took the very last layer of me, the only thing protecting my soul, the worst thing he could possibly do to me.

Rage was rising in me. I was shaking with it under his hands, my lips drawn over my teeth.

"We're the same," Regan said. "Are you starting to feel it?"

He came within range. I had been waiting.

I jutted my head forward and grabbed his bottom lip in my teeth, snapped my jaws shut. His gasp and then howl sent my blood rushing hot and wild through my body. Regan tore himself away, and I spat his blood on the ground.

While he was distracted, I made my move, backing into the beam with my arms out behind me as far as they would stretch. In one swift, hard motion, I leaped forward, tugging my arms forward against the beam. It didn't work the first time. My wrists banged against the corner of the beam, the cable tie holding fast.

Regan watched, confused by my purpose. I tugged the cable tie tighter, the final few clicks of hard plastic pulling taut, so tight my eyes were watering, then attempted the move again.

With an audible snap, the plastic tie broke on the corner of the beam, and my hands were free.

Regan smiled. He set his feet, ready for me to come at him.

I took a moment to shake the blood flow back into my fingers.

"Oh, I've been looking forward to this," I said.

CHAPTER 104

HE'D SPENT FIFTEEN YEARS in prison learning to fight. That much was clear from the beginning, when he failed to approach me, letting me come to him, putting me at a disadvantage.

I faked and he pretended to fall for it, then ducked when I swung at him, twisted and brought his elbow up and into my face. I felt my teeth crunch together. The blood was immediate, warm as it fell down my chin and dripped onto my exposed chest. I stepped back, zipped my jacket up, and wiped my mouth on the collar.

He waited for me to come again, but I refused. As he came charging toward me, I bent and ducked out of the way, gave him a hard, short jab in the ribs as he passed.

The anger was all-consuming, urged on by my exhaustion, the pain in my bleeding wrists and wounded leg. I needed to breathe, think of him as just any other opponent, and not the man who had destroyed my brother. Not the man who would unleash all of my worst nightmares on me if I let him subdue me again. I needed to ignore the horrific plan Regan had laid out for me, the one I saw in his eyes as he bent toward my mouth. His Harriet, finally captured. His to draw along on a string, just like Vada, his to break down and experiment with as his sick desires dictated.

Regan grabbed at my shoulder, tried to land a punch in my midsection.

There was no time. I swung wildly at his face, not even a punch but a furious scratch. It was a lucky shot, right across the eyes. While he was blinded, I landed two hard, heavy punches to the side of his head.

As he went down, he grabbed my calf in his enormous hand and pulled. We fell together, his arms around me suddenly, thick and hard as tree branches. His giant hand pinned my head against the ground. The other grabbed my wrist as I tried to swipe at him again, squeezing so hard, I could feel the bones bend. There was a neat line of teeth marks between his bottom lip and chin.

"No one's coming for you, Harry," he said. "It's you and me. You have to face what you are now. You have to see. Sam didn't get that chance."

I roared at the sound of my brother's name, scraped the side of my boot hard down his shin. He tried to steady his position on top of me, but I used his weight to keep him rolling, then jabbed an elbow into his stomach. I got up and staggered away from him. He rose, fists clenched. I'd made a mistake, rolling him right into the pallets where he had been sitting when I arrived. His gun clattered to the floor, and he swept it up and pointed it at me.

I scoffed absurdly, the outrage coming hard like a slap. He didn't drop the weapon. I couldn't believe what he was doing, gesturing toward the ground with the barrel.

"Coward," I spat, shaking my head. "Fucking coward. You can't pin me with your own hands? Are you that pathetic?"

"Get on your knees," he ordered, gesturing with the gun. "We're gonna see who's weak. Get on your knees and take the jacket off."

My mind rushed, a flurry of bad ideas. *Throw yourself at him again. Try to knock the gun away. Scream for help. Try to dive, roll, run for the door.*

And then I started laughing. A heavy, wet, bloody laugh that rippled from the back of my throat. Regan wasn't expecting the sound. His brow creased.

"What…" he began, trailing off.

He followed my gaze over his shoulder. And took in the sight of Tox Barnes edging up behind him, a pistol gripped in both hands.

"Remember me, arsehole?" Tox smiled.

He shot Regan in the stomach.

CHAPTER 105

REGAN COLLAPSED ONTO his knees, the gun falling from his hands.

Tox kicked the gun away and leaned over Regan as the big man held his stomach, writhing in pain.

"Yeah, that fucking *hurts,* doesn't it?" Tox tapped the barrel of his gun against Regan's forehead. He reached into the killer's back pocket and took the knife, threw it across the room as he came to me.

I hadn't seen Tox in a long time. Since before I learned of my brother's death. He looked terrible, smelled worse, and wore a mask of determined brutality as he came to my side. He was exactly the man I remembered.

"You'll have to make it quick," Tox said, glancing toward the open door of the barn, the dark field beyond, and the distant black mountain. "The tactics guys over in the next valley would have heard that shot. Do what you've gotta do and let's get outta here, Harry, okay?"

He handed me the gun.

Regan was bent forward, steadying himself against the ground, a hand clasped against the wound in his stomach. He raised his head and looked at me, and I leveled the gun at his forehead.

It was time to take my revenge.

CHAPTER 106

MY HAND WAS SHAKING, the aim of the gun wavering across Regan's bloodied face. His eyes were steady, knowing, unafraid. These were eyes that had looked upon so many as they died. The last face so many innocent souls had seen as their lives were ripped from them. I couldn't breathe. My free hand rose to my throat, raking my fingers through my hair, trying to find the calm I needed. I ran my finger up and down the curve of the trigger.

"You won't do this, Harry," Regan said.

"I wouldn't be so certain." I flicked the safety off with my thumb. "You . . . You killed my brother. You can't go on. I won't *let* you go on. I came here to end you, Regan. For all those girls you took. For their families."

"Are you sure?" he asked. "You really came here to do good, to make the world safe again?"

My mind was fragmented. Reaching for traction. I felt hot all over. I tried to get a grip on the gun, but it felt slippery in my hand. I couldn't pull the trigger. Not while my mind raced helplessly with questions. Had I really come here to kill this man?

I had abandoned and endangered the people I loved for this. Me, the good friend. I'd thrown in my job, run and crawled and hidden from police. I'd committed a host of crimes. Me, the good cop. I'd brought pain and suffering on anyone who'd tried to help me, some of it decades after I'd wandered in and out of their lives. Me, the good kid.

Maybe I hadn't come here for vengeance at all.

Maybe I'd come for answers.

I looked at Regan. Every cell in my body was on fire. But did I hate Regan for what he had done to me? Or did I hate him because he had discovered something about me that I was only just now coming to understand?

Maybe it was a much greater desire that had brought me all the way here. I looked at Regan, and I realized what he was saying—what he had been saying all along.

He had been telling me that he was a soul that would never fit, an outcast doomed to wander on the edges of the world, finding pleasure wherever he could. That he'd been born and had grown without feeling love, not even for his parents. That something inside him not only rejected people but sometimes enjoyed hurting them.

That he wasn't good, but empty inside.

And so was I.

We *were* the same.

I hadn't come all the way here to kill him. I'd come

because I was curious to see if I had finally found someone just like me.

Without realizing it, I'd turned the gun away from Regan. It was still in my hand.

But now it was pointed at my head.

CHAPTER 107

REGAN SMILED. He wasn't desperate for me to drop the gun from my head, worried and sickened by my aim. He was curious. Excited. It was all a game to him. No expression crossed Tox's features. He didn't ask what I was doing. Tox Barnes, my loyal friend, seemed to know from my face what I was thinking. Yet he put his hands in the pockets of his filthy jeans and watched me. His calm only tightened the muscles pulsing in my jaw, drove my heartbeat faster and faster. When I tried to speak, my voice shook with the tremors running through my body.

"Is he right?" I asked. Tox shrugged. I needed him to be shocked, appalled, to try to stop me. Anything but the expectation I could see in his face, the resigned look of someone who had known, all along, that I would eventually burn myself out. The tiger born in captivity, trained to walk on a lead, and yet unable to deny that natural instinct always whispering in the pit of its mind. Once I realized what I was, I would have to destroy myself. Regan's smile was rigid with pain, but he held it, knowing that I was finally seeing through his eyes.

"You tell me right now." I kept my eyes on Tox. "Tell me the truth. Is he right about me? He is, isn't he?"

"Harry," Tox began.

"I'm a killer." My voice was trembling on the edge of sobs. "I'm a punisher. I tell myself I only hurt bad people, but isn't that just bullshit? Isn't that just a cover-up for something really bad inside?"

"You're not going to shoot yourself," Tox said.

"I can't live if I'm like him. I can't. What if this is the beginning of me ending up like that? What if he's opened the door to something, Tox? Something I can't control. People aren't safe from me. They haven't been safe from me for a long time."

"You're going to put the gun down, Harry," Tox said. "That's a fact."

But I was on a road now that had no exits. Faster and faster, the realization was coming over me. My words came in a furious stream. "My own mother didn't want me. I was a mistake. My whole life's a joke. It's not *real*, Tox. Nothing I've ever done can cover up what's really in here." I tapped my chest furiously. "I'm bad *in here!*"

"I don't think so," Tox said, clicking his tongue, dismissive. "He's just got into your head. It's what he does. You may be a freak, but you're not all bad inside, Harry, and you don't deserve to die."

"How do you know that?"

"Because he isn't all bad, either." Tox gestured to Regan.

I looked at the killer kneeling before us, a man who had wrought unimaginable pain on the world since he was a child.

"Don't get me wrong," Tox said. "He's a miserable, vicious shitbag who deserves to be drowned in a vat of acid. But he came here looking for you. He spent all this time trying to convince you that he knows the real you. That you're the same. That you belong together. He tried it out the first time with your brother. And now he wants you. It's because he's lonely."

Regan was watching Tox as the shaggy-haired man gestured to him.

"If he's as evil and empty as he says he is, why is he so afraid of being alone?"

I looked at Regan. The blood from his belly had soaked his legs, the earthen floor. The breath in my chest was coming easier. Tox watched me. He was unafraid. He knew I wasn't going to shoot myself. As he approached me, I thought about his words.

Regan had been right about so much. I had few friends, yes. I was selfish, violent, messed up. I'd been a problem to the world from the moment I was born, and I grew up honing my skills to be a bigger, more offensive problem. There was a lot of bad in me, and stripping away any goodness I'd managed to cover it up with had been easy. I was like Regan in so many terrifying ways.

Inside me, there wasn't a great ball of warm, glowing, righteous goodness.

But there was a tiny spark. And there was a tiny spark in the man on the ground before me. As vile and merciless and depraved as he was, he was human. He felt loneliness. He wanted to find comfort with someone as unredeemable, as profoundly worthless, as he saw himself. He'd tried to show me that we were as bad as each other, deep down inside, and I'd come here to find out if that was true.

It was not.

CHAPTER 108

I DROPPED MY AIM.

Blood was seeping from between Regan's fingers. He steadied himself against the ground with one hand, his expression unreadable. It would have been too easy to take his life then. I was exhausted. My resolve was gone. All I wanted was for Regan to be gone from my life, taking all the pain he had brought with him.

But it wasn't going to happen like this.

"I can't do this," I said. "I can't kill a wounded, unarmed man on his knees in a fucking barn."

"I can," Tox suggested, taking the gun from me.

"Don't even think about it," I said. "Help me tie hi—"

A crash split the air, so sudden and loud it made all three of us jump. Vada's head was turned toward me, the bullet hole in her cheek running blood over the side of her face, a grotesque half-mask of red. Her hand was still on the leg of the foldout table that she had yanked backward, causing the table to fold in on itself and crash to the floor.

As we watched, Vada's unfocused eyes fell closed.

In her last act, she had caused a desperate distraction. The shock of the noise was enough to draw my and Tox's attention away from Regan for just a second.

That was all the time he needed to escape.

CHAPTER 109

A FIERCE WIND had risen outside the barn, whipping the long grass, dragging smeary clouds across the moon. At first, I saw no sign of him, my night vision ruined by the light inside the barn. But then I caught a flicker of movement through the forest. I had to take a chance.

Tox ran beside me, grabbed my wrist, and pulled as he noticed Regan turn in the darkness ahead. I was worried that with my wounded leg, my friend would get ahead of me, that I'd be leaving Tox to capture Regan by himself.

But Tox wasn't running on full strength, either. Now and then a hand braced against his abdomen, his breath coming too hard as he sprinted through the bush.

A desperate thought pulsed with the rhythm of my feet on the forest floor.

You let him go. Now he'll kill again. You'll never exonerate Sam. Regan will continue his sick game until he wins.

Tox stumbled on a tree branch and gave a growl of pain.

"Are you okay?" I yelled against the wind. He didn't answer. I stopped with him in the blackness, both of us panting heavily. We held each other. Not a hug, but the fierce grip of two allies glad to be within arm's reach of each other.

"We can't lose him," Tox said, his eyes searching the forest around us. Suddenly there was a gust of wind, carrying the thump of a chopper. I could feel its beat in my chest. A white light swept the forest, looking for Regan, for us. In its wake, I spotted a figure moving through the trees.

"There!" I dragged Tox along, then let go of him and sprinted up the incline. Tox overtook me. Regan appeared from behind a tree and smashed a branch into Tox's face.

Tox went down hard, Regan sprinting away from him. The chopper light darted again through the forest, and I caught a flash of my partner's face. He was out cold. As the light disappeared, I fumbled on the ground around him, looking for the gun he had dropped, feeling only rocks and branches, his warm jacket and hard chest.

I was unarmed. It was dark, I was on my own now, and the tactical team would be heading toward me, most likely with orders to shoot me on sight. The smartest thing to do would be to wait with my injured friend and surrender when the police eventually found us.

Instead, I ran after Regan.

CHAPTER 110

I CAME TO the clearing suddenly, a small patch of treeless sandstone reaching out over a shallow valley. Regan had stopped just short of the cliff edge, taking a moment to glance over its rim before he noticed me standing there. His lower half was soaked in blood from the bullet in his guts, and yet he carried on, a machine built for violence.

He didn't wait. Regan strode to the edge of the forest and grabbed my throat, slamming me into the rocks in one swift motion. My brain was still tangled up in the idea of finding him and was unprepared for what I would do now that I had.

I reached up and punched him hard in the head, twice, three times, but his strength was inhuman. A frantic thought pushed through the madness, that perhaps our fight in the barn had just been play. He was serious now. I had turned away from him. I had betrayed him. I had failed to be that perfect other he'd been searching for, to surrender to the lessons he'd been trying to teach me. He had been lonely, just as Tox said. And now he was enraged.

Regan straddled me, pinning my legs with his, and wrapped both hands around my throat.

I scratched and clawed at his hands, grabbed at his ears and face. The cartilage in my throat was creaking and crunching, and my eyes flooding with tears. I was only seconds without air, too early for hallucinations. But I was sure that what I was seeing was not real when Edward Whittacker's face appeared behind Regan's shoulder.

The knife in Whitt's fist came down hard, the blade sinking into Regan's shoulder. Whitt tried to yank the blade back, but it snapped at the hilt.

Regan rolled, staggered to his feet, holding the wound.

Whitt and I moved together, a silent agreement made. We ran at the big man at the cliff edge.

Our hands met at the center of his chest, a hard shove, both our bodies almost rocketing over the cliff with him.

Regan fell into the darkness.

CHAPTER III

WHITT AND I collapsed at the edge of the cliff, still struggling for breath. He held my arm as though to stop me from falling as we peered into the blackness below. The drop was long, at least a hundred feet. I could see a pale, twisted shape below on the rocks but couldn't tell if it was Regan or the fallen trunk of a young ghost gum. I slid back from the edge and knelt, and Whitt folded his arms around me.

I was taken back to the moment, seemingly years ago but really only weeks earlier, when this man had held me in the airport after telling me my brother had been killed. As I clung to Whitt, my fingers gripping at his sweat-damp shirt, I remembered thinking that my brother's death had been the loss of all that I had in the world. I'd been wrong. I squeezed Whitt and he squeezed me back, a strangled laugh coming from his chest.

"What are you doing here?" I said, catching his laughter. "What are you *doing here?*"

"All my friends were in the same place." He shrugged. "I thought I'd join the party."

We walked back through the darkened forest, Whitt's arm around my shoulder. He reeked of Scotch. Whitt had been driven back to his addiction. I realized, as we moved through the forest, just how much of the man I had known was gone. He pulled me close, surprised perhaps by how long I'd let him touch me. The few attempts he'd ever made at hugging me were always a risk. Maybe I was changing, now that I'd discovered that the real me Regan had spent so long unraveling wasn't empty, or completely bad.

We reached the place where I was sure Tox had been hit and knocked out, but there was no sign of him. I stopped and pulled away from Whitt, scanning the dark for any sign of the man.

I thought I saw him coming out from behind a tree, but as the forest exploded with light, I knew I was wrong.

CHAPTER 112

THERE WERE TEN of them. Fifteen, maybe. The bush around me was suddenly alive with people, too many to count behind the torchlight, the screaming voices. I heard the ominous sound of a dozen rifles engaging. I threw my hands up, my shout of terror inaudible among the voices all around me.

"Don't move! Don't move!"

They had authority to fire, and every reason to do it. I was a rogue. A dangerous woman. I'd shown myself to be willing to kill, and was covered in my own blood and the blood of my enemy. I probably looked like a fiend in the torchlight. There was a pause, and I could almost see the decision to end my life rushing quickly through the crowd around me. Flickering through scared, hardened faces.

I braced for a shot. But none came.

Someone shoved me onto the ground. I lay still and silent as I was cuffed.

CHAPTER 113

THE NEXT FEW HOURS came to me in fragments, a film now and then blurring or skipping as I lost focus. I remember nothing of Whitt and me being led out of the woods in handcuffs. But I distinctly remember a plump, freckle-faced paramedic trying to untie my boots as I sat on a gurney in the back of a parked ambulance. The laces hadn't been untied in days, and the boots were caked in mud and blood.

"Girl," she said, shaking her head in dismay, taking a scalpel to the laces, "you're one hell of a mess."

I waited in the ambulance to be taken away, but it seemed they wanted to keep me on site until they had determined what had happened to Regan. Officers I didn't recognize came and barked questions at me, took my answers without acknowledgment, and left. I caught a glimpse through the ambulance doors of Tox and Whitt—who was now uncuffed—the two of them walking shoulder to shoulder. Tox was holding a hand to his broken nose.

"Just get one of the paramedics to look at it," Whitt was pleading.

"You nag like an old woman," Tox growled.

I didn't realize I was falling asleep until the man I recognized as Deputy Commissioner Woods appeared at the bottom of my gurney, flanked by two tactical officers with rifles. While I'd drifted, my body responding to the softness of the pillow under my head and the relative safety provided by the crowd beyond the ambulance doors, the paramedic had inserted an IV drip in my vein. My handcuffs had been removed and my good ankle secured to the gurney frame. I looked at the chain connecting me to the chrome rail and supposed the sight was something I would have to get used to.

"Regan's body has been found," Woods said. "He's dead."

I smiled and let my head fall back onto the pillow.

Woods turned to the officer beside him. "Note for the record that upon hearing of Banks's death, Detective Blue reacted positively."

"Positively?" I laughed. "That's the understatement of the year. I'm fucking elated. I want a picture with the body so I can get it framed. Can someone save his head in a jar for me? I'm gonna put it on my coffee table."

"Detective Blue," Woods said, "they told me you were an expert on digging holes for yourself. Let me assure you, there's no need to make this one any deeper.

You set out, with foresight and premeditation, to murder Regan Banks, and you've done just that. It doesn't matter to me what kind of danger he was to society. You were a police officer, and when you went vigilante, you broke the law."

"Strip me of my badge," I said. "I don't care."

"Oh, I'm going to do much more than that." Woods laughed humorlessly. "I'm going to see that every charge you racked up in this stupid, selfish mission of yours is presented fully. We've got four people dead tonight, and a fifth on the way. You're gonna be sorry Regan's gone so he can't share some of the shit I'm about to rain down on you."

I hardly heard Woods's last sentence. My mind was rushing. Regan and Vada were dead. That made two. And I assumed Vada had killed the officer she'd stolen her uniform from. Her knife had already been bloody when I'd seen it on the edge of the well as she bound my wrists. I knew that the tactical teams had most likely paired up. That made four. I'd just seen Tox and Whitt walk by my ambulance, arguing like a married couple. They were fine. So who was the fifth casualty?

"Who's number five?" I asked Woods.

The officers by his side looked grave, but Woods only glared at me with disgust. He nodded to the paramedic beside me. She walked in a crouch to the end of the ambulance and started to pull the doors shut.

"Wait," I called, but Woods and his guys were already turning. "Who's the fifth casualty?" A desperate feeling was growing in my chest. I tried to shift upward, and the cuff around my ankle clanged as it held me in place. I turned, wild-eyed, to the paramedic as she gave the driver the signal to go.

"Who's the fifth casualty?"

"An older man." The paramedic hushed me, trying to push me back onto the pillows. "You don't have to worry about that now."

ONE WEEK LATER

CHAPTER 114

IT WAS CLEAR to me by the second day in hospital that I was getting special treatment. With no television allowed in my room, and no visitors, I'd amused myself in any way that I could. I lay watching the people passing the door of my single room for hours, counting the breakfast, lunch, and dinner trolleys going by. Breakfast seemed to be little plastic bowls of oats and wafer-thin slices of fruit, jugs of pale orange cordial. When mine came, however, it was not on a plastic tray but in a styrofoam container, and it was fried eggs and thick toast, strips of bacon and a cappuccino. I asked questions, but the nurses only smiled and shrugged, having been directed by the two thuggish police officers outside my door not to speak to me. When dinner came, there was even a slice of pecan pie for dessert, my all-time favorite. I'd stopped wondering about all the strange benefits I was getting until I heard one nurse in the hall outside my room explain to another, "She's a friend of Mr. Handsome."

I didn't know what that meant.

Being a friend of Mr. Handsome had more benefits than just the upgraded hospital cuisine. On the third night, one of the nurses caught my eye as she brought in my dinner tray, setting it on the stand beside my bed. She had a funny look on her face, like a practical joke was about to go down and she wanted me to be aware of it.

"Ward C, room 8," she whispered.

"Huh?" I asked. She winked and disappeared.

As I ate my dinner, I noticed that dessert tonight was one of the regular little tubs of colored jelly that all the other patients got. That was odd. I examined the tub, noticing the surface of the jelly was uneven and cracked. I tilted it up and saw that a key had been pushed into the jelly and lay at the bottom of the tub.

A handcuff key.

At about midnight, two nurses walking by suddenly became very interested in the officers outside my door. There was a lot of smiling and laughing, and I saw one of the women put her hand on one officer's chest, slapping him as though he'd said something cheeky. As they all moved off down the hall, I unlocked the cuff around my ankle and slid off the bed.

CHAPTER 115

THE BULLET WOUND in my calf had been badly infected when I came in, but since then, it had been hit with every drug known to modern medicine. Still, I limped as I made my way down the darkened hall to the elevator, past rooms full of sleeping men and women and blinking machines. The hospital lights had been dimmed, so I walked in a soft gold glow toward ward C, checking the room numbers as I went. The nurses on this floor hardly glanced at me. I turned toward room 8 and pushed open the door.

Pops was lying on his back, propped uncomfortably against the high pillows, both hands folded over his round belly like he'd fallen asleep reading a book. I stood looking at him for a while, at the machines all around him and the whiteboard above his head. When I closed the door, he woke but didn't seemed alarmed by my presence. As I curled on the blanket beside him, he put an arm out and smiled, shifting his head to give me more room on the pillow.

"Sneaky, sneaky, sneaky," the old man said.

"I had to see you before there's bulletproof glass between us," I said, patting Pops's chest. "How's the ticker?"

"It's still going. They've sent me a nice little booklet on retirement from the police force and all the benefits I'll get. They're subtle, the top brass."

I'd learned from a doctor when I arrived at the hospital that Pops had suffered a heart attack. There had been a team of people around me, trying to hold me down so that I could be prepped for surgery on my leg. But I'd made a hysterical fuss about knowing Pops's fate. The doctor had been so troubled by my screaming and kicking that he'd had an intern go down to the emergency room to check on Pops's progress. They'd told me he was stable.

Pops had since been given a single bypass. It would be a long road to recovery, the doctors had told him. The chances of him clearing, or even being allowed to attempt, a compulsory police fitness test were practically nil.

"They gave me a list of things I'm not allowed to eat," he said. "Since I've been here, it's been nothing but carrots. Carrot salad. Boiled carrots. Carrot sandwiches. I hate carrots."

I didn't mention my gourmet menu in ward D.

"I'll try to visit again tomorrow night," I said. "I think they're taking me on Thursday."

"You didn't get bail?"

"No," I said. Pops's hand was cupped around the top

of my arm. He gave the muscle a squeeze, and a stressed sigh emanated from his chest.

"You'll do jail time," he said. "You'll have to. Resisting arrest, the assaults. Disarming that tactics kid. The department will have to save face, but they're not sticking a murder charge on you. No way. I'll pull in every favor I can, and I have favors owed going back decades."

"Don't worry about it," I said.

We lay in the quiet together.

"I haven't heard anything about charges against Whitt," I said eventually. "I tried to tell them it was me alone who killed Regan, but Whitt was honest in his statement. They're going with his version. Are they going to go after him?"

"No." Pops shook his head. "He was off his head. Self-defense, defense of a colleague. It's your head Woods wants on his den wall."

"I'm surprised he hasn't visited me to gloat," I said.

"He hasn't visited me, either." Pops said. "I thought he would have delivered the retirement pamphlets himself."

"Weird." I shifted closer to him.

"You need to speak to Tox Barnes about the remand center," Pops said. "Whichever one they send you to. He'll have women in there who can look out for you. He knows those kinds of people."

"Pops, don't worry about it. *I'm* not worried about it, so you shouldn't be, either."

The old man settled back against his pillow. He seemed calmer.

But we both knew I was lying.

CHAPTER 116

I SAT IN THE police wagon and looked at the cuffs on my wrists, the rubber floor beneath my sneakers. I'd been in this type of six-prisoner transport wagon before, but I'd never sat on the steel benches here, never ridden in the back while the vehicle was in motion. I was on the dark side of the moon now, existing in a bizarre place where I was the bad guy. I couldn't decide if it was the smell of the bleach the wagons were hosed out with, motion sickness, or nerves making me nauseated. There were no windows. I supposed windows were a luxury I was done with now.

The wagon had picked me up from the Prince of Wales Hospital, and I was now on my way to Stillwater Women's Remand Center, on the edge of the western suburbs, where I would await legal proceedings. I'd heard that Deputy Commissioner Woods was personally going to make sure I got as much jail time as possible, but the man himself hadn't been in contact with my lawyer. That had surprised me. I'd stolen Woods's quarry, and that had seemed like a personal insult to him the last time I'd seen him, standing at the end of my gurney at Bellbird Valley, his lip curled in disgust. I'd have thought my eternal damnation would have been first on his to-do list.

The wagon stopped and started, working its way through the traffic on Parramatta Road. I could hear the radios of cars on either side of my enclosure, one pumping rap music, another blaring out jazz. Every sensation was painfully vivid, my mind set to record these tiny realities, knowing soon they'd all be locked away from me.

I silently tried to calculate what Woods could throw at me. A common assault charge against any of the people I'd fought off in my pursuit of Regan Banks carried a maximum of two years in prison, and that's if Woods didn't have the charges bumped up to reckless wounding or wounding with intent. He would probably be able to get me for breaking and entering, and certainly for stealing vehicles from members of the public. I might have been able to soften the onslaught of legal proceedings that was owed to me if they had been first offenses, but in my teenage years I'd been in and out of police stations frequently for the same kinds of write-ups. A good lawyer, which I couldn't afford, might have been able to get the jail terms for all those charges to run concurrently with a charge for killing Regan. But even if I convinced the court I was remorseful (which I wasn't) or that I had good character (which I didn't), I figured I was looking at a minimum of six years.

I didn't notice that the wagon had stopped at a police station until three other women climbed into the back with me. I shuffled along the bench to allow for them, but they all sat together opposite me. I kept my head down, didn't speak as the wagon lurched into motion. In time, I realized one of the women was staring hard at me.

She was a young dark-skinned woman, missing her two front teeth.

"You that cop, huh?" she said.

"Excuse me?" My stomach twisted harder into knots. I told myself there was no reason to panic. My face had been all over the news for the better part of a year. Of course the women in prison were going to recognize me. Even though I'd killed Regan Banks, a killer of women, a cop in prison was still a cop. I would be universally hated by everyone there. But that didn't mean I was going to be in danger. Surely the remand center's staff would put me in segregation straightaway, rather than leaving me to be ripped apart by dogs in the yard. Surely that was something that had already been organized.

As I tried to convince myself of this, the woman jutted her chin at me and repeated her question.

"You that copper woman from the news?"

"That's me," I said.

"Oh, baby." She laughed and looked at her friends. The two women in chains beside her joined in. "This is gonna be fun."

"What's gonna be fun?" I asked.

"Watching the girls inside fight each other to be the one who kills you," she said.

I sneered, brushing the comment off. But by the time the wagon stopped again, all my bravado was gone.

The doors opened, and I looked up at the prison walls.

ABOUT THE AUTHORS

JAMES PATTERSON received the Literarian Award for Outstanding Service to the American Literary Community from the National Book Foundation. He holds the Guinness World Record for the most #1 *New York Times* bestsellers, and his books have sold more than 380 million copies worldwide. A tireless champion of the power of books and reading, Patterson created a children's book imprint, JIMMY Patterson, whose mission is simple: "We want every kid who finishes a JIMMY Book to say, 'PLEASE GIVE ME ANOTHER BOOK.'" He has donated more than one million books to students and soldiers and funds over four hundred Teacher Education Scholarships at twenty-four colleges and universities. He has also donated millions of dollars to independent bookstores and school libraries. Patterson invests proceeds from the sales of JIMMY Patterson Books in pro-reading initiatives.

CANDICE FOX is the coauthor of the *New York Times* and *Sunday Times* number one bestseller *Never Never,* the first novel in the Detective Harriet Blue series, which was followed by *Fifty Fifty*. She won back-to-back Ned Kelly awards for her first two novels, *Hades and Eden*, and is also the author of the critically acclaimed *Fall*, *Crimson Lake*, and *Redemption Point*. She lives in Sydney, Australia.

POLICE DETECTIVE BY DAY, CELEBRITY FOOD TRUCK CHEF BY NIGHT, NOW CALEB ROONEY HAS A NEW TITLE: MOST WANTED.

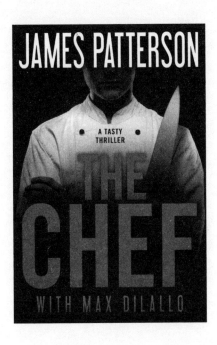

BY JAMES PATTERSON WITH MAX DILALLO

FOR AN EXCERPT, TURN THE PAGE.

"GIMME TWO scoops, three waddles, and a shake!"

Marlene is standing a few feet away from me, yelling out the next order because of the damn noise. Like the clanging of the manhole-sized skillet I'm using to sauté a fresh heap of diced onions, celery, and bell peppers. The popping and crackling of our deep fryer, louder than hail on a tin roof. The roar of the exhaust fan, straining to suck out all the smoke.

And that's just inside our sweltering little food truck.

Outside, a line of hungry customers stretching twice around the block is starting to get rowdy, yelling out encouragement and menu demands. Midday traffic with its engines and horns is rumbling up and down Canal Street, along with rattling trolley cars. And seemingly out of nowhere, a five-person roving brass jazz band has appeared on the corner, blaring a toe-tapping tune, causing some in line to snap photos with their phones to pre-serve yet another memory of their trip to this enchanted place.

A collision of food, music, history, passion, chaos... yep, that pretty much sums up New Orleans for you. "Nawlins," as us locals say it. NOLA. The Crescent City. The Big Easy. Different names for the same magical, one-of-a-kind place. My hometown of three-and-a-half decades. The capital of the world, as far as I'm con-cerned. A city where anything can happen, and nothing is *ever* as it seems.

Sometimes that's a good thing.

Other times—and I refuse to go there at the moment—it's a bad thing.

A very bad thing.

"Two scoops, three waddles, one shake!" I call back to Marlene, parroting the culinary shorthand we've developed running Killer Chef together these past few years. The work is grueling. Endless. Exhausting. But I love every second of it, doing something so simple yet so satisfying, providing great food at good prices to hungry and eager customers.

And with Marlene, I couldn't imagine having a better partner in crime, even though we've been divorced for years.

From the stack of empty paper serving boats beside me, I take six and fan them out along my prep space like a poker dealer flicking cards. From a plastic baggie sticking out of my back pocket, I grab an organic green jalapeño chili pepper and pop it into my mouth for a spicy pick-me-up. It's an unusual habit, I know, but better than a lot of *other* chefs' vices—trust me. Then I get to work.

I start with the "scoops." I fill two paper boats with mounds of fresh, piping-hot cheese grits. I top each with a healthy—well, *unhealthy*—dollop of softened butter, followed by a huge scoop of *grillades.* That's a thick, fragrant Cajun stew made with seared veal medallions, onions, garlic, beef broth, and red wine.

Next come the "waddles." Into three serving boats go generous portions of "dirty rice," the grains the color of caramel, thanks to the spiced chicken giblets they're cooked with. Then, from the sizzling griddle in front of me, I add to each one a gator *boudin,* a succulent smoked sausage made with the meat of that legendary bayou predator. (The first time I ever cooked one for Marlene, years back, she said it tasted so fresh and juicy, she half-expected it to waddle off her plate. The name stuck.)

Last, I make the "shake." I dump a batch of twisted strips of raw dough into the metal deep-fryer basket, then plunge them into the scalding vat of oil. Once they're golden brown and perfectly flaky, I slide them into a serving boat and dust them with precisely six shakes of powdered sugar. Most New Orleans joints serve *beignets,* a similar, more common regional pastry. But I've always preferred these, known as angel wings. And I've never been one to follow the crowd, either here or in my other career.

"Order up!" I cry, sliding the six steaming paper boats over to Marlene.

She grabs them without looking, bundling each with

napkins and plastic cutlery. Then she hands them down through the service window to a gaggle of attractive women, already tipsy despite the early hour, each wearing a bright sash over their shoulders and tiaras in their hair. A bachelorette party, if I had to guess, which is about as common in this city as air.

"Thanks, Killer Chef," one of the ladies says to me, twirling her colorful beaded necklaces around her finger. She adds with a coy giggle, "It sure looks...*yummy*."

Most of our customers come to us for the incredible food. Can I help it if a few also want to flirt? And truth is, all sweaty, covered with food stains and smelling of cooking oil, I love the attention.

But before I can respond, Marlene answers for me—with a blatant eye roll.

"Oh, honey," she says, her voice dripping with experience and sarcasm. "Don't let Caleb's two hundred pounds of hunkiness fool you. That man's a lot like the sun. Plenty hot when he shines on you, but try to get close and he'll burn you to a crisp. Believe me. I know."

Good old Marlene. Opening this truck with her was one of the best decisions I ever made. But walking down the aisle with her? Eh, not so much.

I'm just about to tell these gals how my ex-wife is a lot like a lemon—sweet-looking but truly bitter—when something outside catches my eye.

And chills me, despite the sweltering heat inside my truck.

Down the block, four white boys in their mid-twenties are leaning against the hood of a black SUV, a Ford Explorer with new, shiny chrome rims. They're passing around a bottle of liquor in a paper bag. Whispering among themselves. Watching the traffic go by. Watching the morning tourists stroll past.

But most of all, watching me.

I don't recognize their faces, but I do recognize their clothes. Each is wearing something yellow. A yellow bandana. A yellow baseball cap. A yellow hoodie.

Gang colors.

They're part of the Franklin Avenue Soldiers, an up-and-coming crew based out of the St. Roch neighborhood, a good four miles from here. I wasn't expecting to see any of them this far from their turf. In fact, I was hoping that working this busy brunch shift would distract me, would help keep all that bullshit out of my brain for a few hours.

I should have known they'd find me.

Especially today.

"Hey, fall asleep at the stove again?" Marlene barks, jolting me back to reality. "I need four waddles, two shakes, and three scoops!"

And so goes the rest of our morning. I try to stay focused on cooking our food. On pleasing our customers. On flashing a devilish grin at the pretty ones. But every time I glance through the service window, those gang-bangers are still out there. Glaring at me. Waiting for me to make my next move. Waiting for me to step out and away from all these potential witnesses lined up at my truck.

"And that's the last of 'em," Marlene finally says long minutes later, as the last two happy customers stroll away, leaving the sidewalk clear before us. She wipes her hands on her apron. It's stained with so many different colors, it looks like some kind of abstract painting.

I've already untied my own apron—and stripped off my sweaty black T-shirt with the Killer Chef logo as well. I wet a clean towel with cold water and rub down my chest, belly, and arms, trying to get most of the sweat off. I reach for a black duffel bag in the corner of the truck. I unzip it and start rummaging inside. Marlene clicks her tongue, annoyed.

"You're really not gonna stick around and help me prep for lunch, huh? Slacker."

"Trust me, Mar, I'd much rather keep slaving away over a hot stove than get dragged over the hot coals that are waiting for me down the way," I say, taking out a stick of deodorant that I liberally apply to each underarm. "Even if it means listening to you yammer on while I do it."

My ex-wife snickers. We're just busting each other's chops. The truth is, I *would* rather do just about anything right now over what I'm about to. And she knows it, too.

"Caleb," she says softly, putting her hand on my bare chest. "Good luck."

"Thanks," I answer. Then I remove from the duffel bag a folded blue dress shirt, along with a plastic ID card dangling from a cloth lanyard.

It reads: ROONEY, CALEB J.—DETECTIVE—NEW ORLEANS POLICE DEPARTMENT.

I have a badge, too. I swear. And a gun.

But currently, they're not in my possession.

Long story.

I slip on the collared shirt, stuff my ID into my pocket, then look one more time through the service window at those gangbangers.

To my surprise, they're gone.

I should be relieved, but I'm not.

I know at the time and place of their choosing, they'll be back.

And they won't be lining up for my famous food.

I STEP out of the food truck and suck in a deep breath of fresh air from the sidewalk.

The temperature probably topped triple digits inside that metal sardine can, but out here it's balmy and delightful. Folks are walking around in shorts and T-shirts. The palm trees lining Canal Street are gently swaying from the slight breeze. Anytime is a perfect time to visit New Orleans, if you ask me, but February can't be beat, especially if you're from some frozen place like Maine or Minnesota.

I start walking north away from my truck and ex-wife. After a few steps, I hear a metallic screeching and clattering coming up behind me. Turning back, I see a distinctive red and yellow vintage streetcar slowing down as it nears its next stop. If I broke into a jog, I could probably catch it. I'm going in that direction anyway. But I decide not to. I'm in no rush. Besides, I want to use the mile-and-a-half walk to do some thinking.

And ponder that visit from the Franklin Avenue Soldiers.

So I keep strolling, taking in all the sights and sounds. Preparations are well under way for Carnival, the two wild weeks leading up to Mardi Gras, the single greatest party on the entire planet—at least in my totally biased opinion.

It kicks off tonight and you can feel it in the air, see it everywhere you look. Shopkeepers have started hanging up purple, green, and gold streamers, flags, and other decorations in their windows. Eager, excited tourists have already begun trickling in. And at various key intersections around the city, the NOPD has started placing Delta barriers—big, white, mechanical traffic barricades that keep cars off designated parade routes and pedestrian paths. Things can get pretty crazy when the festivities are in full swing, but law, order, and safety are always top priorities.

Right now, I'm thinking about my own safety.

In more ways than one.

As I keep moving, scanning the streets for any lurking Franklin Avenue boys, I mentally rehearse how this whole thing is going to play out in just a short while.

I know what I saw. I know I did the right thing. And I know what I want to say.

So why do I still feel like I'm walking the plank?

Soon I'm hooking a left onto South Broad Avenue. I keep going until I cross Tulane—the thoroughfare, not the university. Up ahead is the Orleans Parish criminal court, one of the ugliest buildings in this otherwise beautiful city, a hideous concrete fortress surrounded by barbed-wire fences.

After I cross Gravier Street, my destination comes into view. Set back from the road by a wide courtyard, it's a place I've spent hundreds of hours of my life and been a part of some extraordinary investigations. But today, the New Orleans Police Department headquarters feels different. Strange. Foreboding. Uninviting.

I consider whether to enter through one of its side doors, or maybe via the staff parking garage. Both would avoid a possible scene.

But that would also make it look like I had something to hide.

Screw that.

I take a final moment to compose myself. Then I march straight through the courtyard and up to the main entrance. As I expected, a flock of reporters is there waiting. They spot me, and the feeding frenzy begins. They'd all showed up at Killer Chef earlier, but Marlene screamed that she'd ban them from the truck forever if they didn't leave us alone. That took care of them.

"Detective Rooney, Detective Rooney!" they yell. "Any last words before you—"

"Last words?" I ask wryly. "This isn't an execution. Just a firing squad."

A shout comes from the rear of the journalist scrum. "Is it true you've waived your right to have a police union official or other counsel represent you?"

"You're looking at an innocent man," I firmly say.

I've nearly reached the glass front doors. I'm almost

inside. So the questions come even faster, in a frantic jumble, like they're desperately trying to trip me up.

"What outcome are you expecting this afternoon, Detective?"

"How do you respond to critics who claim this whole proceeding is a sham?"

"Do you regret any of your actions?"

"Do you have anything to say to the victim's family?"

Grasping the metal door handle, I turn back and face the thick throng of reporters, some I know intimately from investigations past. You'd think they'd show me some courtesy, some consideration, not be part of a baying pack eager to bring me down.

But you'd be wrong.

To them, I'm a story now. Strictly business. Nothing personal.

The reporters finally quiet down, waiting, their cameras and phones ready and rolling.

I want to say plenty. To everyone involved.

But not here. Not now.

I give the crowd a nod and head inside, knowing that when I eventually leave this huge building with so many memories, I won't be the same man who came in.

Which both frightens and exhilarates me.

TYPICALLY, THE NOPD Use of Force Review Board hearings are handled internally on the third floor, inside a stuffy conference room furnished with a beat-up oval table and a bunch of uncomfortable chairs. I know this because over the course of my fourteen-year career with the department, I've testified in three such proceedings on behalf of fellow cops.

But in this, my fourth appearance before the Board, I'm the focus.

Not a great feeling.

Usually the hearings are kept confidential and closed to the public, except in cases where the department is looking to make an example of someone and try and look good to the public.

Like this one.

I'm kept waiting for nearly twenty minutes in the

hallway outside the spacious ground-floor briefing room co-opted for today's event. The uniformed officer acting as the hearing's sergeant-at-arms—a kid barely out of the academy, with a face so pink and boyish I bet he gets carded at R-rated movies—tells me the committee must first address some "administrative matters."

"Sounds like a bullshit excuse," he adds under his breath. He's clearly trying to buddy up to me, gain some macho props. "This whole *thing's* bullshit, if you want the truth, Rooney. Everybody knows it, too. Your shot was cleaner than a nun's ass."

I pity-chuckle at the officer's attempt at humor, but smile with genuine thanks for the support. I couldn't agree with this kid more. Every police shooting should be investigated thoroughly, but what the department's making me go through is ridiculous. It's all politics. Pure PR.

But that's the job. Sometimes it's your turn to be "made an example of," and my number just came up.

It pisses me off so much that some nights I can't sleep, just replaying the events over and over again in my mind: the chase, the gunshot, the aftermath.

Each time I think it through, I know I made the right choice.

But facts aren't going to matter today.

Appearances will.

Finally, the young officer opens the door to the briefing room and I walk in. Five NOPD brass are seated behind a polished wooden table up at the front. They range in rank from lieutenant to the big cheese, Deputy Superintendent of Field Operations Charles Bossett, a burly African-American man whose mere presence projects authority.

About two dozen people are crammed into the gallery. As I take my seat by myself at a separate table, I give the crowd a scan. It's a mix of spectators, reporters, a few department colleagues and police union reps, as well as the friends and family of the late Larry Grant.

His death last month by my use of a department-issued sidearm—which is currently being kept inside a locked steel cage deep in this building's evidence room, alongside my silver badge—is why we're all here today.

"For the record," Deputy Superintendent Bossett begins with a stern voice, "Detective Caleb James Rooney has joined the proceedings."

"Good afternoon," I respond with a respectful nod.

Bossett continues. "We now return to the matter of the detective's use of lethal force in the line of duty against Lawrence Christopher Grant, age twenty-nine, at approximately 11:43 p.m. on the night of January 10, 2018—an episode, we are all aware, that has been the subject of ample media coverage, both local and national."

No shit, I think. *That's* why the department is making such a big spectacle out of this. Not because of the facts of the shooting, which was about as by-the-book as could be. But to try to regain some shred of public respect after all the negative press over the past years.

Grant had been on my radar for a couple months. He was a mid-level Franklin Avenue Soldier and well-known drug dealer. But he was also a devoted husband who coached his little cousin's youth basketball team and took night classes at nearby Delgado Community College. Not exactly your typical criminal lowlife.

And I'm not exactly your typical police, either. Just try to find another major crimes detective anywhere in the country who moonlights as an award-winning chef and runs a popular food truck in his spare time.

The blogs and papers had a field day with that. The story spread far and wide. The headlines practically wrote themselves. KILLER CHEF TURNS KILLER COP. NOPD IN BOILING WATER AFTER FOODIE FLATFOOT FIRES FIRST. PUBLIC TO CITY: 'COOKING COP MUST FRY.'

I've never tried to keep my double life hidden from anybody. Not from the community, not from my superiors. Killer Chef even catered the policemen's ball three years running, and the wedding of my chief's niece. I understand police use-of-force policies are being put under a fresh microscopic examination across the nation. So overnight in my hometown of New Orleans, I'd become an embarrassment to the entire department. A liability. Any support I might have gotten from my fellow cops and senior officers dried right up.

So here we are.

"This board has had the opportunity to read your official statement regarding the events of that evening, Detective," Bossett says. "Before we begin our questioning, is there anything you'd like to add to your story? Now is your chance."

My *story*. Like I was a suspect hauled in for questioning! What a shit-show. What a *betrayal*.

But I know if I ever want to get my gun and badge back, I have no choice but to play along.

I take a breath, knowing everything—my life, my future, my dual careers, hell, even the possibility of a prison term—rests on what I'm about to say.

BOOKS BY JAMES PATTERSON

FEATURING ALEX CROSS

Alex Cross—Stop Me Please • *The People vs. Alex Cross* • *Cross the Line* • *Cross Justice* • *Hope to Die* • *Cross My Heart* • *Alex Cross, Run* • *Merry Christmas, Alex Cross* • *Kill Alex Cross* • *Cross Fire* • *I, Alex Cross* • *Alex Cross's* Trial (with Richard DiLallo) • *Cross Country* • *Double Cross* • *Cross* (also published as *Alex Cross*) • *Mary, Mary* • *London Bridges* • *The Big Bad Wolf* • *Four Blind Mice* • *Violets Are Blue* • *Roses Are Red* • *Pop Goes the Weasel* • *Cat & Mouse* • *Jack & Jill* • *Kiss the Girls* • *Along Came a Spider*

THE WOMEN'S MURDER CLUB

The 17th Suspect (with Maxine Paetro) • *16th Seduction* (with Maxine Paetro) • *15th Affair* (with Maxine Paetro) • *14th Deadly Sin* (with Maxine Paetro) • *Unlucky 13* (with Maxine Paetro) • *12th of Never* (with Maxine Paetro) • *11th Hour* (with Maxine Paetro) • *10th Anniversary* (with Maxine Paetro) • *The 9th Judgment* (with Maxine Paetro) • *The 8th Confession* (with Maxine Paetro) • *7th Heaven* (with Maxine Paetro) • *The 6th Target* (with Maxine Paetro) • *The 5th Horseman* (with Maxine Paetro) • *4th of July* (with Maxine Paetro) • *3rd Degree* (with Andrew Gross) • *2nd Chance* (with Andrew Gross) • *1st to Die*

FEATURING MICHAEL BENNETT

Ambush (with James O. Born) • *Haunted* (with James O. Born) • *Bullseye* (with Michael Ledwidge) • *Alert* (with Michael Ledwidge) • *Burn* (with Michael Ledwidge) • *Gone* (with Michael Ledwidge) • *I, Michael Bennett* (with Michael Ledwidge) • *Tick Tock* (with Michael Ledwidge) • *Worst Case* (with Michael Ledwidge) • *Run for Your Life* (with Michael Ledwidge) • *Step on a Crack* (with Michael Ledwidge)

THE PRIVATE NOVELS

Princess: A Private Novel (with Rees Jones) • *Count to Ten: A Private Novel* (with Ashwin Sanghi) • *Missing: A Private Novel* (with Kathryn Fox) • *The Games* (with Mark Sullivan) • *Private Paris* (with Mark Sullivan) • *Private Vegas* (with Maxine Paetro) • *Private India: City on Fire* (with Ashwin Sanghi) • *Private Down Under* (with Michael White) • *Private L.A.* (with Mark Sullivan) • *Private Berlin* (with Mark Sullivan) • *Private London* (with Mark Pearson) • *Private Games* (with Mark Sullivan) • *Private: #1 Suspect* (with Maxine Paetro) • *Private* (with Maxine Paetro)

NYPD RED NOVELS

Red Alert (with Marshall Karp) • *NYPD Red 4* (with Marshall Karp) • *NYPD Red 3* (with Marshall Karp) • *NYPD Red 2* (with Marshall Karp) • *NYPD Red* (with Marshall Karp)

SUMMER NOVELS

Second Honeymoon (with Howard Roughan) • *Now You See Her* (with Michael Ledwidge) • *Swimsuit* (with Maxine Paetro) • *Sail* (with Howard Roughan) • *Beach Road* (with Peter de Jonge) • *Lifeguard* (with Andrew Gross) • *Honeymoon* (with Howard Roughan) • *The Beach House* (with Peter de Jonge)

STAND-ALONE BOOKS

Liar Liar (with Candice Fox) • *The House Next Door* (thriller omnibus) • *The 13-Minute Murder* (with Shan Serafin) • *Juror #3* (with Nancy Allen) • *Texas Ranger* (with Andrew Bourelle) • *Triple Homicide: From the Case Files of Alex Cross, Michael Bennett, and the Women's Murder Club* (thriller omnibus) • *Murder in Paradise* (thriller omnibus) • *The President Is Missing* by Bill Clinton and James Patterson • *Fifty Fifty* (with Candice Fox) • *Murder Beyond the Grave* (Murder Is Forever book 3) • *The Patriot* (with Alex Abramovich and Mike Harvkey) • *Murder, Interrupted* (Murder Is Forever book 2) • *Home Sweet Murder* (Murder Is Forever book 1) • *The Family Lawyer* (thriller omnibus) • *The Store* (with Richard DiLallo) • *The Moores Are Missing* (thriller omnibus) • *Murder Games* (with Howard Roughan) • *Penguins of America* (with Jack Patterson and Florence Yue) • *Two from the Heart* (with Frank Costantini, Emily Raymond, and Brian Sitts) • *The Black Book* (with David Ellis) • *Humans, Bow Down* (with Emily Raymond) • *Never Never* (with Candice Fox) • *Woman of God* (with Maxine Paetro) • *Filthy Rich* (with John Connolly and Timothy Malloy) • *The Murder House* (with David Ellis) •

Truth or Die (with Howard Roughan) • *Miracle at Augusta* (with Peter de Jonge) • *Invisible* (with David Ellis) • *First Love* (with Emily Raymond) • *Mistress* (with David Ellis) • *Zoo* (with Michael Ledwidge) • *Guilty Wives* (with David Ellis) • *The Christmas Wedding* (with Richard DiLallo) • *Kill Me If You Can* (with Marshall Karp) • *Toys* (with Neil McMahon) • *Don't Blink* (with Howard Roughan) • *The Postcard Killers* (with Liza Marklund) • *The Murder of King Tut* (with Martin Dugard) • *Against Medical Advice* (with Hal Friedman) • *Sundays at Tiffany's* (with Gabrielle Charbonnet) • *You've Been Warned* (with Howard Roughan) • *The Quickie* (with Michael Ledwidge) • *Judge & Jury* (with Andrew Gross) • *Sam's Letters to Jennifer* • *The Lake House* • *The Jester* (with Andrew Gross) • *Suzanne's Diary for Nicholas* • *Cradle and All* • *When the Wind Blows* • *Miracle on the 17th Green* (with Peter de Jonge) • *Hide & Seek* • *The Midnight Club* • *Black Friday* (originally published as *Black Market*) • *See How They Run* (originally published as *The Jericho Commandment*) • *Season of the Machete* • *The Thomas Berryman Number*

BOOKS FOR READERS OF ALL AGES

Maximum Ride

Maximum Ride Forever • *Nevermore: The Final Maximum Ride Adventure* • *Angel: A Maximum Ride Novel* • *Fang: A Maximum Ride Novel* • *Max: A Maximum Ride Novel* • *The Final Warning: A Maximum Ride Novel* • *Saving the World and Other Extreme Sports: A Maximum Ride Novel* • *School's Out—Forever: A Maximum Ride Novel* • *The Angel Experiment: A Maximum Ride Novel*

Daniel X

Daniel X: Lights Out (with Chris Grabenstein) • *Daniel X: Armageddon* (with Chris Grabenstein) • *Daniel X: Game Over* (with Ned Rust) • *Daniel X: Demons & Druids* (with Adam Sadler) • *Daniel X: Watch the Skies* (with Ned Rust) • *The Dangerous Days of Daniel X* (with Michael Ledwidge)

Witch & Wizard

Witch & Wizard: The Lost (with Emily Raymond) • *Witch & Wizard: The Kiss* (with Jill Dembowski) • *Witch & Wizard: The Fire* (with Jill Dembowski) • *Witch & Wizard: The Gift* (with Ned Rust) • *Witch & Wizard* (with Gabrielle Charbonnet)

Middle School

Dog Diaries: A Middle School Story (with Steven Butler, illustrated by Richard Watson) • *Middle School: From Hero to Zero* (with Chris Tebbetts, illustrated by Laura Park) • *Middle School: Escape to Australia* (with Martin Chatterton, illustrated by Daniel Griffo) • *Middle School: Dog's Best Friend* (with Chris Tebbetts, illustrated by Jomike Tejido) • *Middle School: Just My Rotten Luck* (with Chris Tebbetts, illustrated by Laura Park) • *Middle School: Save Rafe* (with Chris Tebbetts, illustrated by Laura Park) • *Middle School: Ultimate Showdown* (with Julia Bergen, illustrated by Alec Longstreth) • *Middle School: How I Survived Bullies, Broccoli, and Snake Hill* (with Chris Tebbetts, illustrated by Laura Park) • *Middle School: Big Fat Liar* (with Lisa Papademetriou, illustrated by Neil Swaab) • *Middle School: Get Me Out of Here!* (with Chris Tebbetts, illustrated by Laura Park) • *Middle School, The Worst Years of My Life* (with Chris Tebbetts, illustrated by Laura Park)

Confessions

Confessions: The Murder of an Angel (with Maxine Paetro) •
Confessions: The Paris Mysteries (with Maxine Paetro) •
Confessions: The Private School Murders (with Maxine Paetro)
• *Confessions of a Murder Suspect* (with Maxine Paetro)

I Funny

The Nerdiest, Wimpiest, Dorkiest I Funny Ever (with Chris
Grabenstein) • *I Funny: School of Laughs* (with Chris
Grabenstein, illustrated by Jomike Tejido) • *I Funny TV*
(with Chris Grabenstein, illustrated by Laura Park) • *I
Totally Funniest* (with Chris Grabenstein, illustrated by
Laura Park) • *I Even Funnier* (with Chris Grabenstein,
illustrated by Laura Park) • *I Funny: A Middle School Story*
(with Chris Grabenstein, illustrated by Laura Park)

Treasure Hunters

Treasure Hunters: Quest for the City of Gold (with Chris
Grabenstein, illustrated by Juliana Neufeld) • *Treasure
Hunters: Peril at the Top of the World* (with Chris
Grabenstein, illustrated by Juliana Neufeld) • *Treasure
Hunters: Secret of the Forbidden City* (with Chris
Grabenstein, illustrated by Juliana Neufeld) • *Treasure
Hunters: Danger Down the Nile* (with Chris Grabenstein,
illustrated by Juliana Neufeld) • *Treasure Hunters* (with
Chris Grabenstein, illustrated by Juliana Neufeld)

House of Robots

House of Robots: Robot Revolution (with Chris Grabenstein,
illustrated by Juliana Neufeld) • *House of Robots: Robots Go*

Wild! (with Chris Grabenstein, illustrated by Juliana Neufeld) • *House of Robots* (with Chris Grabenstein, illustrated by Juliana Neufeld)

OTHER BOOKS FOR READERS OF ALL AGES

Cuddly Critters for Little Geniuses (with Susan Patterson, illustrated by Hsinping Pan • *Unbelievably Boring Bart* (with Duane Swierczynski) • *Not So Normal Norbert* (with Joey Green) • *Jacky Ha-Ha: My Life Is a Joke* (with Chris Grabenstein, illustrated by Kerascoët) • *Give Thank You a Try* • *The Injustice* (with Emily Raymond; also published as *Expelled*) • *The Candies Save Christmas* (illustrated by Andy Elkerton) • *Big Words for Little Geniuses* (with Susan Patterson, illustrated by Hsinping Pan) • *Laugh Out Loud* (with Chris Grabenstein, illustrated by Jeff Ebbeler) • *Pottymouth and Stoopid* (with Chris Grabenstein, illustrated by Stephen Gilpin) • *Crazy House* (with Gabrielle Charbonnet) • *Word of Mouse* (with Chris Grabenstein, illustrated by Joe Sutphin) • *Give Please a Chance* (with Bill O'Reilly) • *Cradle and All* (teen edition) • *Jacky Ha-Ha* (with Chris Grabenstein, illustrated by Kerascoët) • *Public School Superhero* (with Chris Tebbetts, illustrated by Cory Thomas) • *Homeroom Diaries* (with Lisa Papademetriou, illustrated by Keino) • *Med Head* (with Hal Friedman) • *santaKid* (illustrated by Michael Garland)

For previews of upcoming books and information about the author, visit JamesPatterson.com or find him on Facebook, Twitter, or Instagram.